THE

GHOST ORCHID

MURDER

A JILLIAN BRADLEY
MYSTERY

Book 2

NANCY JILL THAMES

To Holly Miranda Thames, who caused me to wait until I was ready to write. I love you, daughter.

Editors: *Donna K. Montgomery, Jennifer Steen Wendorf, and D.A. Featherling*
Cover Photo: *Mick Fournier*
Author Photo: *Glamour Shots Barton Creek*
Yorkshire terrier: *"Romeo"* Courtesy: *Dan & Sara Olla*
Special thanks to *Stel Montezuma* for technical support

ISBN 1453607927
EAN-13 9781453607923
Category: *Christian Fiction/Mystery & Detective/Women Sleuths*
Language: *English*

Chapter 1

I took off my glasses, rubbed the bridge of my nose, and glanced down at my Yorkshire terrier, Teddy, curled up asleep on his pillow next to my desk. This was a long session. The words on my computer screen were jumbling together.

"I need a break, Teddy. Would you like to go outside for a minute?"

Like a kid eager for ice cream, Teddy jumped off his pillow and headed toward the back yard. That meant a path from my office through the conservatory. It took him no time to reach his destination and soon he scratched on the door, begging to roll on the lawn.

So much for work.

"All right, all right." I followed him through the house. "Here you go." I opened the door and Teddy darted outside. The yard was green and beautiful with a smell of freshly cut grass. Gorgeous weather. Working any more would prove hopeless.

For my own rest break, I took some cottage cheese, pineapple slices, and cold roast chicken I keep on hand for protein boosts from the refrigerator. It would be a succulent mid-morning meal.

"One last addition…a nice glass of cranberry juice

and I'll be all set."

I smiled, placed the food and juice on a floral tray, and added a napkin and a set of silverware. I would feast in the conservatory where I could view Teddy frolicking in the yard, chasing dead leaves in the breeze. Warm sunlight gleamed in beams streaming through the glass. The conservatory. It was the perfect place to get my daily fifteen minutes of vitamin D. But, there was something about the room...something missing. Another painting perhaps on the adjacent wall to accentuate the beautiful garden view. I sat on the rattan sofa contemplating the sort of piece I wanted as I ate.

After the last bite of chicken and final sip of juice, I set my glass down and let out a sigh.

"Break over."

Opening the door I called, "Come on in, Teddy. Work time."

Work...I didn't hate it. But today had been especially stressful. Glued to my computer with a fear that put fire into my typing fingers, I had searched through numerous news releases since receiving a call from a friend of mine, Arthur Wingate.

A few weeks ago, Arthur approached me to help him win an important research grant from a wealthy couple who happened to be in my circle of acquaintances. The Hansens were devoted to the preservation of rare American flora on the verge of extinction. My degree in horticulture, my Master's in botany and years of experience working as a contributor for various gardening magazines gave Arthur the impression I might bring a few interesting sidelights to the work he was doing.

He had invited me to attend a ceremony at the Sanctuary Resort and Spa in Scottsdale to hear the winner announced. My bags were packed, the garden weeded, timers for watering were set and the neighbors had graciously agreed to pick up my morning paper.

Then the dreadful news came.

It had been a shock and surprise. Of course I would do all I could to help him. A technical assistant on the competing team had been found dead in one of their offices in Phoenix just yesterday. Arthur discovered the body upon arriving for work. The light was on. He peeked inside and was horrified at the bloody scene.

Arthur described the man lying on his back, arms outstretched. Someone had placed what looked like a white ghost orchid over his heart, right on top of the bullet wound. Arthur called the police immediately.

They arrived a short time later and soon the homicide detective and the coroner had sized up the crime scene, zeroing in on the orchid.

After he gazed it for some moments, the detective commented on how real it looked.

Arthur told me due he was badly shaken and could barely speak due to the shock of seeing a colleague in such a state. My friend explained to the detective that the ghost orchid only bloomed in the early summer and this was November.

My friend said the detective seemed puzzled when he pulled on his gloves and carefully lifted the thin, delicate flower from the body, discovering that the orchid wasn't real. Instead, it was a lifelike piece of porcelain.

***

I focused on the screen. Demanding discipline from myself, I clicked on one more Wikipedia article that promised answers.

The American ghost orchid is a rare and beautiful species of orchid found in the southwestern part of Florida and Cuba. The flower roots grow deep in the moist, swampy forests on the trunks of the bald cypress tree. Their roots blend in so well with the tree, the flower often seems to float in midair, hence its name "ghost orchid." These orchids are so rare that when a giant one surfaced in the Corkscrew Swamp Sanctuary in 2007, a flood of observers from all over the world flocked to southern Florida to view the specimen which contained eleven flowers on one stalk. Each bloom was the size of a hand.

I glanced at my hand, and allowed my fingers to uncurl from the keys. *A bloom...as big as a hand.* What a sight that must be. Well, surely that was enough. I clicked 'send' on the e-mail that contained links to the information. Hopefully, it would be of some help to him. As far as I knew, no one had canceled the award ceremony.

After watering the plants on the porch and in the conservatory one last time and placing Teddy in his crate, I locked up the house. While loading Teddy and my bags into my Jeep Cherokee, I felt a sense of foreboding. The skies had grown overcast and the brightness of the day seemed to dwindle. Surely, it was nothing. Everything would be fine. Now, on to the airport to meet Cecilia.

Cecilia Chastain, my personal assistant, was my right arm. An extra right arm was needed for a person like me so I could be two places at once. Teddy required constant care, but I couldn't take him everywhere. Cecilia was indispensable, not only in my work, but also in caring for my precious canine companion as well. She and I were to fly into Phoenix together.

I kept running over in my mind how a man like Arthur Wingate could possibly be involved in a murder. I thought about how jovial he was, always making us laugh when we became a little overheated about a subject like deforestation or insensitive land users.

He and his wife Diana had been colleagues prior to their marriage twelve years ago. Before that, Arthur never had the time for relationships outside of work. He was certainly the workaholic type. When he met Diana, however, they fit hand-in-glove, and the chemistry between them happily resulted in marriage.

I was looking forward to seeing them again, but the murder cast a pall over our visit.

***

Teddy was grateful to climb out of his carrier after being stuffed under the seat for two hours. I attached his leash to his red rhinestone-studded collar and our little party marched through the airport to retrieve our bags. Heads turned to watch Teddy prancing along and wagging his tail.

After giving himself a good shake, he blew a tiny sneeze to clear his sinuses and looked up at me.

"This exercise feels good after being cooped up so long," he seemed to communicate to me as he often does.

I scooped him up, and gave him a squeeze. Cecilia and I piled into the rental car and headed into traffic.

Phoenix is, admittedly, the largest city in Arizona at around 4.3 million people, boasting some of the hottest temperatures and some of the best southwestern food you'll ever taste. Right in the middle of the metropolis sits majestic Camelback Mountain, looking just like its name—a large rust-colored dromedary camel towering over the city. Fabulous palm-studded resorts nestle at the mountain's base with casitas, swimming pools in the shape of camels, spas, golf courses, and exclusive shops available for tourists with money to spend. How nice that included Cecilia and me.

Cecilia was such a Godsend. We'd met eight years before while she'd worked as a hotel housekeeper to earn her way through college. Through the years, we'd stayed in touch and worked out an arrangement for her to be my personal assistant.

Besides her strong work ethic, I was impressed with her being one of the few people I'd ever met who never used the "five Cs." Because she never complained, compared, condemned, criticized, or cursed, she certainly had my respect. We became fast friends.

Today, she wore her long auburn hair straight with bangs curved to the side and sported a cute pair of glasses and hat for the Phoenix sun. Typical for tourists like us.

The rental car gave us a smooth ride through the sights. Towering saguaro cacti and a few yuccas were still in bloom sending tall white stalks high into the air. To the north side of the mountain, the gated communities of Paradise Valley sprang into view. As we turned right off 44th Street, custom million-dollar homes of every style and shape dotted the mountainside. A sign for the Sanctuary on Camelback Mountain Resort and Spa entrance marked our way. We turned into the winding desert path to Guest Reception. Three valets in gold polo shirts and tan slacks opened our car doors and welcomed us to the Sanctuary. All of the grant contenders would reside here through the ceremony.

"This is really different, isn't it?" Cecilia stepped out of the car and paused to gaze up at the entrance. The building was art itself.

Influenced by Frank Lloyd Wright, the Asian-inspired architecture incorporated the natural desert setting. Winding brick and flagstone paths ran in between each casita and each of them had a unique desert garden. I had to agree with her; it was definitely different from the green rolling hills of San Francisco.

I checked us in at the small reception area. Original art lined the walls, all excellent works, and all were for sale. This, of course, intrigued me.

The young receptionist interrupted my musings. "You have a message waiting in your room, Mrs. Bradley."

I noted her name badge. "Thank you, Rebecca."

"If you need anything or have any questions, please don't hesitate to ask." She smiled.

Before climbing aboard the golf cart loaded with our luggage, Teddy pulled on his leash, leading us to a nearby mountain laurel that he wanted to sniff. He wagged his tail indicating he was thoroughly going to enjoy his stay.

"We have a dog lawn if he needs to pay a visit," the young valet offered.

"Thanks."

Teddy barked a tiny "yip" as an affirmation that he knew exactly what had been said. This trip was going to be delightful.

The young driver, whose name badge read "David" made small welcoming talk and recognized my name from *The San Francisco Enterprise*.

"Yeah, my mom reads your column all the time. Says she learns more about gardening from your answers than from any gardening book. You should see her collection of plants.

"I guess you know what you're talking about because my mom's garden is really something, Mrs. Bradley. Would you like to get a tour of the grounds sometime while you're here? If you want, I could set it up for you."

David was trained to be chatty, I'm sure, to put guests at ease.

"I'd love a tour. Thank you. Perhaps I'll call once my schedule becomes clear."

Arthur's message was an invitation for dinner just after a private meeting on the Jade Bar patio. The representatives of the contending project teams would be there and the facilitator, Herbert Jamison as well, who represented the grant donors. This was all going to be so fun.

I settled into my comfortable earth-hued room. The design made the dramatic views of Camelback Mountain even more spectacular. Various travel and shopping magazines beckoned next to a tray on the nightstand. Perhaps those would make good reading later. Hopefully, I might get to do some shopping, while I was here, in neighboring Scottsdale.

A comfortable over-sized chair and another long chaise holding colorful throws paired well with an armless geometric print chair and a small brass table. Tiny lights hung from the ceiling, interspersed among the dark wooden beams. There were even candles.

I flipped the switch next to the lava rock fireplace. Flames rolled up and their crackle accented the classical music station I found on the clock radio. I unpacked my bags and made sure Cecilia was comfortably settled.

After seeing that Teddy had fresh water and a dog treat for being so good on the plane, I placed a towel at the foot of my bed to protect the comforter and settled him on top for a nap. He seemed grateful. He gave a little sigh and put his head down on his tiny paws.

The provided robe was royal blue and plush. I threw it on in a surge of haste and tucked my hair up in a clip, for a quick bubble bath. Time to unwind. Dinner would come soon enough and I felt a little nervous about meeting the new team members.

"Cecilia?"

"Yes?" She opened my bedroom door slightly. "I know, tea, right?"

"Bless you, child!"

"I'll order room service along with your tea so I can get to bed early. Let me know when you need to leave for dinner and I'll come watch Teddy."

Cecilia was such a blessing, such a pleasure.

A few moments later the tea arrived. "Do you want me to fix you a cup?" she asked.

"Thanks, dear. Just what I needed, thank you."

I took a small sip. *Earl Grey...delicious.* I brought the tea into my room, sprinkled bath salts into the over-sized bathtub and filled it with extra hot water. After placing the cup carefully on the edge of the tub, I stepped in and immersed myself in mounds of aromatic bubbles. Heaven.

***

"How's Walter Montoya these days?" I queried Cecilia after I emerged from my refreshing bath. He was a sweet young man from a trip I'd taken to the Ritz-Carlton in Half Moon Bay, California. He'd worked with her there and they were roughly the same age. "Have you heard anything about how he's doing?"

"Jillian, it's incredibly odd that you ask me. I was just texting him. He wanted to know if everything went okay with our trip."

"Oh...so you do keep in touch?"

"We do."

"How is he then?"

"Walter's actually doing quite well. He got his degree in criminal justice and then went through the police academy. Graduated with honors." She blushed. "He's been working with Chief Viscuglia on the force for the past three years and now he's applied to become a detective. Should be hearing back any day now. That business in Half Moon Bay a few years ago really inspired him to want to catch bad guys."

"Well, good for him. I'd love to see him again. He was such a sincere young man. I really liked him."

"I like him, too." Cecilia voice was quiet.

Now that was interesting. I smiled. "Well, I must be off to dinner."

The sun was beginning to set as I strolled past the other casitas. A few guests sat on their balconies enjoying appetizers and drinks. I could hear snippets of conversations and an occasional laugh. A slight chilly breeze came up and I pulled my black leather coat closer around me as I meandered along the flagstone paths.

Pausing at the giant saguaro cactus to figure which way to walk, I turned left and followed alongside the deep-blue infinity-edged pool. A blazing fire rising from a giant stone bowl at the far end created a truly unique setting.

The huge red rock formation of Camelback Mountain reflected the magnificent sunset and created a dramatic fiery orange backdrop. I noticed, not for the first time, a small outcropping high up on the right side of the formation, standing alone and aptly named, *The Praying Monk*. The figure could be seen from a small clerestory window in the entry of the hotel, as well as from any casita that had a view. Clearly, a touch of Frank Lloyd Wright.

If the murderer was someone involved with the grant contest, perhaps he or she felt the eyes of God looking down through this edifice, even right this moment.

Arthur Wingate was a head taller than most men so it made it easy to spot him. His black hair was only slightly grayed at the temples and he was in great shape for a middle-aged man. I couldn't help but smile at his attire which was typical professorial buttoned-down blue shirt, topped with a tan micro fiber sports coat, Dockers slacks, and tennis shoes. He spoke in a strong bass voice that I loved hearing.

Upon spotting me he boomed. "Jillian, it's so good to see you."

"It's good to see you, too. You look well, all things considered."

"Thanks, it's probably due to the fact that I'm mostly a vegetarian. I also work out at the fitness center close to my office."

"I work out only when I feel guilty!"

We both laughed.

"You look wonderful as always. How was your flight? Did you bring Teddy?"

"Yes, he's back in the room with Cecilia. The flight was quick and uneventful so Teddy did just fine."

Arthur became a little less animated and I could sense an undercurrent of tension as he spoke. "I want to thank you for coming considering the circumstances."

"Well, my bags were already packed. How is Diana holding up through this awful ordeal?"

"She'll be all right. I'm worried about *me*. I've never seen a dead body before and what's worse, I knew him."

"It must have been horrible. You told me he was part of the Florida team?"

"That's correct. Let's get something to drink and I'll fill you in."

A smiling young server dressed in a black shirt and slacks came to wait on us.

Arthur ordered a glass of Cabernet and I stuck with cranberry juice with a twist of lime. The bar was almost empty so we had privacy to talk. The only people nearby were a couple of young women in the restaurant area having an early dinner. They were smiling and talking, probably friends catching up.

Arthur stood. "Let's take our drinks outside. It looks like there's no one on the patio right now and I want you to enjoy the view."

We watched the magnificent sunset spread out behind the majestic purple mountains. Deep oranges, reds, gold, and grays filled the canopy as the sun slipped quietly over the mountain's rim, silhouetted darkly against the sky. Soon we were overlooking the twinkling lights of Paradise Valley.

Arthur Wingate was a gentleman in every way. Comfortable with who he was, he never put on airs. He knew botany like no one else and loved and respected mother earth. Although he was fifty-seven, he acted like a man of forty, with all the energy and passion of a man of twenty who had just discovered what he enjoyed doing and couldn't wait to get started. Every new species Arthur learned about garnered his full attention, but when a rare and endangered species was in his sights, he focused so completely one had to believe his sheer will would keep it from dying out.

"We have just a few minutes, Jillian, but here's what I know so far. I told you how I found Rene. He was quite dead of course, but there was a look of surprise on his face."

"You mean like when dead people meet their Maker?"

"I know you're a believer, Jillian, and it could have been that, but when I saw him, it reminded me of that program where the expert can tell if a person is lying or not by their body language. I don't know. It was just strange. And as I've said, I've never seen a dead body before."

"I've seen two dead bodies and they didn't look surprised at all. You may have something, Arthur. Did you tell the police?"

"Yes, but when I mentioned it, the police didn't act as if it was important. I don't think I'll ever be able to forget seeing his face."

"I know it must have been a terrible shock. Have the police found any motive yet?"

"I don't think they have any idea why he was murdered or who could have murdered him. Nothing was taken from the office and there wasn't evidence of a break in, so it had to have been someone he knew or someone who was there that day or that night."

"I'm sure you've told the police who was there at the time, haven't you?"

"That's the trouble. I left shortly before everyone else and there were about seven or eight people still there after our meeting with the grant people."

"Why did you leave early?"

"Can't talk now. Here comes the group."

One by one, Arthur introduced me to everyone, and the server led us to a large secluded table overlooking the patio. An affable gentleman named Herbert Jamison sat next to me. Herbert was the grant facilitator.

"Arthur tells me you're a columnist for the *Enterprise*, Jillian." He picked up his water glass and waited for me to comment.

Wow. Self-confident and charming. "I write the 'Ask Jillian' gardening column every week."

"Yes, I read it every week online." Mark Russell nodded his head. He seemed to approve.

Arthur had introduced Mark as his main research assistant and the systems administrator for the Arizona team.

Everyone seems so young! How is that possible? Guess I'm getting old.

"I'm flattered, Mark." I noted the nice way he was dressed in a black turtleneck and tweed sports jacket. He wore his medium brown hair closely cropped and his skin had the pale tone of one who sat at a computer all day.

Being the consummate matchmaker, I also noted the lack of a wedding ring on his finger.

The server took our orders and made sure our water glasses stayed full.

I turned to the man on my right and said, "Dr. Fontaine, I've followed your work in Florida for years. It's an honor to finally meet you."

"Why, thank you, Jillian. But I think you probably outrank me in notoriety with your gardening column."

Everyone chuckled. The ice had been broken.

Dr. Fontaine's eyes seemed to twinkle. "That article you did on the demise of the blue agaves was most interesting. Pesky weevils. I suppose if you tried to eradicate them some irate weevil-loving group would get a protection law passed."

I blushed at his compliment. "Well, I'm sure they'd meet with resistance from the tequila makers *and* their growing markets. Tequila is big business, you know."

Everyone nodded in agreement. I thought I could tell by certain expressions who the tequila lovers were. I surmised Dr. Vincent Fontaine was one. A real sanguine kind of person I figured—expressive—life of the party, no doubt. However, he was likable and kept the conversation light and amenable.

The woman sitting next to him jumped in. "My father is our consultant from the Florida Department of Agriculture. He knows more about endangered plants in Florida than anyone alive."

Dr. Leah Fontaine was the Director of Research for the Preservation Society of the Florida Everglades and head of the Florida project. She had the thin figure of a model and wore her jet-black hair sleekly up, crowning her lovely oval face. She wore a striking blue camisole with her charcoal gray business suit. Ironically, I had almost bought a camisole just like it a few weeks ago but thought it too expensive.

"He's pretty amazing." Tori DeMarco, the young woman introduced to me as Leah's administrative assistant, agreed.

Nothing really stood out about Tori except for her blue eyes, peering out against her beautiful olive complexion. She wore her ash blond hair in a simple ponytail. Tori seemed quiet, but maybe this was not unusual. Perhaps she just kept to herself owing to a melancholy temperament.

Leah commented at one point that Tori was an

excellent administrative assistant, highly efficient down to the smallest detail. Even though Leah had been complimentary, there was still a distinctive undercurrent of tension between the two women. I decided to find an opportunity to acquaint myself with both of them as soon as I could.

Vincent Fontaine's voice brought me back to the present world of the dinner. "My dear colleagues, I appreciate your endorsements, but I think we should wait until the winner of the grant has been announced before singing my praises."

Arthur smiled. "No matter who wins, I think what's especially important is that we find ways to protect those species that can't protect themselves against the human element."

"You're right of course, Arthur." Vincent nodded. "Too bad we can't discuss our projects in such a friendly atmosphere as this, but the grantors do have their rules in this competition."

"Well," Herbert interjected, "everyone is welcome to discuss both projects as soon as the grant has been awarded. It seemed the only fair way to go about funding two million dollars. You must understand that most research competitions are cutthroat. I think it's rare that both of your teams have collaborated in the past and are as comfortable with each other as you are."

Everyone had their drink orders so Herbert raised a toast of good luck to the winner of the Peter and Elise Hansen Grant for the Preservation of Endangered Flora.

"Cheers." The room echoed with the toast.

"And a toast to Rene Parker, may he rest in peace." Vincent Fontaine added a sobering note.

"To Rene," everyone repeated.

The server brought a delicious spiced soup to start. Others had the mixed field greens with jicama and cilantro vinaigrette. The food was a combination of Asian and southwestern fare, but I played it safe by ordering the roasted free range organic chicken breast on top of mashed sweet corn pudding and creamed spinach. To keep my weight down I only ate half-portions. I saved a few morsels to take to Teddy.

Soon the conversation turned to the murder. It began with Richard Sanchez, head of field studies for the Florida team. His tousled brown hair kept to what was in fashion for the young men of today. He must have spent most of his life outdoors by the look of his handsome tanned complexion.

"Well, Arthur. Have the police found out anything about who killed Rene?"

Before answering, Arthur took a healthy sip of water and wiped his mouth. "I only wish they had found something out by now. It's been two days. I'm meeting with the detective tomorrow. Maybe he'll know something by then."

"I can't believe he's gone." Leah sighed.

"How long had Rene worked for you?" I had to ask.

"For two years." She looked at me, thoughtfully.

"I'm truly sorry, Dr. Fontaine."

"Thank you, Jillian."

"Rene was really good at what he did." Richard spoke up. "He was a top notch researcher and we really depended on him for our tech support."

"It will be hard to replace him with someone with his unique skill set." Leah shook her head. "In the meantime, I'll have to depend on Tori and Richard to fill in until we can hire someone else."

"At least your project was submitted before all this happened." Herbert took the dessert menu the server was distributing around the table.

"Yes, that was fortunate, wasn't it?" Leah smiled.

The idea of the Grand Marnier crème brulee with fresh berries and whipped cream set my mouth watering. I ordered one accompanied by a favorite of mine, cappuccino.

The man sitting on my right was Warren Burkett. The only person who hadn't spoken all evening had me intrigued and I turned toward him. He was Arthur's assistant director and was certainly worth knowing.

"You've been awfully quiet all evening, Warren. Are you feeling all right?"

He gave a wry smile. "Oh, I'm fine. I just keep wondering who the last person to leave the office was before Rene was murdered. I know I left before Tori and Richard."

"And I left before Mark." Herbert added his comment. "Because I remember he said he was going out to celebrate and needed to call a taxi."

Arthur turned toward Mark. "I suppose you were going to celebrate posting the final submittal."

I wanted to head off a confrontation. "I think we'd better leave the details to the police for all concerned."

"Jillian's right." Leah's father added. "Let the police figure it out. I don't know about the other team, but I'm exhausted after this whole thing. We'd better call it a night."

He stood, and as if on cue, Leah put her napkin to the left of her plate, glanced around and said goodnight to everyone. Richard Sanchez and Tori DeMarco stood up, thanked Herbert for the dinner and bade us goodnight. Since Herbert did not seem to be in any hurry, the rest of us lingered over our dessert and coffee, making small talk.

Herbert commented about how difficult it must be for everyone to have a murder hanging over their heads along with the stress of the ceremony. Losing a much hoped for injection of funds for research could mean a lot to an academic career.

I finally stood, thanked Herbert for a lovely dinner and told Arthur I would see him in the morning at eight sharp.

Ah, jet lag. I was beginning to feel it. Since it was an

hour later here in Arizona, the thought of not having much time for sleep made me weary. When I returned to my room and ran my passkey across the lock, Teddy barked furiously.

After I let myself in, I scooped him up gently—all four- and-a-half pounds—and gave him a hug and a kiss on top of his sweet little brown head, right between his long, silky, perked up ears. I often thought his hair looked like I had streaked it on purpose because of the blond highlights.

Cecilia was still up.

"Hi, Cecilia, has Teddy been out?"

"I just let him out. How was the dinner?"

"Well, it was interesting meeting everyone. The only one I didn't meet was Arthur's administrative assistant because she was just getting over the flu. But he said she'd be at work in the morning so I'll meet her then. I brought Teddy some leftovers."

"What would you like me to do tomorrow?"

"Why don't you book me that gardens tour in the afternoon? I'll also need you to take Teddy for a walk after breakfast and after his afternoon nap. Afterward, you're free to do anything you like, as long as Teddy is with you. I haven't let him out of my sight since Half Moon Bay."

"I totally understand, Jillian. Don't worry—I'll take good care of him. I have some articles to go over for my editor, so I'll keep busy here in the room. See you in the morning."

"Goodnight, Cecilia, pleasant dreams.

"Let's go to bed, Teddy. We have a big day tomorrow. I'm going to have to look at where that poor man was murdered. Then there's the garden tour."

I put him gently down and he laid his head on his paws ready to go to sleep. After I crawled between the smooth sheets and pulled the down comforter close, I felt as if I was sleeping in a cloud.

I flicked off the lamp, but lay awake on my back. It was hard to imagine any of those people shooting a colleague, but I suppose anything was possible. *If* there was enough of a motive. Rene must have terribly upset someone. Maybe tomorrow I would learn more.

My eyelids grew heavy as I thought about Mark's comments regarding who left the office after him. I thought about Leah Fontaine's apparent composure after the ghastly affair, since it had taken place only a few short days before. Of course, she still might be in shock. That had happened to me after receiving the news of my husband's death in Vietnam. All I felt was numbness. Couldn't function. So empty...alone.

I miss you, my darling, but I will see you again...in Heaven.

Chapter 2

Teddy licked my cheek the next morning as I slowly became conscious. I gave him some love pats and a kiss. "Good morning, Teddy, time to get up and at 'em!" I stretched my arms to help cirulate the blood flow through my body. I heard Cecilia knock on my door.

"Jillian, are you awake?"

"Yes, come in. What's going on?" I was still half-asleep.

"I think you should read this." She handed me the morning paper. I put on my glasses and sat up in bed as Teddy jumped down to greet her.

"Well, look at this!"

Mr. and Mrs. Peter Hansen have informed the contenders of the Peter and Elise Hansen Grant for the Preservation of Endangered Flora, worth two million dollars, that the grant will not be awarded until the murder of Rene Parker is resolved in full. When asked if the Hansens had any ideas of who they thought was a suspect or had a motive for the murder, they declined further comment.

"Interesting." I handed the paper back to her. "I wonder how this news is going to affect everyone. This grant was extremely important to both research groups."

"It will be interesting to see their reactions then."

"Cecilia, did you get the information on this Hansen grant I asked you for before we left?"

"Indeed I did. The grant has been awarded only two times before this current competition. The first one was in 2003, to the Dwight M. Rinehart Foundation for the Preservation of Endangered Flora of Hawaii, in the amount of one-and-a-half million dollars, and the most recent one in 2006, to the Katharine B. Moss Restoration Society for the Flora of South Carolina, for one and three quarter million dollars."

"Sounds like an awful lot of money for a grant. The most I've ever heard of was $450,000 and that was from the government. I'd say this is unusual, especially in the world of plant enthusiasts. Have you found out any more about these donors? "

"Ran out of time. I'll get you the information as soon as possible. You have an appointment at three o'clock for the tour with the head groundskeeper. Hope that's a good time."

"Sounds perfect, it'll give me a chance to rest a little before dinner. I'm driving over to the Wingate's. Diana insisted on seeing me and she said to bring Teddy as well, so it looks like you're free tonight."

"Hmm, mind if I rent a Pay-per-View tonight?"

"Be my guest!"

"Thanks, Jillian. You'd better get ready! It's almost seven o'clock. And don't worry—I'll get that information on the Hansens tomorrow first thing."

***

I followed Arthur's directions to his office complexes, which, like many Phoenix businesses, were renovated concrete block buildings. I understood using the concrete material because nothing kept out the hot sun better in the summertime. I was just happy to be here in November.

I pulled up in front of a small office with three cars parked in front and got out. There was no landscaping around the premises. Watering was probably too costly. There was a larger rear building attached to the front office with ample parking. Perhaps it was the lab.

The door was open. I found myself in a partial reception area which included a few partitioned office spaces. The walls were wood-paneled and the floor spread out before me in an emerald green ceramic tile. The décor seemed quite appropriate for a plant office. A busy receptionist nodded acknowledgment of my arrival and motioned for me to sit down. I did as she said and waited patiently for her to finish.

The nameplate on her desk said Helen Morningstar. Seeing no one else around, I assumed she was Arthur's office manager. Her wide smile conveyed friendliness.

My watch said eight o'clock sharp. I waited patiently, listening to her conversation on the phone. It was an assortment of "Yes, that's rights," or "No, you got that entirely wrongs."

Talking to a reporter, no doubt. I glanced around and thought how different offices were in Arizona compared to California. It then dawned on me what was missing: surveillance cameras. Hardly anyone in California trusted anyone else, but things seemed different here. It might prove difficult to find a murderer with no video tapes.

The receptionist finished her call. After making a few notes, she raised her head, seeming to see me for the first time.

"May I help you?"

"My name is Jillian Bradley. I have an appointment with Dr. Wingate at eight o'clock."

"Hello, Mrs. Bradley, I'm Helen Morningstar, Dr.

Wingate's administrative assistant. Sorry to keep you waiting, but it's been crazy around here." She extended her hand. "It's a pleasure to meet someone famous like you."

I laughed. "I'm happy to meet you too. I heard you had the flu yesterday. Are you feeling better?"

"Much better, thank the Lord. It was not fun. Thanks for asking. Dr. Wingate said to bring you right in so if you'll just follow me?"

We wound through several office cubicles until we reached the back. Arthur's office was the first one on the left. Warren Burkett lounged at his desk in the next office. I waved a friendly hello. He smiled and waved back.

The police had sectioned off the last office with crime scene tape but a light was on. I looked forward to getting a look soon. I could see a door at the end of the hall marked "Lab" and assumed it was where they conducted experiments.

"Jillian, come in!" Arthur gave me a friendly hug.

"Good morning, Arthur. How are things going? I heard the news about the grant being postponed."

"Yeah, I received an e-mail from Herbert Jamison last night. Why don't you sit here? He offered me a chair. "Would you like some coffee? I was just going to get me a refill."

He headed toward the small coffee bar set up outside his office door.

"Thanks. I take it black."

He returned with the coffee and I took the cup from his hand.

"I assume you're relieved to be finished with the grant proposal."

"I'm relieved that it's finished, yes. In fact, I did the final perusal and gave it to Mark to submit the day before Rene was murdered." Arthur took a sip of his coffee.

"Mark submitted the proposal the day *before* Rene was murdered? That's interesting."

"You see, this grant was different from most because Elise Hansen was going to select the winner personally after reading the summaries. Her minions had already done the homework on our labs and credentials, so all she had to do was decide which one she thought had the most merit. She's an educated woman and fully capable, I'm sure.

"She insisted the proposals be short, only fifteen pages, so it wouldn't take her long to decide. I don't know how well it will stand up against the one Leah submitted, but I must tell you, I think it will knock their socks off."

"It sounds like you have a good chance to win."

"Our team did a phenomenal job with the research findings, and what's more important, the plans we submitted to preserve the species will undoubtedly work, *if* we can get the funding. I just don't know what's going to happen now that we have this murder on our hands." He looked gloomy.

"I suppose only time will tell. There isn't much you can do at this point."

"Jillian, when I looked into that office and saw Rene sprawled on the floor, I could tell he was dead. I remember running back to my office and calling the police because I knew I shouldn't touch anything anywhere near the body. Felt like I was in a dream. The whole project just started to melt away at that point. How could this happen? I can't believe all our hard work will be for nothing." He sat down dejectedly.

"Now listen to me, Arthur. You can't give up. I'm sure everything will work out, especially if your team has done nothing wrong."

"We haven't. I have such great faith in this project. It's as thorough as any project could be. Of course, the Florida team may have one just as worthy."

"Perhaps they do. I hope my input helped a little. It didn't seem like I did much...."

"Jillian, I think your support article on the blue agaves is one of the main reasons ours will win. It goes beyond our species and exposes the potential danger to all agaves."

"I'm glad I could help." I took a sip of my coffee. "How is the investigation going?"

"The detective is supposed to be here any moment. He's kind of a hardhead, but he seems intelligent enough to get the job done. Want a peek at the crime scene?"

I smiled. "I thought you'd never ask!"

We walked down the hall to the room entrance, which was cordoned off. A large chalk outline of Rene's body colored the floor. There was a bloodstain on the carpet where the wound had been, right beneath Rene's heart.

Arthur pointed. "You'll notice by the wall the chair was turned over. The police left everything the way it was."

"Whose office is this?"

"It's Mark Russell's. He's using the two cubicles you saw when you came in now with a laptop, since the police confiscated his computer."

"Arthur, why in the world would two teams competing for a two million dollar grant meet in one of the competitor's offices? I'd think the security would be easily compromised. I don't understand."

A man dressed in a charcoal gray suit poked his head around the cubicle surround, then came into the room.

"Hello, Dr. Wingate. Actually, I was wondering the same thing, sir."

"Good morning. We've been expecting you. Detective, may I present Mrs. Jillian Bradley, a dear friend and colleague of mine. Jillian, meet Detective Jack Noble."

"It's my pleasure, Mrs. Bradley."

"Do call me Jillian, Detective. 'Mrs. Bradley' sounds like I'm your mother," I laughed.

"As you wish, Mrs. Bradley."

Was he listening?

The detective struck me as being about as serious as they come. He was a smaller man, not more than 5'8", but he had a presence. His suit was well-tailored, though not necessarily expensive, and he wore an unobtrusive blue and gray tie. He didn't smile, didn't look friendly, and his small dark brown eyes appeared to not miss a thing.

Arthur spoke. "Why don't we go to the conference room and sit down? Helen, would you please bring in some coffee?"

"Right away, Dr. Wingate."

The conference room was to the right of the entry area behind a closed door. The room was spacious and furnished with a large wooden table surrounded by twelve padded chairs. Walls painted in warm earth tones held a few excellent desert botanical prints. Wall-to-wall carpet helped to create a relaxed atmosphere for conversation.

Arthur pulled a chair out for me. He gestured for Detective Noble to sit.

After Helen brought in the coffee, she closed the door and left the three of us. Detective Noble began.

"Let's cut to the chase, Dr. Wingate. I want to know why the two teams were together in your offices the night Rene Parker was murdered." Detective Noble's tone seemed brusque, but Arthur responded politely.

"Look, Detective. It's true we're competing for a grant worth a lot of money, but our teams are still after the same result—the protection of endangered species. Besides, we've been colleagues together before on projects of the same nature."

"Like what, for instance?"

"Well, like the comparative studies of their *Ribes echinellum* with our *Tumamoca macdougalii* just last year."

"Say that in English, Doctor."

"Sorry. The comparative studies of two endangered species, the Miccosukee gooseberry in Florida, *Ribes echinellum*, and our Tumamoc globeberry, *Tumamoca macdougalii* here in Arizona.

"Please understand we scientists don't have many opportunities to share our knowledge unless it's through periodicals. We rarely socialize. We're always heavy into research and I mean hours and hours of work.

"Often our forays for knowledge go into the night until we finally have a breakthrough of some kind. Understand—breakthroughs don't happen often."

"Arthur." I jumped in. "Whose idea was it to meet here and what was the purpose? Surely you were concerned about security for your projects."

"It was both my idea and Dr. Fontaine's." Arthur showed embarrassment. "Sometimes we scientists like to see other working environments. I had been to their lab last year when we worked on a project together. We thought it would be good for them to see our lab when they came to Arizona. It's really pretty simple. We had no idea someone would get murdered here. I still can't believe it." He shook his head.

"Which Dr. Fontaine?" Detective Noble didn't wait to continue his questions.

Arthur turned back toward him. "The committee head, Dr. Leah Fontaine. Her father is only a consultant. He's here to be with Leah. She's not well, I understand.

"Detective, the offices were locked. The lab was locked except for the tour I personally led during the first hour we were together. Helen, as the last person to exit the lab, made certain everyone was accounted for. No one had a chance to see any confidential research of any kind, I swear to it."

"So you didn't trust everyone, huh?" Noble looked thoughtful.

I decided to help out. "I think what Arthur is saying is that precautions were taken to prevent any tampering with the Arizona project without seeming to be hostile, Detective."

"Maybe. But maybe somebody took advantage of the good doctor's hospitality here and wound up getting involved in murder. We're going to find out what happened because I smell a rat."

"That's great." I leaned toward him a little. "And I've got a good nose too, so why don't we share what we find and maybe we'll catch the rat together?"

Detective Noble didn't seem to know whether I was serious or not.

I assured him I was and asked him to get on with his questions. His next was to me.

"I take it Dr. Wingate let you look at the crime scene?"

"I saw where the body was found and he pointed out the overturned chair."

"You know, of course, that you're not supposed to release any information that would jeopardize any leads."

"I understand completely. I happened to be involved first hand in a murder case eight years ago."

"That so?" Noble acted rather surprised. "Did you solve the case?" His tone mocked.

"As a matter of fact, she did." Arthur answered for me. "You may have read about it. The murders of several people in Half Moon Bay, California, all related, and all solved with the help of Jillian Bradley, here."

"I'm impressed, Jillian." The detective finally relaxed. He must have made a decision to trust me because he contiued. "To be frank, we don't have a clue regarding motive. The means is obvious—a .22 caliber gunshot wound to the chest—but we haven't found the weapon."

"What about the porcelain ghost orchid you found over the wound?"

"So you know about that, huh? Guess Dr. Wingate here told you. No one else knows that little detail and I would appreciate your keeping it under your hat."

"Not a problem. You were saying...?"

"The problem with the porcelain ghost orchid is that it could have come from anywhere. It will take time to have someone track it down. By the way, in case you're wondering, the little souvenir was wiped clean. I'm having some of my men check out possible places where people can buy stuff like that. Reminds me of the junk my mom used to keep on her tables in the living room."

"Detective, have you questioned everyone who was here at the time? We need to discover who the last person was to see him alive."

"Look, we've interviewed the whole lot. Most of them don't have good alibis. No one claims to have seen him last because they probably think it will incriminate them, and it would. I personally think someone has to be lying, but trying to figure out who is not going to be a picnic."

Arthur cleared his throat. "Detective, I'm sure Jillian can help you if you'll let her. She can talk to these people as a botanical insider and maybe find out things they'll never tell you."

Detective Noble looked at me warily, then sighed. "I'll ask my superiors. I don't care if you follow along, lady, but just don't get in my way. Murderers aren't the nicest people in the world, you know. In fact, they can be dangerous to your health if you know what I mean." His smile came off more as a sneer.

"I'll help in any way I can and I promise I won't get in your way. Although, I do have a question for you."

"Yeah? Shoot!"

"We noticed the overturned chair. Now that would indicate a struggle of some kind, wouldn't it? Which means the murder was not pre-meditated."

"Yeah, we thought of that. Means the victim may have known the person who shot him and tried to defend himself."

"Or maybe the person who shot him was trying to defend himself or herself." I spoke gently but decisively.

"Hey, that's pretty observant, Jillian. You may be of some help after all."

I laughed, taking no offense.

He excused himself from the table. "I'll let you know when I get word from my superiors. And Dr. Wingate, don't plan to go anywhere. I'll be in touch."

Arthur shook the detective's hand. Noble had one more request.

"I'd like a word with your secretary before I go."

Arthur nodded. "Certainly...certainly."

With a curt sort of respect, the detective nodded in return and headed for Helen's station.

Arthur watched him out of sight, then turned toward me. "Jillian, I need to have a meeting with Warren. We're going ahead with the project as best as we can whether we win or not."

"Please go right ahead. I'll see you tonight for dinner. What time would you like me to be there?"

"I think Diana said seven o'clock."

"Seven is fine. I'll see you then."

Arthur went into Warren's office and closed the door.

Detective Noble had evidently finished with Helen, because he joined me as I started to leave.

"I need to be going too. I'll give you a call as soon as I square it with my boss for you to be in on this investigation, Mrs. Bradley."

"Please call me Jillian, Detective. I insist."

"Whatever makes you happy, lady." He gave me a

small salute and walked out the front door. A tough sounding little man. I could only hope his bulldoggish personality would assist in solving the crime.

"Looks like they'll be in there for a while." Helen poured herself a cup of coffee. "Would you care for a refill? I can make a fresh pot if you want."

"I think I'd like that, if you don't mind."

"I don't mind at all. That's one reason I'm on the payroll."

"You say you're Dr. Wingate's administrative assistant...."

"Administrative assistant, office manager, secretary—whatever they want to call me, it's really all the same to me." She smiled a little.

"I'm sure you know everything that goes on around here, Helen."

"I do, and I don't. I've been working here for six years, and I'll tell you there's not a finer man to work with than Dr. Wingate. He's top of the line."

"I totally agree. How did you land this job, anyway?"

"You mean, how did a Native American girl like me land a swanky job like this?" She laughed.

"I wasn't implying...."

"Oh, it's okay. I'd probably wonder too, if I were you sitting there."

We talked for a few minutes about our families and places we had lived.

Then the phone rang again. After answering Helen handed it to me. "It's for you—Detective Noble."

"Thanks. Jillian here, Detective. What's going on?"

"I called the chief and he says to get all the help I can, so it's official. Can we meet somewhere so I can catch you up on what we know so far?"

"Sure. I'm staying at the Sanctuary, but since everyone else is too, we'd better meet somewhere a little less conspicuous, don't you think?"

"Yeah, I guess you're right. How about ZuZu's over

at the Valley Ho? You know where that is?"

"Yes, I've stayed there before. What time? I'm free until three o'clock this afternoon."

"Chief says I can treat you to lunch, so let's say noon. That all right with you?"

"Fine, see you then." I heard a click and surmised he'd hung up.

"Nice guy!" I laughed. "So Helen, you were saying how you got this job?"

"After twenty-five years, I retired from social services. During the last few years there, I took a few courses at the university in plant studies. I was fascinated with desert plants, particularly succulents and cacti, and I would go on hikes and tours of gardening centers in and around Phoenix.

"I even ventured to Sedona where I fell in love with the red rocks. Sedona is noted for its mystical qualities, and I felt it calling to me. It must be the spirit of my Pima grandfather. I enjoy the quiet peace that surrounds me whenever I make the journey. " She paused for a minute, her eyes seeming to gaze at a distant memory before she continued. "I'm sorry, Jillian. I'm digressing."

"Oh no! It's quite all right. You make me want to go there right now."

"Anyway, I met some friends of Dr. Wingate on these hikes of mine so when the job of administrative assistant came along, they recommended me. Dr. Wingate decided to hire me and here I am."

"Did you get to know Rene Parker at all before he died?"

"I only talked to him a little. He was friendly, confident, nice looking. I thought he got along with just about everyone."

"You say, *just about everyone*?"

"Well, I did notice a little friction when he was working with his team. You know how you can just feel stuff like that?"

"I think I know what you mean. Kind of like vibrations."

"Exactly."

My cellphone rang. I answered, surprised to hear Detective Noble's voice again.

"Jillian, we've had a development."

"What happened?" I lowered my voice.

"The Sanctuary has reported a missing security guard by the name of Simon Collier."

"How long has he been missing?"

"He was last seen when he reported for duty on the night after Rene Parker's murder. No one's seen him since."

"That's not good." Questions streamed through my mind. "Have they searched the area yet?"

"They begin this afternoon. Our men had to find out if anyone had seen him first, just as a precaution, but it doesn't look good. Jillian, keep this confidential until we do the search, just in case."

"I understand perfectly. Are we still on for lunch? I really need something to eat."

"Might as well, I can't get my team together until four o'clock because we're swamped with other cases."

"All right, I'll see you in about an hour. I'm leaving right now."

"What happened, Jillian?" Helen placed her hand on my arm.

"Oh, just police business, Helen. I'm not at liberty to say, but I'm sure we'll know more soon. I've got to go. I enjoyed getting to know you. And Helen, keep your eyes and ears open for me here."

"It will be my pleasure, Jillian."

Chapter 3

As I pulled into the hotel driveway, the valets were huddled together in front of the check-in stand. They were probably discussing the disappearance of the security guard.

I stopped the car and immediately two of the men approached, opened my door, and welcomed me back to the hotel.

"I'll need my car again at 11:30 am"

"No problem, Mrs. Bradley." The older of the two forced a smile as I gave him a tip. "Would you like a ride to your casita?"

"Yes, thank you."

He raised his hand and motioned for another valet to bring a golf cart from the end of the lot.

The young driver was quiet and since I had a lot on my mind we rode in silence, looking straight ahead until we had almost arrived at my casita.

Finally, he spoke. "Did you hear about our guard?"

Being careful not to divulge the fact that I knew he was missing, I acted casual. "What happened?"

"He's been missing for two days. His wife is worried sick. The police have been questioning people all over the place including us."

"I'm sorry about that. Was he ever gone before? I mean absent from work?"

"Old Simon?" He sounded defensive. "Not him. For one thing, he loved his job. Took his night guard shift quite seriously. He has a keen eye for anything suspicious going on. Gee, I hope nothing's happened to him. It would kill his wife. He has six grandkids. Talks about them all the time."

"I'm sure the police are doing everything they can. Let's pray that this is just some sort of mix up."

We pulled up to my casita.

"Here we are. Have a nice day, Mrs. Bradley."

His voice sounded heavy and concerned. I truly felt sorry for him. I tipped him and he drove the cart back down the hill.

I unlocked the door with my passkey and smiled when I heard Teddy's yips.

"Hello, boy."

I put my purse down on the glass entry table and picked him up.

"What's been going on around here this morning?" I looked at Teddy but directed my question to Cecilia as she stood up to greet me.

"We've had a little excitement. Did you hear about the missing guard?"

"Yes. The valet told me."

Cecilia picked up the room service tray and placed it outside the door. She came back and sat down facing me.

"I took Teddy for his walk, and we met the cutest little Maltese dog who's staying here."

Teddy's ears pricked up at the word *dog*.

"You'll never guess who it belonged to."

"Someone we know?"

"Indirectly. I did some research on our grant friends, the Hansens, and found out that this hotel is one of their regular haunts."

"That's amazing, Cecilia. And this dog belongs to them?"

"That's how I found out they own The Sanctuary. The guy walking Lila and I got to talking and he told me they were the owners and were staying here."

Teddy jumped down from my lap and ran to the door. He started scratching for a potty break.

"Jillian, I just brought him in. I don't think he needs to be let out."

"He doesn't want a break, Cecilia. This talk of Lila has him riled up."

Teddy became even more insistent at the mention of her name. I told Cecilia from now on we had to spell the name L-i-l-a to keep him calm.

"What else did you find out about the Hansens?"

"Just some basic facts—like Peter Hansen is a successful Wall Street investor with some highly successful business ventures on the side. He's a millionaire no doubt. His wife is from Arizona and holds a doctorate in education from the University of Arizona. They met when she got her first job in a company he owned. Evidently, they're happily married. He makes the money and she gives it away."

"On things like two million dollar grants for endangered species preservation."

"Endangered *plant* species to be specific." Cecilia grinned.

"Right, I suppose there's nothing unusual about wanting to use your husband's hard-earned money to support a worthy cause. Thanks for getting the information for me. Doesn't seem like there would be any motive for murder where the Hansens are concerned."

"I agree. I think I'll make some coffee." She moved to the bar, and started a pot with the supplies provided. Soon she was back for conversation.

I smiled. "The coffee smells wonderful. I think I'll

join you. Maybe a cup before I leave for lunch."

"I'll get it." Cecilia waved me toward the sofa. She poured fresh brew into two mugs, then brought one over and handed it to me.

I took a sip and thought for a minute. "Listen, after lunch I'll take Teddy on the groundskeeper's tour with me. I miss being with him and he'll have had his nap."

I picked up the newspaper. "At least the weather is nice today. I'm wearing my gardening hat, though. Taking no chances with sun damage."

The front-page carried a headline about the murder. There was an article about the Hansens on page two.

"You didn't tell me there was a picture of them in here. She's nice looking. He seems to be rather ordinary, but I guess he must be special to have earned all that money. It says here that the grant *was* to be awarded this coming week."

I rested the paper on my lap. "We just *have* to find the killer before they decide to leave."

***

The highly-acclaimed Valley Ho Hotel had been renovated in an original art deco style but with a contemporary twist. The color scheme was a tantalizing bright orange with touches of blues and greens. The focal point of the lobby was a long sleek fireplace filled with crushed white quartz covering the entire right wall. Guests conversed seated in comfortable chairs positioned in front of the fire. In one of the chairs, Detective Noble sat waiting. When I walked in, he stood to greet me.

Café ZuZu was located at the other end of the lobby. As we passed by the long, curved, granite bar I noted the clientele and surmised that this was where Scottsdale's younger professionals hung out. We reached the restaurant. A host led us to a booth along the wall facing the view of the pool and patio.

"This is nice of you, Detective." I glanced around to see what people were ordering.

"Welcome to Café ZuZu." The server handed us menus and took our orders for drinks. "I'll be back in a jiffy."

"The meatloaf looks excellent." I'd seen several orders at other tables. "I'm going to try it."

The server returned with our drinks, took our orders and left.

Detective Noble took out a small notebook from his pocket. "Thought I'd catch you up on everything we know so far, Mrs. Bradley."

I tried to ignore the fact he refused to call me Jillian.

"The victim was Rene Michel Parker, born in Ocala, Florida, age thirty."

"Michel?"

"Yeah, you know, it's French for Michael."

"I suppose he *was* French with a name like Rene. Please go on."

"Found dead at 8:00 am on the morning of Thursday last from a gunshot wound to the chest. The bullet removed was from a small .22 caliber handgun. The gun itself was not found on the premises. A small porcelain replica of a ghost orchid covered the wound. A chair was overturned. Fingerprints found were of the deceased and the occupier of the office, Mark Russell."

"Do you know about what time he was shot?"

"I'm coming to that. Time of death was determined to be somewhere between six and ten o'clock on that evening. There was a meeting with eleven colleagues, one of whom left before the others. That was Dr. Arthur Wingate.

"One Helen Morningstar stated she locked up after everyone left but doesn't remember if Rene Parker was among them. She states the time as 5:15 pm sharp.

"The lab workers had already left as well since the

lab closed at five o'clock. There were no cars parked out front when Helen left. All the lights were off and all the office doors locked according to her. She claimed she checked them personally. No one heard the shot."

"Did you find anything on Rene's body?"

"Yep. We found his wallet, car keys, and a note with directions to the office. And this is the best part, Mrs. Bradley, a key to Mark Russell's office."

"I see. This doesn't look good for Mark Russell, huh?"

"I'm afraid not. In fact, things look rather bad for him."

The server brought our food. She smiled. "Will there be anything else?"

"Not now, thanks." Noble picked up his sandwich and took a bite.

I silently thanked God for the food and asked for guidance as our meeting continued. I had a gut feeling about Mark Russell. I thought he seemed like a thoroughly nice young man, but I suppose I could be a bad judge of character. Anything's possible.

It was my turn for a question. "What did Mark say when you quizzed him about the key?"

"He seemed flabbergasted. Told me Rene had never even been near his office before that day as far as he knew. Said he was just as surprised as I was."

"Did you believe him?"

"I don't believe anybody, Mrs. Bradley. I only believe hard evidence. And I'm telling you—the fact that we found that key on Rene's body strongly suggests Mark gave it to him."

"Well, I think he must have been in Mark's office for some reason. Perhaps after Rene was murdered, Mark got scared and denied having given him the key. It's certainly possible, isn't it?"

"Oh, anything's possible. But people who lie are usually covering up something and I'm going to get the truth out of Mark Russell sooner or later."

"Detective, did you search Rene's room?"

"That was one of the first things we did, but all we found of interest was his laptop which we're going over with a fine-toothed comb."

"That's bound to turn up something interesting." I nodded in approval.

The server swept by and refilled our water glasses.

I had another thought. "What about Warren Burkett's alibi?"

"His actually checked out. He said he went home as usual and had dinner with his wife. They watched Extreme Home Makeover, a two-hour special, Jay Leno, and then the news. After that they went to bed."

"That sounds perfectly normal. But again, his wife could be covering for him."

"Yeah, but there's one thing that corroborates his story. He said he started receiving scam calls about 6:00 pm and the phone rang on and off all evening. Said he talked to several customer service people at the phone company. The records verify his story."

"So I suppose that lets Warren out. Besides, we have to think of a motive. Would someone on the Arizona team have a plausible reason to kill someone on the Florida team?"

"You want a motive? Ha! What do you call two million dollars? I call that a big motive."

He casually looked around the room.

"What are you looking at, Detective?"

"Just force of habit. For instance, I bet you didn't notice who came in a few minutes ago and just finished ordering—and please, don't look around."

"All right, I won't look around. Just tell me."

"It's Richard Sanchez and Tori DeMarco, the ones who *didn't* have dinner together that night."

"You think two co-workers having lunch together is suspicious, but not dinner?"

"Maybe. Looks like they've seen us. Richard just nodded, and now Tori is looking this way."

"We'll have to stop by their table on the way out," I said. "Now let's get back to the facts. I was wondering about alibis. Have you talked to all of the suspects yet?"

I took a bite of the delicious open-faced meatloaf sandwich covered with fontina cheese and mushroom gravy, flanked by Yukon mashed potatoes.

"So far, everyone on the Florida team says they came back to the hotel. The grant guy, Herbert Jamison, said he and his assistant went out to eat right after they left and then came back to the hotel around 8:00 pm. They went to their rooms and didn't see each other until the next day. We checked their stories and they pan out."

"Still, there are those two hours unaccounted for."

Detective Noble nodded. "Richard Sanchez and Tori DeMarco said they ate at the hotel but not together, and again they said they merely went back to their rooms to kick back."

"What about the Fontaines?"

"Vincent Fontaine said he and Leah came straight back to the hotel. However, they didn't eat together. Leah said she was under the weather and had her heart set on a little room service and bed. Vincent said he did the same."

"So far, no one has an airtight alibi that I can see."

Detective Noble had almost eaten his entire sandwich. Without looking up he said, "Now you see our problem."

"What about the Arizona team? I know Arthur said he went home early. Did you find out why?"

"Said he promised his wife he'd take her out to dinner and couldn't be late. He told me he had been working such long hours he felt bad about having to ignore her so much. I can relate to that with my own wife."

I smiled. "That sounds like Arthur. And what did

Helen Morningstar tell you?"

"Now there's a character. Helen lives with her sister over in Mesa. She told me they always go out and get something to eat on Friday nights and afterwards head over to this neighborhood joint where they listen to live music and watch people dance. Doesn't seem like the type."

"I guess anything's possible nowadays." I chuckled.

"We had no trouble making sure their story checked out. Seems they're well-known and everyone loves them."

"I'm glad for Helen. I really like her. But I like Mark Russell, too." I pushed my plate away. "I'm full. That was delicious meatloaf. This was the perfect choice for lunch. I appreciate you inviting me."

"My pleasure. Are there any other questions, Mrs. Bradley?"

"Well, I was just wondering if anyone owned a gun. And if money was a motive, who needed it badly enough to kill someone for it?"

"Excellent questions. As to the first, Richard Sanchez said he owned several guns back in Florida but hadn't brought any with him. Tori DeMarco said she carried a registered handgun to keep her ex-husband at a distance. Everyone else denied owning one."

"I wondered about Tori. That explains a lot. And did anyone need money?"

"That we're still checking on. But some people always need more money, know what I mean?"

"I think I do. For some, enough is never enough. Well, I must be getting back to the hotel. I have things to do before your search team gets there. Where would you like me to meet you?"

"Meet me? Oh, right. How about the front parking lot? That's where the guard was last seen." He motioned for the server to bring the bill. "Check, please."

Detective Noble paid with a credit card and we left

the booth. We stopped by and greeted Tori and Richard. They seemed a little surprised to see us together but kept to small talk and wished us luck in the investigation.

I finally got back to my room. It was nearly two o'clock. Teddy had to smell me all over to see where I'd been. He wagged his tail furiously. "You smell delicious, like meatloaf," he seemed to say. I picked him up and petted him as I sat down on the cozy sectional in front of the fire.

"How was lunch?" Cecilia acted interested.

"You'd love ZuZu's. Great meatloaf. Good thing I'm going on a walking tour this afternoon."

"Did you learn anything?"

"Unfortunately, it looks as though Mark Russell may be a prime suspect."

"Why him? Or should I ask?"

"Let's just say they found evidence to connect him. I've been sworn to secrecy not to divulge any details that might impede the investigation."

"I totally understand, Jillian. Walter tells me the police have to be extremely careful with information so they can prosecute effectively."

"Have you talked to him recently?"

"We stay in touch. He almost got married two years ago but she found someone else. It pretty much devastated him, but I think he's over it."

"What about you and that writer you were dating? Wasn't it this past summer?"

"Oh, him. We didn't see eye to eye on a lot of things, so we ended the relationship."

"It was so simple in my day. People fell in love and they got married. No one cared how old they were, or if they had their degrees, or even if there was a war on, which there was."

It struck again. I felt the sadness welling up inside me. I held Teddy closer as I thought of my husband and the war in Vietnam. *Jillian, get hold of yourself!*

"Come on, Jillian." Cecilia sounded soothing. "Don't worry about me. I'm only twenty-six. Besides, I love my job at the paper and I love working for you. I'm sure I'll meet someone eventually, but I do hope it's before I'm thirty." She winked at me. "Hey, you'd better give Teddy to me while you get ready for your tour. It's almost three o'clock."

***

With Teddy on his leash, I put on my wide-brimmed straw hat and we walked down to the Sanctuary Spa Patio where I was to meet the groundskeeper and begin the tour. I only had to wait a minute.

The ruggedly handsome groundskeeper greeted me.

"Mrs. Bradley? For the three o'clock tour?" He smiled. "And I see your little dog is coming along.".

"This is Teddy."

"And I'm Jeff Gorman, the groundskeeper here at the Sanctuary."

"Nice to meet you, Jeff."

He was in his forties I guessed, with sandy blond hair and skin that was a bit on the weathered side from being outdoors all the time.

He spoke in a quiet, friendly manner. "I feel a little intimidated showing someone of your gardening fame around. I hope you'll enjoy the tour."

"I always enjoy seeing plants in their habitats, especially these desert flora specimens. I've been admiring them since I arrived."

We meandered through the cart paths and walkways as Jeff pointed out the various plants he so lovingly cared for.

"You'll notice the desert spoon here in front of the mountain laurel." He pointed. "All of these desert trees and shrubs are producing seedpods at this time of year which are eaten by birds. The birds digest the seeds and excrete them into the soil which produces the seed culture to grow a new plant."

"The cycle is quite amazing."

We proceeded along the granite path until we came to a century plant that had recently bloomed.

Jeff pointed to the smaller plants coming from the base. "The century plant is an exception to the seedpod rule. The plant dies after blooming, but it leaves pups which then become the new plants."

He pointed out native foothills palo verde trees, some of which were over one hundred years old, and ironwood trees used by the Indians to build their homes. Jeff explained that ironwood was such an extremely hard wood that it was used to make everything from durable homes for the Indians to airline propellers. My favorites were the sweet acacias and Chilean mesquite trees with their tiny fairy-like fern leaves.

My tour guide pointed out magnificent organ pipe cacti, Argentina torch, palm canyon Mexican fan palms, giant bird of paradise, pencil cactus, purple prickly pears, beaver tail, old man and fish hook cacti, and numerous other plants growing on the property. We talked about their different characteristics as we walked.

The conversation made me want to make a return trip in the spring to witness the blooming season. I let Teddy walk along from time to time to enjoy the different smells but kept a close eye on him.

Jeff showed me the pet lawn and then we walked over to a charming patio terrace in between the restaurant and meeting rooms where they held small weddings. I wondered if Mark Russell would ever have a chance at happiness like that. I also thought of Cecilia and hoped for a wedding in her near future.

"Here's something I think you'll find interesting." Jeff gestured as we came to a large casita.

Teddy began to bark and I had to shush him to be quiet.

"This is one of our private residences we rent out on occasion to VIPs. If you look in the back yard you'll see a beautiful garden surrounding the pool. And over here," he pointed toward the picture window, "grows a boojum tree."

"Those are extremely rare, aren't they, Jeff?"

"Extremely. This one is worth between $10,000 and $15,000. The value depends on the height of the trunk. The previous guests wanted it cut down because it blocked their view of the pool until I told them what it was worth."

He smiled in satisfaction at having rescued the rare tree.

"Who's staying there now?" I asked. "The Hansens, perhaps?"

He looked truly surprised. "How did you know?"

I laughed. "Our dogs have met."

"I see. So you've met Lila have you, Teddy?"

It was too late. Teddy heard the name and started barking so I suggested we get on with the tour. Jeff showed me a magnificent easter cactus that he was particularly proud of and apologized that it wasn't in bloom. After about forty-five minutes we came out onto the front parking lot.

"I wanted to share something really unique." Jeff gave a warning glance. "You'd better pick Teddy up and hold him for the next plant I'm going to show you."

I did, and we walked past the golf carts to where the pavement met the desert.

He pointed to a hairy looking cactus covered with thick yellow and black thistles. "This specimen is the cholla cactus, or some people call it, the *jumping cholla.*"

I inadvertently blurted out, "*Cylindropuntia fulgida!* I've never seen one up close."

"That's just the point, Mrs. Bradley. You don't *want*

to get close to this plant. Golfers swear that the plants attack them as they walk by on the course if they're anywhere near one. Actually, that's why we planted this one as far away from the hotel as we did. Let me show you."

Jeff slowly moved his shoe close to a piece of cholla that had fallen off on the ground. The thorny piece seemed to attach itself to his shoe immediately.

"The plant discards lower limbs from time to time, and the limbs attach themselves to animals passing by. The animals carry them to a site where, after they are dropped off, they propagate themselves in the new ground. The thistles on the main plant protect it from predators that eat the fruit. They seem to be reaching out. An illusion, of course."

Teddy began barking and shaking a little in my arms. I stroked his fur, trying to soothe him.

"Shhh, Teddy. That cholla's not going to get you."

Jeff looked up and pointed to the top of the cholla. "He might sense that nest up there belonging to a cactus wren family. They protect their nests from predators by hiding it in the cactus's foliage. Most other animals know better than to approach the dangerous spines. The cactus wrens are about the only ones who can get anywhere near this plant."

Teddy continued to shake and bark, so I decided to stop. I thanked Jeff for such an informative tour. He gave me his business card and offered to help in any way. He was quite kind, so I took the card and placed it in my pocket.

Teddy was still shaking when I returned to the room. I explained to Cecilia what had happened. She laughed, but assured me she would distract him with a treat or two and put him down for a nap. I took Jeff's card from my pocket and placed it in my wallet for safekeeping. I only had a few minutes to put my hat away, run a brush through my hair, and grab a jacket in case I needed one on the search. I felt a foreboding as I headed back out the door.

"Lord, please help us find Simon and please let him be alive."

Several police cars, including a jeep, had pulled up in front of the hotel as I arrived.

Detective Noble stepped out of the jeep dressed in a brown jumpsuit with "Police" marked in yellow letters on the back of it. I wore sensible shoes, jeans, and a sweatshirt. He nodded at me approvingly.

Two men leading search dogs joined him.

"Ready, Mrs. Bradley?" He introduced me to Sergent Bryers and Sergent Niemi and to the dogs, Robo and Sam.

"Please call me Jillian." The men nodded without smiling.

Detective Noble looked at his watch. "Let's go, men."

We walked over to the carts, and the police gave the dogs one of Simon's shirts to smell to get his scent. The dogs barked and whined then started sniffing the carts. Within minutes, Robo let out a loud bark soon joined by Sam.

"It looks like we got something, lady. Men, take a look at this cart here in back but don't touch anything."

The men dusted for prints, took tape samples, and tested for blood.

"Looks like this may have been the cart Simon was in that night. It's been parked in back like someone was trying to hide it."

"Look at the tires." I pointed. "They're covered with sand and plant material."

"Sir." Sergent Niemi spoke up. "We've identified the blood sample as human."

"That was fast." I was amazed.

"The equipment does the work, ma'am." The Sergeant grimaced, apparently not willing to take too much credit.

"Well, you work it very nicely."

He blushed. "Thank you, ma'am."

Detective Noble was getting excited. "Look for tracks, men. This cart's been for a ride in the desert." Noble stood at the end of the pavement and looked out into the rugged landscape. "We don't have much daylight left but I don't see any choice except to do a search."

Sergent Bryers ran up to us. "Sir, we found tracks leading in."

"That's good enough for me. We'll follow them to see where the cart's been. Let's go, people."

The men and dogs led the way on foot. Detective Noble and I followed alongside in the jeep. The horizon was flat desert landscape, but soon a flock of large birds began congregating over something, circling in the sky.

"Look over there." I pointed. "Over there, where those birds are circling the rocks."

He shouted for the men and dogs to get into the jeep and we headed to the spot.

"I'm calling for backup, Jillian." Detective Noble took out his phone.

Chapter 4

It wasn't what I'd hoped to find. Poor Simon's body lay face up with sightless eyes. Hungry birds circling overhead had taken their toll.

"Lord God, please have mercy on his family." My response was heartfelt.

Detective Noble placed a hand on my shoulder as we stood in the open field. "It doesn't seem fair, does it? He was just doing his job and someone bashed his head in."

"No." I was at a loss for words. "No, it's not fair."

"Well, we're going to get whoever did this. Criminals always mess up sooner or later."

I felt an overwhelming sense of bitterness. "Let's hope for his family's sake they mess up sooner, rather than later."

The back of Simon's head had suffered blunt force trauma causing a large loss of blood. He looked so small lying there, surely no match for a crazed killer. Someone had attempted to cover the body with a few rocks and brush but the birds found him anyway.

The ambulance arrived with flashing red and white lights. The detective and I stepped into the background while they worked to confirm it a death. For crime documentation purposes, the police took photographs, placed the body in a zippered bag, then on a gurney. The ambulance doors slammed shut with finality and drove away, its tires crackling on the dry desert rocks.

I felt so sorry for his family. Surely, they would be grief stricken.

We got in the jeep and headed back with the search dogs in tow. Sergent Bryers and Sergent Niemi would stay behind with the forensics team to collect evidence.

The road was bumpy as we headed back onto the main road.

"Are you going to tell his family, Detective?"

"Yeah, it's part of my job. The worst part, I might add."

I returned to my room and told Cecilia the bad news.

Teddy comforted me and gave me a warm lick on my cheek.

"Thanks, boy."

Cecilia hugged me. "I'm sorry, Jillian."

Sirens blared and lights flickered through our window as the police did their job.

"You think this is tied to Rene's murder, don't you?" Cecilia's gaze was penetrating.

I wiped my brow. The search had been exhausting. Now my adrenaline was returning to normal.

"The time frame sure fits. The murderer is probably staying here at the Sanctuary. I don't think anything will make sense until we find out the reason for the first murder.

"I keep asking myself, 'What was he doing in Mark Russell's office at that time of night?' If he was going to meet someone, why meet there?

"Rene must have been doing something on Mark's computer and I'll bet it had something to do with the Arizona project. The Florida data wouldn't be on Mark's computer. So far the police haven't mentioned finding any entries of interest but they'll keep looking."

"Maybe someone stopped Rene by killing him."

Cecilia walked over to the window and looked out.

I sat down and considered. "Anything's possible. I have to start talking to the Florida people if we're going to get anywhere but I'm exhausted from this afternoon."

"How does a pot of tea sound?"

"Like exactly what I need. Thank you. I probably should start getting ready for the dinner tonight. I don't want to go, but I promised Arthur and Diana I'd come at the first opportunity."

"It will do you good, Jillian. Perhaps it will at least clear your mind a little and well, you have to eat. You said you were taking Teddy along, didn't you?"

"Yes, as a matter of fact I am."

"Great. That will give me a chance to do some work for the paper."

She sat down at the desk and began to write.

I picked Teddy up, set him next to me and opened my laptop. I lovingly stroked his fur and he melted some of my tiredness away. After spending a few minutes catching up on e-mails I read an interesting question regarding bulbs. They mentioned them as a way to have something always blooming in your garden. It distracted me for a bit but soon enough the depression returned.

I logged off and laid my head back on the sofa.

Cecilia answered the door for room service and set the tray down on the ottoman in front of the sofa.

Teddy looked up at me and said, "I'm hungry now. Would you please feed me?"

I accepted the cup of tea that Cecilia proffered. "Thank you. I guess you'd better feed him so he'll be ready to go, although I'm sure he'll do his share of begging when we're at the Wingate's."

Cecilia prepared his dinner of ground turkey, mixed vegetables, rice, fruit, and shredded cheese. She poured him a tiny cup of milk, set it on the floor, and gave him a fresh bowl of water.

I drank the delicious jasmine tea, so nice and hot. This depression got me nowhere. It was time to work. Hard work and determination were the only way to solve this, and solve it I would.

Dinner would be soon. With more care than usual I began to dress in my pink and black crewel jacket and black skinny jeans. I topped off the outfit with a black boa scarf for warmth. Since it had been a gift, it would be a reminder of God's support. I would have to get tough. I would have to be impartial. I had to do it for poor Simon.

After I inserted my shiny black earrings, cleaned my glasses, and applied a spritz of perfume on my neck and wrists, I was all set. On to the Wingate's.

**

Overlooking the Fort McDowell Indian Reservation was the newer neighborhood of Fountain Hills. The homes were not as expensive as those of Paradise Valley, but they were nice. People were just now discovering their exclusivity and snapped them up whenever they went on sale. Arthur and Diana had done just that and considered themselves most fortunate to have purchased their home before the prices had really gone up.

I turned into a circular driveway and parked at their front entrance. The beautiful desert landscaping was illuminated with solar lights. The number of integrated varieties of cacti as well as desert grasses was impressive.

Diana was happy to see me when we arrived and gushed over Teddy, which he loved. She had a gorgeous tan that set off her turquoise jewelry exquisitely and wore her short blond hair in a style that conveyed a weekly visit to a stylist.

She worked as a concierge at the Royal Palms Hotel.

She was great with people and really enjoyed her job. Once she told me she worked solely to have money to spend on her wardrobe. Her tastes were expensive. She never expected Arthur to pay for her extravagances and so Arthur never complained.

Delicious aromas from the kitchen filled the air. This was my first visit to their home and I was impressed with its sophisticated southwest décor.

Arthur took me outside on the large, covered patio with a magnificent view of the sunset and proceeded to give me a short tour of the back yard. He had planted a stunning garden full of statuesque cacti and desert trees highlighted with the same solar lighting as in front. Magenta bougainvillea and orange, yellow, and lavender lantana meandered through the rock and gravel paths. I thought these gardens were certainly a contrast to the almost non-existent landscaping surrounding his office.

We had just finished the tour when Diana brought out a tray of drinks and appetizers. She placed them on the glass patio table as we sat down on the comfortably padded wrought iron chairs. We enjoyed polite conversation as we sipped our drinks of sweet tea and munched on jalapeño stuffed mushrooms. I helped myself to some mixed nuts and realized I was hungry even after the hearty meatloaf sandwich I enjoyed at ZuZu's.

"Dinner's almost ready, Jillian." Diana started to go back into the house, but then she turned and looked straight into my eyes. "We heard they found that security guard. It was on the news. Just dreadful. Arthur said you were working with the police."

"I was there when they found him. It was horrible, Diana."

"I understand, Jillian." Arthur shuddered. "Finding Rene dead like that was something I'll never be able to forget. Sometimes I wake up dreaming I'm finding him all over again. I have a hard time getting back to sleep, I'm telling you."

"Well, we're going to find out who did it." I thought of Simon's family.

Arthur went to Diana's side, and placed his arm around her waist as if to steady her. "This has been a terrible strain on both of us, Jillian. We've gone over who could possibly have committed such a heinous crime and so close to home. Vincent? Leah? Tori? Richard? None of them seems likely, and yet one of them must have killed him. None of our people even knew Rene that well."

We all walked back into the house and Arthur escorted me into the dining room. Diana excused herself and went to the kitchen to put the finishing touches on our dinner. He pulled a chair out for me and scooted me toward the table. After he seated himself, I peered at him and shook my head.

"Arthur, I think we seriously need to look at the possibility that the answer lies in the grant. Now if you won, how were you going to spend the two million?"

"We had this plan. The donors would have distributed the grant over a period of two years with $250,000 given at the first of each quarter. We had planned to purchase land with the first check — that would get us started. Then we would put in a visitor center to act as a natural deterrent to predators that are causing the species extinction."

"I assume the Florida team has a spending plan as well."

"That was part of the submittal. We had to have a plan in place to spend the grant if we won."

We both looked up as Diana wheeled in a serving cart loaded with a platter of baked ham accompanied by bowls of Cabernet-infused cranberry relish, cheese-scalloped potatoes, and steaming fresh sautéed green beans with almonds. A basket of warm crescent rolls and a dish of butter sat on the bottom shelf.

"This looks absolutely delicious." Teddy sat at attention by my chair. "God bless you for preparing this meal, Diana."

"Why, thank you, Jillian." She passed me the platter of ham. "We're just grateful you're here to support us."

After I filled my plate and started eating, from time to time I slipped Teddy a morsel or two. We were halfway through the meal when the phone rang in the kitchen. Diana rose to get it.

"Thanks, honey." Arthur took a bite of the cheese-scalloped potatoes.

Diana came back with the phone in her hand. "Arthur, it's for you. It's Helen and she sounds pretty upset."

She handed him the phone. We watched his expression turn to shock and concern as he listened.

"What's the matter?" Diana's question blended with Arthur's reaction to the call.

"Is everything all right?" Apprehension chilled me.

Arthur put the phone down on the table and looked first at Diana and then at me. "Mark Russell is in the emergency room. He's just been in a terrible car accident and they're trying to stabilize him. Helen just got there. She says he's hurt badly and is unconscious. She's waiting for the doctor to tell her what his chances are."

"Does Mark have any family here? I thought I remembered he wasn't married."

"I don't think he has anyone living close by. He probably listed Helen as his emergency contact."

The phone rang again and Arthur picked up immediately.

"Yes, Helen. He's at the NextCare Urgent Care on Shea Boulevard. Got it. We'll be right there."

"Jillian, I think you'd better start praying." Diana looked concerned.

"I already have. Come on Teddy, we're going now."

I scooped him up and grabbed my purse from the back of the chair. "I'll follow you, Arthur."

"I think I should stay here." Diana sat down. "Why don't you leave Teddy with me? I'll take care of him until you get back, then you and Arthur can drive over together."

"I hope we won't be long. If they put Mark in ICU, we won't even be allowed in since we're not relatives."

"Let's go. Sorry the dinner was spoiled, darling." Arthur's tone was loving. He placed a kiss on her cheek.

"I'm just sorry for Mark — you both get going. I'm sure Helen needs you to be there with her. Jillian, I'll see you later."

"Thanks again for everything, Diana. We'll be back soon, Teddy."

Arthur drove as fast as he could without going over the speed limit. We sat in silence. I wondered what we would find once we arrived.

Helen was waiting in the clinic lobby for us, still wearing her coat and carrying her huge black purse which looked more like a briefcase.

"Thank the Lord you're here. I'm still waiting for the doctor to tell me about his condition."

Arthur put his arm around her small frame and told her to sit down and tell us what happened.

We each took a chair.

Helen began at the beginning.

"I got a phone call from the receptionist here asking me to come down because Mark had been involved in an automobile accident. I started asking all sorts of questions, but she suggested I come get the facts. That way, she said, I would be able to talk directly to the doctor taking care of him. I came as soon as I could. When I got here, Mark was in the emergency room. The doctor said he was in a coma and they were trying to determine if they could save him or not. That's what I'm waiting to find out."

"Helen, what about the other car? Did they say what happened?" I had to wonder.

"Yeah." She swallowed hard. Before going on she looked first at Arthur, then at me.

"Head-on collision. The other driver and a passenger were killed on impact. Some nurses were talking. They said they didn't even live long enough to get to the hospital. And…." Helen started to cry.

Arthur and I tried to console her.

"No, I must tell you." She caught her breath. "It was a mother and her little eight-year old girl."

We decided to let her cry on Arthur's shoulder.

I found a fountain with cups nearby and brought her some water. As I handed her the cup, the doctor came out and walked over to where we sat. He looked young but had a kind and intelligent face.

"I'm Dr. Kelly." He shook hands with all of us.

We introduced ourselves as colleagues and braced for what he might tell us.

"Mr. Russell is presently in a coma, but our tests show he may come out of it within the next twenty-four hours. He's suffered a tremendous amount of trauma to the head. If he hadn't had the air bag or the seat belt I don't think he'd be alive."

Helen stopped crying. "You think he'll pull through, Doctor?"

"Possibly. We have to drain the blood buildup in his brain and that will be touch and go."

"Jillian, we need to pray, right now. Dr. Wingate, do you mind?" Helen had no idea how he would respond.

"Of course not, Helen." He smiled. "Mark is going to need all the help he can get."

Helen and I bowed our heads and took turns praying softly that God would be with the doctors as they treated Mark. We prayed for the woman's family who not only lost her, but a child as well.

Soon we watched them wheel Mark into ICU with IVs hooked up to both arms and his head bandaged from the eyes up. There were cuts and bruises over the rest of his face and his hands from where the windshield had shattered upon impact and cruelly lacerated his body.

We started for the front door. "Do you want us to drive you home, Helen?" Arthur's tone was kind.

"No, I'm going to be all right. The crying helped. I know God is in control. He'll see me home okay." She smiled.

"I'll call tomorrow and check on Mark, and then give you a call, if you like." He held the door open for her.

"I'll give Dr. Kelly my e-mail so we can keep in touch."

Helen nodded once. "Please do. I'll come see him whenever they allow it. You can count on me."

She said goodbye and walked toward her car.

When we got back to the Wingates and gave Diana the news, none of us had much to say. Three deaths and Mark in critical condition all in one day...it was too much.

Teddy jumped up into my arms and looked at me as if to say, "I'm ready to get back home. Can we please go?"

I couldn't help but crack a smile at him, grateful for the small break in my gloomy emotional state.

After thanking the Wingates for their hospitality, I drove back to the hotel with a heavy heart. I'd heard of people going through trials, but I'd never experienced so much heartache in such a short time. In my own experience, nothing could be as heartbreaking as losing a husband...but then, a child....

My thoughts turned to the two victims of the crash and my emotions got the better of me. I took a deep breath and petted Teddy on my lap as we drove. I wondered if the murderer of Rene Parker let their emotions get the better of them and shot him as a result. A thought occurred—strong men don't usually show emotions.

What if a woman had shot Rene? Perhaps getting to know Leah and Tori better would give me some leads. I would find a way.

Arriving back at The Sanctuary, I secured Teddy with his leash and one of the young men drove us back to the casita in a golf cart. The valets were normally groomed for polite conversation so it was obvious he was preoccupied.

"I'm so sorry Simon's dead." I patted his arm. "Have you heard how his family is doing?"

"Mary's taking it pretty hard. Fortunately, the people who own this hotel are going to see that she's taken care of. That's what our supervisor said."

"That's generous of them." Yes, the Hansens were good people.

We pulled up in front of my casita.

"Thank you." I gave him a small tip.

I climbed off the cart and carried Teddy to the front door.

"Goodnight, Mrs. Bradley. Take care of yourself. That murderer is still out there."

I nodded with seriousness. "I know. I will. You do the same."

Cecilia was dressed for bed but sat watching the late night news. She turned her attention to me as I came in.

"Jillian."

Teddy jumped down and ran to her. He hopped up on the sofa and gave her some dog kisses, wagging his tail as fast as he could.

"I'm glad to be home," he seemed to say.

"Do you want me to take him out or is he ready to turn in?"

"I'll take him over to the dog lawn. You're all ready for bed and the walk will clear my head."

She shook her head slowly from side to side in disbelief as I relayed a brief account of Mark's accident.

We sat in silence for a moment afterward.

"This has been a dark day."

"I'll tell you what. I'll make you a spa appointment tomorrow. One of those herbal wraps, I think."

I smiled. "You know me way too well."

"I do. Now off on your walk. You need a little communion with nature." She shooed me, "Go!"

I grinned. It wasn't a frequent occurrence for Cecilia to get bossy. Usually that was my job.

"We'll be back soon."

I left her then and stepped into the dry night air.

The dog lawn was pristine and inviting, nearly the only thing here not desert flora. A woman sat on a bench holding a white bundle. Teddy barked and I assumed he was being territorial. Scooping him up gently, I told him to shush. He just whined loudly as if I was torturing him.

The woman turned. Elise Hansen! Yes, I recognized her from meeting her previously and from her picture in the newspaper article. The white bundle turned out to be a tiny Maltese perched smugly in her lap. The dog was perfectly groomed, including a tiny pink clip with one large rhinestone on the top of her head which held back her long white bangs.

Elise looked only vaguely like her picture. It was the sort of resemblance that a grown woman of forty has to her high school yearbook portrait. She must have had the picture taken it quite a few years ago because she looked about my age, or older, with a short bob of gray hair. She wore a nice navy jogging suit with a pink and navy trimmed shell. The pink and white tennis shoes looked expensive. Even in the dark, her complexion looked younger than the rest of her body. Probably Botox or a facelift.

Most women who have money usually find ways to

spend it improving their bodies.

"Excuse my dog for barking so, but I think Teddy and your dog have met. That is if her name is Lila."

"I'm sure that's entirely possible. I have someone walk my dog in the mornings and afternoons. I like to take her out for her evening time—it gives me a chance to get some fresh air and just be with her...no distractions."

"I know what you mean. My assistant comes with me on trips to take care of Teddy when I'm working, but it's nice to have a few moments alone together. I'm Jillian Bradley."

We shook hands.

"And I'm Elise Hansen. Of course you've met Lila." She smiled.

"Actually, you and I have met once, but it was on another occasion. Teddy was with Cecilia the other day when he met Lila. After that, I've had to spell her name to keep him from barking. I think he has a crush."

Teddy wiggled and writhed and I finally let him loose. Lila jumped down off Elise's lap and joined him on the lawn. They romped as though they were old friends, getting all tangled up in their leashes. We smiled as we tried to untangle them.

"I guess dogs just love to play together." Elise shook her head. "But her coat gets matted so easily. We'd better be getting back. I enjoyed meeting you again, Jillian."

"The pleasure was all mine, Elise. Maybe we'll see each other later while we're here."

"Maybe so. Well, I must say goodbye."

Elise led Lila away pulling her on the leash. Lila kept turning around and barking at Teddy as if to say, "I hope we'll meet again, too."

I looked at my watch and noticed the time—11:00 pm. Except for a couple of people in the Jade Bar, there wasn't another living soul around. We meandered over to the parking lot where our search for Simon had begun. I noticed how dark the area looked. Not really safe to be out so late.

Only one person in the valet stand. Cars seemed to have stopped coming and going for the night. It was eerily quiet and I wondered where the security guard was.

With Teddy calm, I held him in my arms and continued to walk observing what might have occurred around the same time the guard had disappeared.

A voice from behind startled me. "Can I help you, ma'am?"

I turned and saw a man wearing a suit. "You surprised me!"

The man smiled and explained they were keeping a watchful eye on the parking lot to see if anyone would return to the scene of the crime.

I looked around. "This place is truly isolated at night. And I'm sure the later it gets, the more isolated it becomes, wouldn't you agree?"

"We're keeping an eye out here, ma'am. You'd better be getting inside for the night. I'll have the valet run you back."

"Thank you. I was actually rather dreading that hill."

The valet shined his flashlight on the floor of the cart so I could see to get in safely, then drove me back to my casita.

"I don't have my purse with me to give you a tip."

"There's no need. I know you're trying to help find who killed Simon and that's enough tip for me."

"Thank you, young man. I'm certainly going to do my best. Goodnight."

"Goodnight, Mrs. Bradley. Goodnight, Teddy."

Teddy barked, "Goodnight" in return as the cart drove away.

"I guess everyone knows who you are by now. You're one special little dog, Teddy, and I love you."

I took the passkey from my pocket and unlocked the door.

The police are at the hotel.

I would certainly sleep more soundly just knowing that.

Chapter 5

Cecilia was an early riser. This was fortunate since I am not.

"Good morning, Cecilia." I walked slowly to the coffee pot. "I really appreciate your having the coffee ready this morning."

Teddy followed closely behind but acted much too peppy. It was early...pre-coffee early.

I motioned to him. "I'll get your treats in just a second."

"Headed for the gym, I see." Cecilia scrutinized my walking attire. "I have your e-mails up if you care to read them before you go. I noticed one from Dr. Wingate you might want to check."

The coffee steamed and smelled delicious as I poured the dark brew into my cup. "I probably should. Could be important."

I situated myself at the laptop, gave one more morning stretch, and scrolled down to his message:

They've scheduled Mark's surgery for seven o'clock this morning. Helen will be there and will keep us informed. Continue to pray. -Arthur

"Cecilia, keep an eye on my e-mails today. Check them every half hour or so. Call me on my cell if either Arthur or Helen sends anything, will you?"

"Of course. And your spa appointment at nine o'clock this morning?" She fetched Teddy's leash. Time for his morning walk.

"I'll see what happens. Right now, I'd better go exercise or I'll never make it. Order some breakfast for me will you? Something healthy but not that gritty protein drink."

"I'll have it delivered in an hour."

"I'm out the door." I grabbed my gym bag. "See you in about forty-five minutes. Be a good dog, Teddy."

I petted him, gave him a quick kiss, and headed out the door.

***

There were quite a few people already working out as I walked through the fitness center doors and glanced around. I placed my bag on the shelf, along with my jacket, and took a towel from a basket before stepping onto the treadmill. I noticed Leah Fontaine exercising on the elliptical machine so I made friendly eye contact.

Ten...fifteen...twenty minutes at level three. I started to perspire.

Leah turned off her machine. Time for me to quit as well.

My heart rate was in the target range. Good. I got off.

Leah headed into the bathroom so I grabbed my bag and jacket and followed her, making it appear as if I had a reason for being there.

"Good morning, Dr. Fontaine." I smiled.

"Hello, Mrs. Bradley. Nice to see you again." She took a brush from her bag.

I placed my bag next to hers and did the same. "How

is your team holding up with everything going on? You heard about the guard, I'm sure." I sincerely hoped this sounded like nonchalant conversation.

"Yes, we heard. Most unfortunate."

"I heard the Hansens plan to take care of the family which is most admirable, I think. Don't you?"

She placed her brush back into her bag."I didn't know that, but yes, that's good. I believe the Hansens own this hotel, don't they?" She picked up her bag and started to leave.

I wanted to keep this going. "Yes. They're staying here in one of the private homes.

"Dr. Fontaine, I was wondering if you'd like to be my guest for lunch today. I wanted to visit some of these wonderful galleries and would love for you to go with me. That is if you're interested in art." I followed her out the front door.

"Well, I had no plans. I think I would like that, Mrs. Bradley."

"There's only one condition." I smiled.

"And that is?"

"You have to call me Jillian."

"All right, Jillian. And it's Leah."

"Thank you, Leah. I'll meet you in the lobby at eleven-thirty if that suits you. We can take my car."

"See you then." She smiled just a little.

Cecilia had ordered me the most delicious breakfast I've had in a long time: Chicken Benedict with grilled asparagus and tomatoes lightly sauced with a low calorie Hollandaise. The perfectly grilled chicken melted in my mouth. Since I was hungry, I proceeded to eat with enthusiasm.

"Good call, Cecilia." My compliment was sincere. "Have you heard anything from Arthur?"

I took another bite.

"Just checked and nothing so far."

"Well, no news is good news. I'll keep praying."

The spa treatment was heaven. When I returned to my room, I sank down into the plush chair and felt my shoulders totally relax.

Wait. I got up and peered into the bedrooms.

"Cecilia?"

They must have gone out. I moved my laptop forward and checked my e-mail. Thirty-eight new messages, most of them questions for my column. I scrolled down and found one from Arthur. It read:

> *Mark's out of surgery; condition still undetermined. Helen's with him. I'm going to relieve her this afternoon. Will stay in touch.*
> *-Arthur*

I replied, promising to drop by that evening to take a turn and let Helen have a break. Time to dress for lunch and prep for taking Leah around the galleries. A quick browse through the internet gave me all of the information I needed on the places I wanted to visit. I was even able to make a noon reservation for two at the Roaring Fork Restaurant.

I made it to the lobby where Leah waited for me. She wore her hair loose, held back with a fashionable leather headband. Her outfit was simple—a pale yellow, long-sleeved silk shirt worn underneath a brown suede jacket, and jeans. Her low-heeled boots were well polished and she carried a fashionable Coach bag.

"Hello, Leah. Thanks for having lunch with me."

"Hello. I'm ready."

I called for a valet to get my car.

"I hope you like southwestern fare." I wanted to break the ice that had surrounded our previous conversation.

"Oh, that's fine. I like just about anything."

We pulled away from the parking lot. Leah kept her eyes forward peering straight ahead which I found somewhat unusual. Hoping to engage her in conversation I tried again. "How do you like the Sanctuary?"

"The rooms are comfortable, but it's a little too modern for my tastes."

"I think it's indicative of the Scottsdale area. I've stayed at a few hotels here and they seem to have that in common. Have you been on the garden tour that the groundskeeper gives?"

"Yes, that's one of the first things I did when I arrived. I'm captivated by flora of any type." She seemed to warm up just a little.

"I took the tour yesterday afternoon with Teddy."

She finally looked at me. "You must be quite attached to your dog to have brought him with you."

"My husband died right after we were married. Teddy is my companion of sorts. Are you married, Leah?"

She immediately looked away and out the window.

"No."

Hmm, not a good conversational choice when the subject drives her back into herself.

She looked down at her lap for a moment before she spoke. "It's okay, Jillian. I just never had the time, really. I've either always been going to school or working at the Society. I graduated from high school a year early and finished my degree in three years so I could get my PhD in another two."

"What was the hurry?"

"I really couldn't tell you. I just feel at home with research."

"You should be proud of your accomplishments, Leah. After all, not many people your age have done what you have. Just think. You may win a two million dollar grant. Do you mind me asking what you're planning to do with it if you win?"

"Oh, we have plans. I've delegated the funds to my staff equally so each department can implement their work."

"I see, so each department would receive $125,000 apiece in the first quarter. That is if Rene had lived...."

"The money still goes to the Research and Technology division. Richard Sanchez, of course, heads the Field Studies division."

I noticed that Leah became more animated when discussing her work. She seemed to have relaxed a little by the time we pulled into the parking lot of the Roaring Fork. We walked inside and gave our names to the host. Still not knowing which track to take with this sophisticated young woman, I said, "Arthur intimated that your father was here on behalf of your being a little under the weather."

She stiffened a little and looked at me.

"Dr. Wingate told you that?"

She turned back, looked straight ahead again, and said, almost under her breath, "That's interesting."

"Perhaps he was mistaken." I hoped she would respond somehow.

"I'm fine, really, Jillian. I just wonder where he got an idea like that, that's all."

"Maybe from your father?"

"Maybe. I'll be sure and ask him when we get back."

"Leah, one of the best things they have here is...." I pointed to the menu item, because the title included a swear word.

"You should try it with a side of their Green Chili Macaroni and Cheese. Absolutely to die for! However," I perused the menu, "For me...I'm going to try the Boneless Fried Chicken with loaded mashed potatoes and peppercorn gravy. I'm really hungry!"

As if she was ignoring me, Leah only ordered a bowl of tortilla soup and a small salad. I ordered the Fried Avocado with spice crab Remoulade as an appetizer. The server took our orders, acknowledged my request for bringing only half, and left. Leah was difficult to reach…a new tactic was in order, so I asked about her family. The ploy worked.

"Well, you know my father, and that he's worked for the Florida Department of Agriculture since the beginning of time." She smiled. "He's a brilliant scientist and I've always admired him. I've always wanted to follow in his footsteps."

She peered at the tablecloth.

"What about your mother?"

"She and my father divorced when I was a child. They drifted apart because my father was so engrossed in his work. She was jealous and finally had enough, so she served him with papers and he went along peacefully."

"That must have been hard. I always think it's sad when a marriage breaks up, for whatever reason."

The server brought my fried avocado and Leah's salad. "Do you have any siblings, Leah?"

I took a forkful of the delicious fried avocado and crab. *Delicious!*

"Yes. I have two younger brothers. They're both successful in business, but they're always out of the country. I never see them."

I took a sip of water. "I'm sure that's hard on your father, not being able to see them."

"Oh, I don't think he minds too much. He has me, you know." She brightened. "And he has his work."

She began to look for the server to bring our lunch. Perhaps a sign that I had asked enough personal questions. The delicious looking fried chicken dinner was set in front of me and I immediately set some aside.

"I'll take this home to share with Teddy."

Leah asked the server to remove her untouched salad and then he replaced the empty plate with a hot steaming bowl of tortilla soup. She looked at it but didn't make a move to pick up a spoon.

"You don't seem hungry," I said. "Is something

troubling you?"

"I'm not hungry, actually. This business with Rene's murder and the uncertainty of the grant has taken my appetite."

"Not to mention Simon's death."

"Who's Simon?" she asked finally taking a spoonful of her soup.

"He was the security guard found murdered at the Sanctuary. I was there when they found him, you know."

"I didn't know." She really looked at me for the first time.

"You know, the police are having a difficult time trying to figure out why Rene was killed, let alone who killed him. I personally think whoever killed Rene might have killed Simon."

"Why would you think that?" She took another bite of her soup.

"I just think that Rene's murder probably had something to do with the grant, and that means someone involved with either team would have the best motive. It's only a hunch."

I picked up a piece of chicken.

"Perhaps, but the only ones staying at the hotel are our team and you, Jillian."

"Great point, Leah." I smiled.

After eating the rest of our lunch, we made small talk about how delicious the food was, and then I asked her about Rene.

She told me he had applied for a job at the Florida Department of Agriculture as a junior accountant and began working there before coming to the Society. He was an outstanding employee, quite skilled at his job and was a team player.

As to friends, she said she didn't know of any. Only that on occasion, he would go to Ocala to see his mother and check on her. She thought he and his mother were close. That's all she said she really knew about him.

"You know," I said, "some people who get murdered turn out to have a secret life of some sort. Did you ever get the impression that Rene could have had one?"

"A secret life?" Leah shrugged. "I suppose it's possible. I don't think he was gay, if that's what you're driving at."

"I wasn't driving at that in particular. You'll let me know if you think of something, won't you? I told Arthur I would do anything I could to help in the investigation, so that's why I'm asking."

"Of course," she said in a polite voice.

We finished our lunch, and after I insisted on paying the bill, proceeded to check out a few galleries, some of which were within walking distance of the restaurant.

"I especially want to go in here." I pointed at the Calvin Charles Gallery. "They've featured many of the paintings in the hotel. I may want to purchase one, but I wanted to see the entire collection of the artist I liked first, if they have any."

Leah followed me inside and began looking at the paintings displayed on the walls and on various easels throughout the gallery. A proprietor came up, offered her services, and said she'd be happy to answer any questions we might have. I thanked her and inquired about the particular artist I had in mind.

Leah paused to look at a certain painting. She seemed transfixed. I walked to stand behind her. The painting was exquisite, reds and rich tones. But, then I realized, she wasn't looking at the painting at all. She was just standing there, staring at the wall. The painting happened to be nearby.

"Is something wrong?"

She started. "I was just looking at the price. $2,500!"

"That's not a bad price for the quality of work," I commented still observing her strange behavior. We stopped by another gallery to view the works, then Leah abruptly stopped me.

"Jillian, this has been nice, but I need to get back to the hotel. I can get a taxi if you want to continue to look at more galleries."

"I don't mind taking you back at all, Leah."

It was just a tiny fib. I would have loved to see the rest of the galleries on my list, but I also wanted more time to talk. We headed toward the car.

"You heard that Mark Russell was in an accident last night, didn't you?"

"Yes, I heard that from my father. How is Mark?"

"We don't know yet. He's still unconscious, but they've performed surgery on him, so we're waiting for the outcome."

"I suppose we should send him some flowers or something."

"I don't know if they allow flowers in ICU. Maybe after he's in a private room. That is, if he pulls through."

I involuntarily thought about the mystery of Mark's key being in Rene's possession. Why would Mark give him a key?

A shame I had to miss most of my gallery tour but there was hope. A few paintings hung in the entry and lobby. Upon returning to the hotel, I decided to look again at those I admired. Just near the conference room area, they'd placed a few works that were less familiar. Here I found a contemporary pair of paintings perfect for my conservatory. They were filled with the sunny yellows I loved so much, and the contemporary design would make a perfect foil for my garden-themed home. Out came my cellphone. I eagerly dialed the gallery but received an incoming call before I could click to ring the number. I answered.

"Jillian?" the familiar voice said, "Detective Noble. Thought I'd let you know an interesting development in the Rene Parker case has emerged."

I hid my disappointment. No, this was good. The

paintings could wait.

"I'm all ears, Detective."

"First of all, Mark Russell came through the surgery. He's still in recovery, so I can't talk to him yet."

"That's wonderful. Thank the Lord," Something positive at last! I walked outside the conference room area to the porch and sat down in a comfortable wicker chair. "So what's the new development, Detective?"

"Seems Rene Parker's mother just arrived by bus from Florida. Came directly to the police station and said she was staying until we released her son's body for burial."

"Wow. When are you going to release it?"

"Just between you and me, I'd like to keep it until we've had a chance to interview her. You know, get whatever information we can that might help us with the investigation."

"I see. I'm sure she wants to have it released as soon as possible, even though this must be heart-wrenching for her. How can I help?"

"I arranged for her to stay at the Sanctuary in Rene's room. She won't be charged, under the circumstances. The management said they'd do anything to help. They want to find out who killed Simon. Here's what I need you to do. I want you to make contact with, let me see here, her name is, Yvette Parker, and find out all you can. Then call me."

"I can do that. I was going to go see Mark but this may be more important."

"Don't worry, I'm monitoring Mr. Russell. He's still unconscious but the doctor says he may come around at any time and he's going to call me when he does."

"Would you call me when you know? I'd really appreciate it."

"Sure. Well, I'll let Mrs. Parker know you'll be contacting her. I told her you were helping in the case and she seemed grateful. I think you'll like her. She seemed pretty pulled together under the circumstances."

He gave me her room number. I would call her as soon as I got back to my room.

When I returned Cecilia and Teddy were out, probably for a walk. I took a moment to call the gallery and told them to hold the two paintings for me. They knew exactly the ones I was talking about when I mentioned they were a pair of sunny yellows. I had been looking for over a year to find something for my conservatory and I was thrilled. For the call to Yvette, I got comfortable on the sofa and dialed. This might be a tiny bit awkward.

She answered with, "Hello, this is Yvette Parker speaking."

Her upbeat demeanor surprised me, but I decided to reserve judgment until I'd met her. "Yvette, this is Jillian Bradley calling. I believe Detective Noble spoke to you about me this morning."

"Why yes, Jillian. Thank you for calling so soon. I'm going a little crazy here all by myself. I'm sure you understand how it is."

"This must be a difficult time for you. These past few days have been difficult for a lot of people. Would it be possible for us to get together, perhaps for a cup of tea?"

"That sounds so good. I don't have anything to do this afternoon. I just got here this morning after a two-day bus ride. I thought I'd be more tired, but quite honestly, until I find out who killed my son and why, I'm not going to…."

Her voice finally broke. The chipper façade slipped away. She regained her composure after a few moments. "Excuse me, but it's so hard."

"There's no apology necessary, Yvette. Let's have tea in my casita. We'll be able to talk more privately and I think you'll be comfortable."

"Thank you, Jillian. What's your room number and

when would you like me to be there?"

"Why don't we say four o'clock?"

"I'll look forward to it. And, Jillian...."

"Yes?"

"Thank you for your compassion."

"You're welcome, Yvette."

I liked her already. I gave her my room number and we hung up. I had my compact out to touch up my makeup when the door opened and Teddy rushed in with a series of exhilarated yips.

Cecilia held his leash tugging him a little from behind. She gave an exasperated sigh, then let go so he could jump right into my arms as I awaited him on the sofa.

After he settled down next to me, I opened my laptop and checked my e-mails. I scrolled down to one from Arthur. It read:

Helen phoned and said Mark has taken a turn for the worse. She's with him, but I think you should come as soon as you can.

I checked the clock. Surely I could make it back before my appointment with Yvette. After a flurry of activity, I was soon in my car making my way down the desert road. Detective Noble called me saying that he was on his way as well. This could really change things. Up the stakes.

All I could do was pray.

Chapter 6

There were a number of people waiting in the lobby of the clinic. A young mother sat holding her small lethargic son, who laid his head on her shoulder. He was flushed with circles under his eyes. He looked dangerously feverish and I felt sorry for her. Hopefully, the doctors would help him.

A few elderly couples sat reading magazines or staring at the floor. They looked lost in thought, possibly apprehensive at what the doctors would tell them. I asked the receptionist where I could find Mark Russell's room. She directed me to the waiting room outside ICU. Arthur was sitting in an uncomfortable looking chair when I walked in. He immediately stood and greeted me.

"Hello, Jillian. Thanks for coming so soon. Helen's with him now. They'll only let us in one at a time."

"How is he?"

"So far, he's just barely conscious. He hasn't spoken and we don't even know if he even recognizes anyone."

Detective Noble entered a few moments later and nodded his head to acknowledge us.

"Hello, Detective," Arthur said, offering his hand.

Detective Noble shook it and looked back at me.

"Did you get in touch with…?"

"We have an appointment at four o'clock this afternoon."

Arthur raised his eyebrows. "Mind if I ask with whom?"

Detective Noble answered with reluctance. "Rene's mother is here. Please keep the news under your hat, Dr. Wingate. I really don't want the murderer spooked if at all possible."

"How would that spook them?" I asked.

"Oh, I don't know. Maybe they'd like to put ideas into her head to throw her suspicions off of them, or maybe they think she might know something that got Rene murdered, and they may decide to repeat their…."

"Okay, we understand." I stopped him before I pictured another murder in my mind.

Helen came in and gave me a hug.

"How is he?" I asked softly.

Her eyes were red from weeping. She took a tissue from the box on the end table, sat down, and dabbed her tears.

"He doesn't recognize me. The doctor came to check his vitals. He said he would let us know when someone else can go in to see him."

"Has he said anything at all to you?" asked the detective.

"Not a word. All we can do is wait."

"Helen, can I get you a cup of coffee?" I asked. "I'm sure they must have some around here somewhere."

"I could really use one. Down the hall on the right. Cream and sugar, please. Thanks."

The doctor poked his head into the waiting room. His glasses slipped down his nose as he whispered, "Mark is starting to talk if anyone wants to come, but only one at a time."

Detective Noble wasted no time in following him. I brought Helen her coffee. We sat together and waited. I looked at my watch. *3:00 pm.*

I still had time to be here. Yvette wasn't until four.

Finally, Detective Noble returned and we all stood, anxious for any news.

"I only got a few words out of him. He didn't remember me and he didn't remember what happened to Rene either. He does know his own name though, so at least we know he doesn't have amnesia. I think his memory will return eventually. Meanwhile, I don't have time to stick around. Could you contact me if any of you can get more out of him? Keep asking him about Rene. I'm telling you, this guy is the key to finding our murderer. If *he* goes, so do our chances of ever finding out anything. So, look sharp, and keep me posted."

We stood there, unable to protest. All we could do was nod goodbye as he quickly made his exit.

"Arthur, do you mind if I go next. I should get back soon as well," I placed my hand on his shoulder as he and Helen took their seats again.

"I'll get your coffee, Helen," Arthur said kindly. "You go ahead, Jillian."

A nurse led me to Mark's room. When she left us, I walked quietly inside and closed the door behind me. I sat in the chair provided and pulled it close to the bed. I wanted to get every word.

"Hello, Mark. It's Jillian Bradley, Arthur's friend."

Mark slowly opened his eyes and raised his right index finger to acknowledge me.

"We're all so sorry about what happened. I want you to know I've been praying for your recovery ever since the accident. Helen has been praying, too."

He raised his right index finger again, letting me know he heard what I was saying. I thought he was blinking, but as I looked closer, I saw tears coming from his eyes. He opened his mouth just a little and said, "I'm—sorry."

"You're going to be all right, Mark. You're going to

get better. It's a miracle you survived, but I think you know that."

He struggled to speak. "I — killed — two — people," he whispered.

The tears starting flowing.

"It was an accident, Mark. Don't think about that now. Please just try to get well. We can all deal with what happened later. We're here for you — Arthur, Helen, and myself."

Mark closed his eyes and opened them again, this time without tears. He turned his head slightly toward me, and spoke.

"They're going to — arrest me."

"Well, not today!" I said. "Mark, I'm here to help you in any way I can, please believe that. Is there anything you want to tell me?"

He closed his eyes, and I thought he was going to sleep, but he opened them again and shifted his gaze to my face.

"Tomorrow, talk tomorrow," was all he said.

The nurse came in and told me to leave. Mark needed rest. He could have visitors in the morning. I conveyed the message to Helen and Arthur when I returned to the waiting room.

We decided to return as soon as visiting hours were open in the morning. I could tell Helen had been under quite a strain, but she told Arthur she had to finish some work before going home. He said he would meet her back at the office.

I got in my car and called Detective Noble.

"Detective," I said, "it's Jillian. Thought I'd let you know that I've seen Mark Russell."

"Well, did he say anything?"

"Yes, he spoke to me. I can't believe you told him you were going to arrest him. What were you thinking? Don't you know what a shock like that could have done to him? I understand your concern about learning the truth, but if he dies, you're certainly not going to learn any truth at all. I'm sorry that I'm so upset but I think you went about this all wrong."

"All right, I apologize. Maybe I was too anxious to make an arrest."

"Thank you. Now I will tell you this. He said two things: 'I'm sorry' and 'Talk tomorrow.'"

"He said he'd talk tomorrow, huh?"

"That's right, 'Talk tomorrow.' He knows he was responsible for killing those two people in the accident and he managed to say he was sorry."

"Did you ask him about Rene?"

"No, but he could barely talk. Listen, the three of us are going to see him in the morning. You can be there if you want, or I'll just call you if I find out anything. Up to you."

"Call me. I'm tied up in the morning."

"Okay, I'll talk to you then."

I took a deep breath and concentrated on my driving, not wanting to get into an accident. I wondered how it had happened, but felt like he would tell us when he was strong enough. My instincts about Mark had been right. He was remorseful—genuinely so. Whatever he had done, I knew God would forgive him. I just wanted a chance to help if Mark would let me.

I only had a few minutes before Yvette would arrive. I told Cecilia to wait in her room with Teddy until I could sense whether he would be an asset or a liability in our meeting. Some people are afraid of dogs and some people are indifferent about them. Others happily connect whenever they encounter one. Perhaps Teddy could comfort Yvette. I hoped so, but I would have Cecilia in the wings to take him back out, just in case.

At precisely four o'clock, there was a knock on my door. When I answered, Yvette stood in the doorway and smiled. Room service was right behind her. I motioned for her to sit down on the sofa by the fire as the server placed the tea tray on the table in front of her. I signed the bill and thanked him.

Teddy was yipping, trying to guard me from whoever entered his territory.

Yvette's face brightened.

She looked surprisingly young for her age which I judged to be about forty-five to fifty. Her firm handshake confirmed that she was self-assured. She sat straight on the sofa with her ankles crossed. Although she was pretty in a country sort of way, the lines around her eyes told of a difficult life, not one of privilege.

High cheekbones spoke of her French ancestry. Like many Europeans, Yvette wore no makeup, only a little lipstick and yet her color looked quite healthy. She wore her shoulder-length blond hair straight and simple. Her clothes flattered her medium built figure. I wondered if Rene had been like her.

Teddy was yipping in the bedroom, trying to guard his territory from the present invader.

"Would you like some tea?"

"Thank you, I'd love some. Just plain, please."

I took my time pouring the tea and stirring in the sugar for mine. I offered her a slice of decadent chocolate cake or a chocolate chip oatmeal cookie. She took the cookie and white linen napkin. We sipped our tea and she told me again how much she appreciated the invitation.

"I would love to meet your dog, Jillian." She placed her cookie on her saucer.

I walked over to Cecilia's room and let Teddy out. He immediately ran over to Yvette and jumped into her lap.

She smiled and began to pet him.

"He's adorable." She rubbed his ears gently and stroked his fur. "I could never give Rene a dog because A.J. said we couldn't afford one. Of course I regret it now, like so many things."

"Is A.J. your husband?" I was glad Teddy was taking to her so.

"He *was* my husband. A.J. died when Rene was a teenager."

"I'm so sorry. What did your husband do for a living?"

"He was a logger." She sighed. "Six days a week he'd take logs from where they fell and load them onto trucks that took them to the mills. A.J. would work twelve hours a day and when he got home, all dirty and hungry, Rene would disappear into another room. The two didn't really mix.

"A.J. and I would have a little time over dinner together where he recapped his day. Then to sleep...early...7 o'clock sharp every evening. The same routine started all over again the next morning."

"He seems to have worked hard to provide for his family. I'm sure you miss him."

Teddy licked her hand as if to say he was sorry she had suffered two deaths now.

"You're a good dog, Teddy. Thank you." She stroked his fur. "Please have your friend come in and have some tea. I feel like I'm encroaching."

I stood. "I'll ask her if she'd like to join us."

I introduced Cecilia. Yvette seemed comfortable sharing her personal life in front of her. I think she sensed I had her welfare in mind and trusted me.

She was hungry to talk to someone, so Cecilia and I listened sympathetically.

Yvette talked for some time, unfolding her life story as we drank tea together. I made sure her cup stayed full.

"I was the daughter of a common shopkeeper who had emigrated from France when I was only three years old. We had moved to Ocala, Florida, where our family ran a small grocery store. After my parents could no longer keep up with the work of running the store, I took over."

Celicia sipped her tea. "So you run a family business. That must take a lot of work."

"Yes. I rarely get a break. We added a couple of gas pumps and turned the grocery part into more of a convenience store. Since tourists stopped by frequently on their way to the Everglades or Disneyworld, I put in a small gift shop section, and it did quite well."

I was curious. "What type of merchandise do you carry?"

"The usual things — greeting cards, souvenirs, stuffed animals, T-shirts, caps, and I even sell books, you know, travel books and books about Florida."

"Do you carry souvenir bells, shot glasses, things like that?"

"Oh, yes. I even carry a few porcelain teacups. I remember my grandmother having quite a collection."

"I collect them myself. I think I'm up to forty-four, last time I counted."

"That's quite a collection." She sipped her tea and took a small bite of her cookie.

"Yvette, would you by any chance carry any porcelain flowers, like Capodimonte flowers?"

"I think I know the ones you're talking about. They're flowers on branches, right? I saw one my friend had sitting on an end table in her living room."

"Yes. They're beautiful and distinctive. Do you carry anything like that?"

"I do have a few flowers, but they're mostly local for the tourists. I carry a few roses because they always seem to sell."

I watched her face closely. "Would you have any orchids for instance?"

Her expression didn't change and she seemed unaware of any significance.

"Orchids? Of course. Florida's full of them. Why do you ask?"

"I collect all sorts of porcelain. I'm really a soft touch for anything out of the ordinary." *Careful. Don't reveal the evidence.* I'd promised Detective Noble.

"I can show you where I order my stock from on the computer anytime you want." She refused any more tea when Cecilia offered.

"Yvette, I know this may be difficult but I must ask. Do you know of anyone who could have killed your son, or do you know any reason someone might have ended his life like that?"

"I've gone over the situation a thousand times in my mind, believe me. Rene had been gone from home for two years when this happened. I can only tell you what I know about his life in Ocala before he left."

"That may help. Right now we don't have a motive. Only the means and a lot of people with opportunity."

"I never met anyone he worked with. He would only come home occasionally to see me, you know, to check on me. He always looked after me even...." Yvette's eyes looked away as if she thought of something.

"You were saying...."

"I don't know. I was just thinking of a time when Rene was particularly upset. He was angry. I don't think I'd ever seen him as angry as that, before or since." She drifted away in thought.

"Yvette, would you mind telling us what happened?" I coaxed gently, hoping she would be as honest and forthright as she had been up until now.

"I'm trying to remember how it all happened. You see, my husband had no intention of being cooped up all day working in a store like ours, so I managed the business myself with Rene's help. Rene had no siblings — we couldn't afford any more. Well, that's not true. I was the one who didn't want more. A.J. didn't care one way or another.

"I think he was just a simple man who only cared about Rene and me. The men he worked with were not the nicest men in the world. I know that a lot of them were homeless, trucked in from Miami and given work to do. Some of them were derelicts who could barely hold a job.

"Before I tell you about what happened, you must understand that I'm a staunch Catholic. I was always faithful to A.J. even though my marriage to him wasn't fulfilling. We always went to mass every Sunday and took communion. I go to confession once a week and I try to be a practicing Catholic."

Cecilia nodded. "We understand. Go on."

"One afternoon when I was taking inventory in the back room Rene had been serving a customer. After they left a man wandered into the area where I was working. He put his arms around me and tried to kiss me and I yelled for Rene."

I interrupted. "Did you know the man?"

"Yes. He was the manager for the logging company A.J. worked for. A man named Ray Ackermann."

"What happened?" Cecilia seemed caught up in Yvette's story.

"When Rene came in Ray stopped and apologized, but he acted like I was the one who had enticed him to act the way he did."

This sounded promising. "What did Rene do?"

"He was so enraged he had no words. Ray Ackermann took his silence as a sign of being a coward. He laughed at Rene and shrugged the whole thing off. He left through the back door."

"That must have been horrible for both of you." I shook my head. "When did this happen? Do you remember?"

"Let me think. Rene started helping me in the store regularly after school when he was sixteen. He was a junior in high school then. This must have happened the next year, because I remember training him for about a year before I let him have much of the responsibility. He was waiting on a customer and ringing them up, so yes; it must have been when he was seventeen or eighteen."

"How old was Rene when he was killed?"

"He was only twenty-four." Yvette almost broke down again. "After high school he got a certificate in accounting at the junior college nearby. He worked for me up until the time he got the job with the Department of Agriculture. He told me he got his *dream* job."

"His dream job, that's interesting. So this incident with Ray Ackermann happened roughly six years ago."

"That's correct."

"I think people like Ray Ackermann should be locked up." Cecilia's anger was apparent in her expression.

I tried to picture how a young teenager like Rene was at the time would react to a man like Ray Ackermann. If Ackerman had done that to me, I might want to see him dead or punished for it. Rene must have felt a great deal of frustration and humiliation when Ray Ackermann laughed at him.

The phone startled me out of my reverie. I asked Cecilia to take the call.

"Yes, I'll give her the message. Thank you." Cecilia hung up the phone.

Yvette placed her cup back on the tray along with the empty napkin and stood.

"You both have been so kind to have me. Sometimes you have to talk to someone when you're going through grief like this." She seemed genuinely grateful for our hospitality. "I know you must be busy, and I think all I want to do is go back to my room and rest a little. The hotel has been so gracious. They said for me to order anything I like, on the house. I didn't think there were still people in the world like this. It has been a life saver."

I wasn't quite through. "Yvette is there anything you can tell us about Rene that would be considered unusual after this event happened with Ray Ackermann?"

"You mean was Rene different in any way?" She glanced away not seeming to look at anything in particular.

"Yes. Did he act differently or do anything different after this happened?"

"I can only describe it as if he had changed somehow. You know, changed from being a child to more of an adult. There was another thing. He started reading magazines and some sort of comic books, I think."

"Were they super heroes or...."

"They were spy magazines like detectives and forensics. I looked at some of them after he left home and wondered why he liked them. That was when he asked me to buy him a camera. I paid him a small salary, so we worked out the payment. He was thrilled to get it and spent a lot of time taking pictures. I asked to see them, but he said they were just pictures of objects he found interesting. He said they were interesting only to him.

"I didn't question him after that and pretty much forgot because I kept so busy running the store. If I'm not mistaken, I think he left the camera in his room when he left home. Do you think this stuff could help the police?"

"Possibly. I'll tell Detective Noble when I see him. We really need a lead right now."

We walked her to the door. Just before she left she turned toward me. "I want you to choose a porcelain flower from my store, Jillian, as a gift. If you'll let me use your computer, I'll show you what I have. Just let me know when there's a time that works for you, okay?"

"I'd be delighted and thank you. I'll be in touch with you tomorrow. Get some rest and have faith that we'll find the answers."

"Thank you, Jillian. At least I have some hope, now. 'Bye, Cecilia, 'bye Teddy."

Teddy yipped as she bent down one last time to pet him goodbye.

I closed the door slowly, looked at the floor deep in thought, then sought Cecilia's face where she sat on the sofa.

I perched on the L-shaped section to face her.

"Well, what do you think?" I really wanted her opinion.

Teddy crawled into my lap and went to sleep.

"She seems genuine enough. Transparent. She didn't act like she had anything to hide."

"I totally agree." I nodded trying to feel confident about the matter.

Cecilia got up and removed the tea tray.

"By the way, you received a message from Vincent Fontaine asking you to have dinner with him tonight. He said to be ready in the lobby at seven o'clock if you'd like to join him, or leave a message in his room if tonight's not good. He said he would keep trying if you weren't able to make it tonight."

"I'll go. Cecilia, please check my messages and see if there's anything I need to attend to."

"Sure, Jillian."

"Thanks."

I glanced at the time. It was only 5:30 pm, which meant there was plenty of time before I was to meet Vincent.

"I'll take Teddy for a short walk. You can feed him when I get back. I won't be long."

I secured Teddy with his leash, left the casita, and wandered down toward the pool and dog lawn. As I passed the giant saguaro cactus once again, my attention was drawn to a couple lying out on some chaises. Even though it was November I noted the air was pleasant. Perhaps it was not unusual for some people to sun themselves whenever the opportunity presented itself. Besides, sometimes even I liked to relax by the pool and read a book, although I didn't enjoy swimming.

The closer I came to the pool area the more familiar the pair looked. To my surprise, I realized they were none other than Tori DeMarco and Richard Sanchez. I waved, hoping they would recognize me. Teddy yipped when I stopped. Richard waved back, but Tori simply looked at me.

Perhaps she thought she didn't have to acknowledge me since Richard did.

I remembered once again that Tori may have a melancholy temperament and wasn't inclined to friendliness. I immediately forgave her for any ungraciousness on her part.

Dogs were not allowed in the pool area so I had to press on. At least I had shown myself to be open and friendly and I hoped this encounter would allow me to speak to both of them sometime soon.

Teddy enjoyed his walk stopping from time to time to smell the plants. He tried unsuccessfully to lead me toward the parking lot.

"What's the matter with you, Teddy? We're going to the dog lawn where trained dogs are supposed to go."

He reluctantly quit tugging away from me at the mention of *dog lawn* and decided to comply.

We walked to our destination and I let him loose. I hovered the way many new mothers do when their toddler takes their first steps. Well, Teddy was my toddler. My fear was he would decide to escape the confines of the lawn.

He scratched the sod, sniffed around and began to wander into a flowerbed filled with rocks and a large Century plant that had just bloomed and was surrounded by new pups.

The day was waning and it would soon be time for dinner. I scooped Teddy into my arms and walked briskly back to my casita, passing by the pool once more. Now, no one was there. Perhaps those two had left for dinner.

There were two messages for me when I returned. One was from Arthur saying he planned to visit Mark at ten o'clock the next morning. The other was from Detective Noble wanting to know if I had learned anything from Yvette.

I asked Cecilia to tell Arthur I would join him the next day. Also, I requested the detective run a check on Ray Ackerman in case there was a lead. I also asked her to have him send me a picture of the evidence; he would know what I meant.

I placed Teddy on the sofa.

"Any interesting-looking questions for my column?"

"Just one, a gentleman wants to know what summer bulbs he can plant."

"I'll answer that one now. Sounds like he wants to get a jump on spring."

I pulled up my column file and explained that summer bulbs were not like the typical fall bulbs we think of such as tulips and daffodils. For instance, gladioli were really corms and when planted at two-week intervals in the spring provided long-lasting vibrant color all summer long. The cannas were actually rhizomes and one should make sure they were crisp and firm when selecting. People prized cannas for their bold foliage and wide range of colors. Dahlias were tubers that came in many colors and petal shapes. They produced impressive blooms, ranging from petite to giant specimens and were some of the most satisfying flowers to grow.

"Excuse me, Jillian, I need to take this text from Walter."

I smiled, glad to hear they were still in touch.

"Go right ahead. I need to get ready anyway. Tell him I said, 'hello,' okay?"

"I will. He loves you, you know."

"And I love him, too. He's a wonderful young man."

I noticed Teddy was asleep on the sofa. He was probably tired from his walk and hungry by now. "Cecilia, you might want to let Teddy rest a little before you feed him. He looks pretty tuckered out."

"I'll keep an eye on him. He usually tells me when he's hungry by staring at me with his ears perked up. He won't leave me until I've set his food and water out."

"Don't forget his milk."

"I never do. Now you go get ready."

I did as I was ordered. After touching up my makeup and running a comb through my hair, I slipped into my new black dinner dress. I loved the way it made me look a few years younger. I took my black fur-trimmed wrap from the front closet.

"I wonder what Vincent has up his sleeve. You may have an admirer, you know." Cecilia's tease was all in fun.

"Maybe, but I bet he has something on his mind. I'm sure I'll find out soon enough. Well, how do I look?"

"That's a killer dress, Jillian." Cecilia covered her mouth with her hand. "Sorry, I didn't mean to blab it out that way."

"That's okay. I'll take the compliment. This dress makes me look at least ten pounds thinner than I really am. Why am I hungry again? Must be nerves. I hardly touched my cake when we had tea.

Listen, I want you to send a message to Yvette for me. Ask her if nine o'clock tomorrow morning is all right for her to stop by and show me the porcelain. I'm going to leave now. You don't have to wait up unless you want to."

"I think I will. I have a couple of things I have to do

for the paper and I really want to learn how your evening went. By the way, Walter says to be careful and treat everyone like they could be the murderer. He says to play it safe and always let someone know where you are—just in case."

"That's sound advice. Tell him I'll be careful and thank him for the tip. I really have to leave now. 'Bye, Teddy."

Teddy didn't move his head, but looked at me with his sweet brown eyes as if to say, "Don't be gone too long."

***

Vincent Fontaine was a formidable man, and handsome in a rugged sort of way. He stood about 6'3" and still had a head of thick black hair slightly tinged with gray. At one time, it might have been the same color as Leah's. His brow was furrowed, but there were laugh lines around his eyes that I found appealing. Leah resembled him in many ways physically, but I thought she must be like her mother in temperament. Vincent was outgoing and fun-loving. Leah seemed closed and serious. He was right on time meeting me in the lobby. His car waited just outside.

"You look stunning, Jillian."

I could tell he was pleasantly surprised that I knew how to dress for a date.

"Thank you, Vincent, and thanks for inviting me to dinner."

"I thought we'd try Trader Vic's over at the Valley Ho because I know how to get there and back to the hotel." He smiled. "Besides, I like the atmosphere and the food and the drinks are wonderful."

"Sounds great to me. I'm always hungry."

"And thirsty, I hope."

"I'm not a big drinker, if that's what you mean. But I

enjoy something exotic once in a while."

"Well, Trader Vic's has the exotic for sure."

It was a beautiful drive with Camelback Mountain lit up with twinkling lights of its wealthy inhabitants. Many of the desert trees and plants were strung with lights as well. I soaked in their delightful uniqueness as we passed.

He parked the car and we entered the restaurant. I followed him into the Island Bar. We sat down in the rattan and leather chairs around a small drum table. A candle flickered in the middle. I thought the whole place was romantic. Bamboo flooring lent a Polynesian flair to the décor. The music was exotic and put me in a relaxed mood, although I planned to find out as much as I could about Rene from this man.

"You must try the Mai Tai. I always order one when I come here."

"How many times have you been here?"

"Oh, Trader Vic's is everywhere. I've been to the one in Atlanta, the one in Chicago, and this one."

"I see. So you travel in your work?"

"Sometimes I do."

The server took his order for the Mai Tai, and I ordered a Queen Charlotte Fruit Punch. How could you not order fruit juice in a place like this? Vincent also ordered Asian Pot Stickers.

We began talking as the bartender made our drinks.

"What took you to Chicago?"

"I attended a conference a few years ago dealing with new scientific experimentation of plant propagation."

I did not ask him what he was doing in Atlanta because it might make me sound like a detective. I wanted to gain his confidence first. I did not have to wait long. He talked to me as if we were old friends. He must miss being with his wife, although I could not see why since Leah said her mother divorced him due to his lack of attention. I decided to approach him through Leah. I knew he cared for her and would probably be interested in anything that had to do with her life.

"Vincent, does Leah have any health problems? The reason I ask is because Arthur told me that you said you were here to look out for her — that she wasn't well."

Vincent looked at the server approaching with our drinks and waited until we'd been served.

"Leah is not what you would call 'delicate' by any means. However, she has been on edge for the past couple of months. Maybe because of all the stress from doing the grant proposal. She won't open up to me anymore."

"I'm sure it's difficult, you being her father. She is, after all, an adult. I can see how you'd be concerned."

Vincent looked uncomfortable and took a sip of his Mai Tai.

"It's never easy, I've heard." I tried to sound sympathetic. "I suppose a parent never stops being concerned for their child."

"Do you have children, Jillian?"

"No, we were never blessed with any before my husband was killed in Vietnam."

"I'm sorry. Why don't we change the subject? Here, have a pot sticker before they get cold." He was quite charming.

I turned on the charm a little, feeling it probably wouldn't hurt, and he seemed to enjoy the flattery.

We carried our drinks into the dining room which was decorated exotically as well.

Tall wooden tiki columns jutted up between white linen-covered tables. An open-pit barbecue area stood behind a glass enclosure for the guests to enjoy watching grillers at work.

Vincent ordered a Caesar salad, a New York steak (cooked medium-rare), grilled spiced corn-on-the-cob, and a loaded baked potato. I had the Barbados chicken soup and shrimp scampi, which was delicious! Vincent had two more Mai Tais.

I knew I would insist on driving home.

We talked about his kids, my dog, his ex-wife, my late husband, and finally got around to our work. I was interested in what he did and fortunately, he was sober enough to tell me.

"My job," he explained, "is to oversee the overall welfare of the Everglades. That includes preservation, the tracking of tourism allowed, allocation of funds for the cataloging of plant species according to botanical orders, and field studies for hands-on interpretation of data collected."

"The job sounds monumental." I was in awe of how much responsibility Vincent really had.

"Didn't Rene Parker work for you at one time?" I tried to sound nonchalant.

"Yeah, he worked for me in accounting before he went to work for Leah. She was prettier than me." His laugh showed he was in a slightly inebriated state.

"Was he a good employee?"

"I didn't come in contact with him much. He was just one of the bean counters. Besides, he only worked for me a couple of months so I really can't say I knew him at all. And I didn't kill him, if you were going to ask me that."

I knew he was still quite alert after making that comment so I shifted gears.

"I was just curious. Are you having dessert?" I hoped to divert his train of thought.

"Why not?" He grinned, and became his amiable self once again. He raised his hand, and a server appeared in an instant. "We'd like a dessert menu please."

"Yes sir, right away, sir."

I chose one of my favorites, Key lime pie, and Vincent had the chocolate brownie sundae. We ordered cappuccinos, and were really enjoying the moment when my cellphone rang.

"Jillian, it's Cecilia. I'm so sorry to bother you, but I think you need to get back. Teddy's acting strangely. I think something's wrong with him. We may need to do something."

I felt suddenly alert. "What's wrong?"

"He's listless, wouldn't eat his dinner, and he's whining like he hurts somewhere."

"I'll be there as soon as possible. Will you call a vet? Check with the hotel for the name of one. Better yet, I'll call Jeff, the groundskeeper. I have his card and he might be able to get in touch with Elise Hansen. Maybe she could refer us to someone reputable. I'll call now. Thanks, Cecilia. Try to get him to take a little water. 'Bye."

"Trouble?" Vincent sounded concerned.

I apologized and explained the situation. He totally understood.

I called Jeff, and he said he would take care of it and for me not to worry.

Vincent paid the tab and said it was okay if I drove. He really was a gentleman.

I pulled into the hotel entrance and the valets helped us out of the car.

"Would you like me to go with you to check on Teddy, Jillian?"

"I think I'll be all right. I have Cecilia, but thank you for offering. And Vincent...."

"Yes?"

"I really enjoyed the evening. Thank you so much for inviting me."

"Let's do it again soon, all right?"

I nodded, said goodnight and then walked as fast as I could to my casita.

There was no barking at the door as I let myself in. Teddy was right where I left him on the sofa, lying on his side with his little head down.

"The vet's on his way over," Cecilia reported. "Jeff contacted Elise Hansen and she was only too happy to help. She wants an update whenever we know something."

After a few minutes, there was a knock on the door.

"It's Dr. Morris. Elise Hansen sent me."

I immediately let him in, thanked him for coming, and led him to Teddy.

"I'll need to examine him. Have you taken him anywhere unusual in the past few hours?"

"I only took him for a walk around the grounds here. We walked over to the dog lawn and he sniffed around a century plant, I remember."

"Let's take a look at you, Teddy." Dr. Morris gently began examining him from tip to toe. When he felt his under belly, Teddy let out a whimper. The doctor examined the spot more closely, and then checked Teddy's eyes and heart rate.

"He seems listless but he doesn't appear to be in a life threatening state. I'm going to take a blood sample and have it tested, and then we'll know more."

"What could it possibly be?" I didn't try to hide my concern.

"At this point, I'd say a possible bug bite of some kind. It could be a scorpion sting."

"Aren't they deadly?" Cecilia came over to Teddy's side.

"They are and they aren't." The vet shrugged. "Scorpions around here bite to either stun as a means of protection or they can inflict deadly venom designed to eat their prey. I won't know which one it is until I can do the test. Until then, I suggest you let me take him to my clinic where we can keep an eye on him. I brought a crate with me, just in case."

"Thank you, doctor."

He gently placed poor Teddy inside.

Teddy looked at me through the small-wired door of

the crate. With those sweet brown eyes he seemed to say, "Don't worry; I have a good feeling about this man."

Somehow, that gave me peace of mind.

"Should I come with him?"

"There's really nothing you can do. I'll call you when we have the tests back. They shouldn't take too long. Don't worry, Mrs. Bradley, I've seen just about everything these little dogs can get into. We'll do what we can to make sure he pulls through. I'll make him as comfortable as I can."

"I'll call you first thing in the morning." I still felt reluctant to part with my dog to a stranger but I had to trust God that he would be safe.

Doctor Morris gently carried Teddy out the front door as I stood helpless behind.

"Lord, please let Teddy get well."

Cecilia stepped up behind me and put her hand on my shoulder. "Amen."

Chapter 7

It's amazing how things change so suddenly. Teddy was gone. I missed his expectant litle face asking me to take him outside for a morning walk. I missed stroking his fur and holding him in my lap.

The next day I roused myself out of bed so there would be time to get organized. The vet clinic opened at eight o'clock so I had an hour to get ready before I could call and see how he was. Cecilia had ordered my breakfast the night before and it arrived promptly. I was hungry, stressed out due to Teddy's condition, so I ate the half-portions ravenously — grilled ham steak, fresh fruit plate with cottage cheese, a raspberry Danish, freshly squeezed orange juice and plenty of piping hot coffee.

I dressed quickly and had just enough time to check my e-mails before it was time to make my call. Yvette was stopping by at 8:30 to let me look at the porcelain flowers. Earlier Detective Noble had sent me a picture of the ghost orchid found on Rene's body.

Arthur and Helen were to meet me at the clinic to see Mark when visiting hours began at 10:00 am. I looked at the time. It was 7:32, just enough time to spend a few moments reading a Psalm and having a word of prayer for my day. I would need it.

All set and ready to face the day, I dialed Dr. Morris.

After getting through the phone tree, a receptionist finally answered and said she would put him on the line. I waited a short time until he picked up the call.

What a relief! Teddy was doing a little better and had actually taken some water. Fortunately, he didn't have to get any IV's put in. The blood sample tested positive for scorpion venom, but it was from a stun bite, not a toxic bite.

"Thank you so much, Lord, for sparing Teddy's life. You're too good to Teddy and me. Thank you."

Dr. Morris said I should be able to take Teddy home the next morning. He still needed time to rest and get back on his feet. I asked if Teddy was wagging his tail at all. Dr. Morris assured me that he was. I thanked him saying that I would call before I came over in the morning. I was so relieved. As I hung up the phone there was a knock on the front door. I glanced at my watch and thought it was a little early for Yvette.

Cecilia made her way over. "I'll answer it if you want, Jillian."

"Be my guest." I sat down at my computer.

"Jillian, look at these!" Cecilia walked toward me carrying a huge bouquet of red roses and lush green ferns interspersed with baby's breath in a beautiful cut glass vase. "They're exquisite!"

"Who in the world would be sending me flowers?" The card read:

> *To Jillian,*
> *Thank you for dinner last night.*
> *Vincent.*

My goodness. What a charming man.

"What happened last night?" Cecilia sat down to drink it all in. "You have to let me in on your secret."

"I'm as surprised as you are, Cecilia. I mean, we had dinner and I listened to him talk. Maybe he just appreciated being able to share with someone. There was certainly nothing romantic going on."

"Maybe not to you, but maybe to him there was."

"Well, I can't think about that right now. I'm expecting Yvette at any minute."

Yvette arrived right on time with a knock on the door. She entered, we all gave each other small hugs, and she slipped off her jacket and placed it on the sofa.

"Good morning, ladies."

"Did you sleep okay last night?" I really cared. "How are you today?"

"I think I'm going to be all right. Thank you for asking. I'm still quite sad about Rene, but I know from losing A.J. that my life will go on. I will be a little sadder without both of them. But knowing that people are working to find out what happened makes it easier. One day at a time is all I have and I give each day to God. He will carry me."

I offered her my computer. Deftly bringing up her supplier's website, Yvette scrolled down to the porcelain flowers for me to make my choice.

I had studied the picture Detective Noble had sent me carefully and right there before me that very orchid came up on the screen. I was absolutely positive it was the same.

"Can you tell me about this one?" I pointed.

"Oh yes, it's a popular piece. Rene had bought one just like it last year, I think."

"Do you know if he still had it?"

"Rene was secretive, but told me he was buying it as a memento for someone he thought would appreciate it."

"Interesting."

Of course, I couldn't buy one myself. It would only remind me of Rene's murder. Instead, I selected a beautiful Double Delight Rose instead. It was one of my all-time favorites, with its luminous white inner petals changing to yellow, and bordered with scarlet-red edges. It would look stunning on the mahogany end table in my living room. Yvette ordered it for me and had it sent directly to my home.

"Your piece will arrive in a decorative fabric box with the authentication number on the bottom. It takes about five to seven business days for delivery."

She was quite the businessperson. I felt she would do well on her own back in Florida.

"I need to be leaving." She rose and put her jacket back on. "I'm going to see Detective Noble to tell him more about Rene. You know the things we talked about yesterday—his magazines and all. I still don't know when they will release Rene's body for burial. I hope it will be soon. I have a lot of details to attend to."

She looked downcast and burdened.

"Yvette, I will pray for you to have strength. I'm also praying for answers which will reveal Rene's murderer."

"Thank you again, Jillian."

Cecilia joined us and wished Yvette good luck.

Yvette stood and began walking toward the front door.

"I must be going. I'll keep in touch, and I hope you'll do the same."

Yvette left and Cecilia joined me for another quick cup of coffee. After the last sip, I stood. "Time to go. Visiting hours begin in thirty minutes."

***

It was a fine morning outside. The temperature was a balmy seventy degrees and the sky was clear except for a few fluffy white cumulus clouds in the distance that promised another gorgeous sunset. Once again, I drank in the beauty of the sculpture-like cacti and slightly swaying palms.

"Lord, thank you for all this beauty even though I know so many people are hurting right now. Father, I pray that You will open doors for us to find Rene's murderer. Please keep us safe from any more harm. I pray for Yvette in her loss. Bless Simon's family. They are grieving. Please provide for their needs. Please help Mark to recover. Comfort the family of the woman and her child who died in the crash, and please help me to minister in any way I can to the people You put in my path."

I arrived at the clinic just before visiting hours started and found Helen waiting.

"Good morning, Jillian. I'm glad you came. Dr. Wingate can't come until this afternoon but at least you and I are here. I hope that detective will give us some time before he lights into Mark again. Mark's a really nice young man. I can't imagine him hurting anyone. It seems so farfetched."

"I hope you're right, Helen." I glanced at my watch. "It's ten o'clock. Let's see if we can go in."

"They've moved him out of intensive care. Evidently they've done everything they can."

After locating the number of Mark's room, Helen and I entered together. The drapes were drawn and Mark seemed to be asleep. We carefully and quietly pulled up chairs on either side of his bed, and waited for him to awaken. Helen began softly talking to him to let him know we were there.

Mark slowly opened his eyes and turned toward her. His lips slowly broke into a smile.

"Hi," he whispered.

"How are you, Mark?" Helen's tone was warm and affectionate.

He winced with pain and fought back a tear or two. "Don't know if I'll make it. No one smiles . . . keep me doped up. . . lots of pain. I'm scared I'm going to die."

I gently placed my hand on his arm, hoping I wasn't

hurting him. "We're so sorry you're going through this. It's still early since the accident happened and at least you're alive. We are all thanking God for that."

He closed his eyes again. "Why did God allow those two people to die and not me? No one would miss me, but that mom and daughter were part of a family. I don't understand a God that would do that."

A few moments passed and then Helen began to speak.

"Mark, I want you to listen to what I have to say." She took a deep breath.

"There was a time in my life when I had little hope, just like you. I have never told anyone what happened to me, but I think now would be a good time."

Helen took another breath.

"We were migrant workers as a family. We worked long, hard hours harvesting sugar beets in Minnesota from the time I was twelve years old until I graduated from high school. My father finally got tired of migrant life and found work as a custodian for a disability treatment center in Mesa. He was able to help me get a job there and I moved on to work for the state of Arizona in the Department for Social Security, in the Disability Division in Phoenix.

"One day, a young man accompanied his mother, who was in a wheelchair, into our office to help her with an application for disability assistance. He and I were taken with each other and after only six months, we got married. We were so happy together—on top of the world. Then tragedy struck. As he was coming home one night from checking on his mom, a big-rig driver suffered an aneurism and veered suddenly into the oncoming lane. Steven was killed. When the state patrol came to notify me of his fatal accident my whole world fell apart."

I sat riveted to her story.

"I fell into a severe depression and was given a leave

of absence to have time to bury him, the love of my life, and somehow get my own life back together. Since Steven's mother had no one to care for her, I decided to move in and live with her. I felt it was what he would want me to do, so I did it out of love for him.

"I became further and further depressed with the added responsibility of taking care of a disabled person round the clock. I was still grieving over my husband's premature death, I was thirty years old, and felt like I was drowning in depression. I had no hope for the future and seriously considered ending my life."

Mark's eyes flickered as if surprised by her confession.

"I took sleeping pills at night to rid myself of the nightmares that haunted me of Steven being hit by the big-rig. The pills were addictive and soon I needed more of them. When I did go back to work, my job performance was poor at best.

"A co-worker noticed how troubled I was and invited me to lunch one day—her treat. I was hungry for friendship, so I accepted her offer. My friend listened to me as I unburdened myself, and after I poured out my heart to her, she put her hand on mine and told me there was hope. She told me God loved me. She said He cared enough for me to send his son, Jesus, to die as a payment for our sins. She explained that we are all sinners and if we asked forgiveness for our sins, He would forgive us and forget it ever happened.

"She said He would take our burdens and bear them, if we would just give them to Him. She explained that this was a gift called salvation and the only way to receive it was to ask Jesus to come into our heart and live as our Savior and Lord. We'd have to relinquish being in charge and let Him guide our life from then on.

"I asked how she could be sure it was real. She told me she believed it was real because God had changed her life from being a worthless, foul-mouthed alcoholic, who had totally messed up, to a different person with a purpose in life. With God's help, she had overcome her alcoholism, and turned from being a failure as a wife and mother.

"I told her that it sounded like what I so desperately wanted. With tears streaming from my eyes, I prayed right then that God would forgive me of all the things that I had done wrong in my life. I asked Jesus to come into my heart and be my Lord and Savior, and Mark, He did. I felt my burden lifted, and a peace came over me. It was a peace I'd never, ever felt before. I wasn't alone anymore. It was as if God was with me, in me, right beside me — all at the same time.

"She explained that when we ask God to come into our life, He gives us His Holy Spirit to comfort and guide us. I felt my life was brand new — a life that came with a promise that it would never end, because you see, when I die, Jesus has promised me that I'll be with Him for eternity.

"When I changed my heart toward God, He changed my life. I still encountered times of depression, but I would pray and God allowed the Holy Spirit to lift the darkness. I was able to get off the sleeping pills with no trouble and the nightmares became fewer and farther apart. I shared what had happened to me with my mother-in-law and she became a believer, too.

"Things began to look better. My mother-in-law's disability qualified her for therapy, and after a year she was walking and able to live on her own again. God showed me work she could do at home and she lived a full life after that.

"I found a church to belong to, so I could be with other Christians and learn how to live the best Christian life I could. We worship together and support one another through thick and thin.

"God told me to share this with you, Mark. Please think about it, and remember, if you reach out to God

He will reach out to you. He reached out to me and I'm so grateful He did."

"Thank you, Helen," Mark whispered.

"Knock, knock." Detective Noble entered the room. "The nurse said I can only stay five minutes since he's had you ladies here for twenty."

"Good morning, Detective." I only gave him a half-smile. "We were just leaving, weren't we Helen?"

She stood up and moved her chair back. "Mark, I'll stop by tonight if you want me to."

"I do."

Helen gently patted his hand. "I'll see you then."

Detective Noble put his hand briefly on my arm. "And I'll be talking to you after I'm through with Mark here, if you don't mind, Jillian."

"I don't mind at all. Give me a call on my cell. And, Detective, be nice."

"Sure thing."

With that, Helen and I left the clinic.

I started back for the hotel, but before I got there, I passed a row of high-end shops and drove a little slower to do a quick perusal of the offerings. A sign caught my eye. Sure enough it was one of the galleries on my list. A parking space opened up and I grabbed it.

The Randall Beckham Gallery displayed just the kind of art I liked. I spent a few minutes looking at the different works and found a painting I couldn't live without. It was oil on linen. The landscape featured all the elements I loved best about Arizona — storm clouds gathering above the peaks of eroded hills; the play of the earth's shadow effect occurring opposite the sunset on the hills and valleys; the ocotillos silhouetted against the background of the overall rich color; it had it all. The price was well worth it. A bargain for only $1,850, even though it pretty well took care of my art budget for the next few months.

I really didn't spend money on anything else. My

needs were simple, my home was paid for, I had a job to cover expenses and pay for travel when I wanted, and my yard was mature enough to only need an occasional replacement of a shrub now and then, and annuals, of course, in the fall and spring.

I arrived back at the hotel at lunchtime and asked Cecilia to join me in the restaurant for something to eat. I knew she probably wanted to get out of the room for a change of pace since Teddy didn't need her. She met me in the lobby and the server seated us almost instantly. I was hungry as usual, so I ordered the grilled green chili turkey burger with a green salad on the side. Cecilia had a regular hamburger with steak fries.

"Elise Hansen called to pay her respects to Teddy from Lila while you were out. She was apologetic about having something like this happen on her property."

"Scorpions live in deserts. I really don't blame the hotel, Cecilia."

"Maybe Elise Hansen might be afraid you'll sue. Why else would she call?"

"Maybe she was really concerned. I'll call her and thank her for thinking of us. Maybe she needs a friend. I don't know."

"Oh, and Vincent Fontaine called. He wanted to know if you were free for lunch tomorrow. I said I'd have you call him. This is getting interesting, Jillian."

"I'll give him a call after lunch. I need to talk to him again anyway."

Our lunch was delicious and filling. We skipped dessert and walked back to our casita. As we passed by the pool I noticed Tori lying out again, this time without Richard Sanchez.

"Let's go say hello."

We used our passkey to enter the pool area then walked to the group of white chaises. Tori had stretched out on one, enjoying the sun. She certainly was attractive in the two-piece white bathing suit she wore.

It set off the tan she was working on beautifully.

Without removing her over-sized sunglasses, she looked at me. "Hi, Jillian." Sitting up and reaching for the sunscreen, Tori looked curiously at Cecilia. "What are you up to today?"

"Pardon me, Tori. This is Cecilia Chastain, my personal assistant. Cecilia, this is Tori DeMarco, administrative assistant to Dr. Leah Fontaine with the Florida team."

Cecilia nodded. "It's a pleasure to meet you, Tori. How are you enjoying Scottsdale?"

Tori ignored Ceceilia, wiped her hands on a towel and closed the top on the sunscreen. Without looking directly at either of us, she shrugged. "On one hand, it's nice to get away for a change of pace. Arizona is much drier than Florida of course, but it's beautiful in an austere sort of way. On the other hand, I can't wait to go home. I don't like being held as if I was a suspect. I wish the police would hurry up and find the murderer."

Finally, she looked at me. "Do they have any idea at all why Rene was even killed?"

"They have some evidence and now they're working on a motive. I believe they get closer every day. It just takes patience."

Cecilia spoke up. "What do you do to keep busy, Tori?"

"Normally I work for Dr. Fontaine. She just happened to give me this afternoon off so I get to read and lay out for a few hours. That's about it."

"Have you been shopping or seen any of the galleries?" I could't believe her disregard for injoying the area's opportunities.

"No. I wouldn't know where to start."

"Why don't you come with me sometime? I'm always poking my head into one shop or another. Looking doesn't cost anything and occasionally I even find something I like. You'll never know if you don't venture out. How about this afternoon? You're free aren't you?"

"I suppose I am. What time?"

"How about in forty-five minutes? I'll meet you in the lobby. We can take my car."

"All right, thanks for the invitation, Jillian. Cecilia, it was nice to meet you."

"It was nice meeting you too, Tori. I hope this investigation is over soon so you can go home."

Tori nodded in agreement, stood up, gathered her paraphernalia and followed us out the gate. We parted and went back to our respective rooms.

Before I could return Elise Hansen's call, Detective Noble phoned to find out any news I might have gleaned in talking with Yvette and Mark. I told him Yvette would visit soon. I would fill him in of course.

I told Cecilia I needed to speak privately, so she went to her room and closed the door, smiling in total understanding. She was a jewel!

"Here's what I've learned, Detective. That ghost orchid porcelain piece belonged to Rene at one time. Yvette confirmed that for me. It was purchased for someone as a memento. Rene didn't tell her to whom he planned to give it. I didn't let on where it wound up — I didn't have the heart, nor did I think you'd want me to tell her."

"I appreciate that, Jillian. Any more surprises before I talk to her?"

"Well, I suppose she'll tell you, but you might want to check up on a person of interest. His name is Ray Ackermann. He lives in the Ocala area. I believe there might be a connection."

"How does he fit in?"

"Ask Yvette. He doesn't sound like a nice man to me."

"Okay, I'll ask her. What else do you have for me?"

"Just that Rene was showing an interest in spy

magazines and purchased a camera right after an incident with this man. It could mean something. It's tied in somehow. I also think you should go over Rene's room at home and his apartment, too, or wherever he was living in Florida."

"I can certainly arrange for that. It looks like we're going to have to dig deeper since no clues have surfaced as to motive. Thanks, Jillian. Nice work."

"Detective, did you speak with Mark this morning?"

"Yeah, we talked for a few minutes before they kicked me out. I asked him about the key again and he clammed up. It's not helping him to get off as number one on my suspect list. Maybe you should tell him that. Listen Jillian, I've got another call, but stay in touch, especially if you learn anything else. I'll talk to you later."

No goodbye, just a click and he was gone.

I put a call through to the front desk to contact Elise. They put me through right away.

"Elise Hansen. Who's calling please?"

"Elise, this is Jillian Bradley."

"Hello, Jillian. How is Teddy doing?"

"Dr. Morris says he'll be fine. I'm picking him up this afternoon. I'm so thankful he's all right."

"We are, too. When he comes around, I think we should schedule a play date, if you'd like to."

"Sounds like fun! I'll give you a call tomorrow and give you an update, and Elise, thanks so much for being there for us last night. I don't know what I would have done."

"I'm just glad I could help. When Teddy gets home, tell him that Lila says hello, okay?"

"I'll do that. I'll talk to you tomorrow."

"Sounds good, Jillian. Goodbye."

I just had fifteen minutes before meeting Tori. It wasn't enough time to call Vincent, but I didn't think it would hurt him to wait. I'd get back to him later.

I quickly checked my e-mails and touched base with Cecilia on some additions to my column for the week. With my makeup refreshed and a comb run through my hair, I was ready for shopping! Window-shopping, that is.

I arrived in the lobby first and was admiring the paintings when Tori came in.

"Hi, Jillian. I'm ready to go."

"Okay. I'll have them get my car."

The heavy spirit remained with the valets. They tried to smile, but it looked forced.

"How's Teddy doing?" One of the valets acted concerned. "We heard he was stung by a scorpion."

"Fortunately it was only a stun; it could have been fatal. I'm picking him up this afternoon. I appreciate you asking about him."

Tori seemed curious about the conversation, so I filled her in after we got in the car.

"Before we go shopping, would you mind if we stopped for something to drink? I'm dehydrated from being outside all morning."

"Sounds like an excellent plan. I could use something to drink as well."

I found a cute little restaurant that advertised specialty coffee drinks and figured they would have cold drinks as well. We walked in and sat at a table in the back next to a window that looked out onto the shops we planned to visit.

"I think we have to order our drinks first." Tori grinned.

"I think you're right." I smiled back.

We ordered from the counter and took our choices back to our table.

"You're observant, Tori."

"Observant enough to know you're working with that detective."

"I'm allowed to help because I'm considered an

outsider. Does that bother you?"

"Not really. What have you found out?" She sounded nonchalant.

"I'm not at liberty to say. The detective has put a gag order on me so it won't jeopardize his investigation."

"I see." She fiddled with her drink straw. "Do you personally suspect anyone so far?"

"To be honest with you, I don't have any idea who could have killed him. Although I must say, hardly anyone has an airtight alibi. What's got me stumped is motive. Why kill Rene Parker? What could he have possibly done to deserve such a thing? I know there are crimes of passion, crimes of revenge, and crimes of the moment, but I don't have any idea which one it could be. If I had just known Rene, known what he was like, known who he spent time with…well, as you can see, there are just too many unknowns."

I took a drink of my raspberry iced tea and waited for Tori to respond.

She didn't say anything for a moment or two but then asked, "What was he doing in Mark's office, does anyone know that?"

"Not really. You know Mark was in that terrible car accident."

"I heard. I should probably go visit him, poor guy. He seemed so nice. Do you think he could have killed Rene for some reason?"

"I'm not at liberty to say."

"So the police think he's a suspect."

I shrugged. It was the only response I could give without ruining my gag order.

"Tori, what did you think of Rene?"

"He was a flirt. At least he flirted with me all the time. I didn't want him to, but he did anyway. I guess you could say he was persistent."

"Did you go out with him?"

"No, I never did. He would corner me when I would

take a break just to flirt. I don't know why he didn't ask me out unless it was because I never acknowledged his flirting with me. I think I was afraid of getting hurt again."

She lowered her head and took a sip of her soda, seeming lost in thought.

"I'm sorry you were hurt, Tori. Did you lose someone you loved?"

She laughed in a cynical way.

"Did I lose someone I loved? You might say someone I loved lost me. I'm surprised you don't know about me, seeing you're doing detective work on all of us."

"Enlighten me. I'll listen."

"I guess it wouldn't hurt anything if you know. I was married for five years."

She started to get emotional but gained her composure again before continuing. "For five years, I was verbally abused and beaten for no reason. My husband would get angry and go on rampages for hours on end. Some little thing would trigger him and off he'd go, yelling and screaming and calling me all sorts of names.

"If I talked back, or tried to defend myself, he'd beat me so badly I couldn't move. One morning, after he had beaten me, I drove myself to the emergency room. I remember how painful the examination was. It almost killed me because I was still in a lot of pain from the night before. The doctor told me that I would never be able to have children because he had damaged my uterus.

"Finally, one night he was in such a bad mood I could see another tirade coming, so I left and found a women's shelter nearby.

"He tried to find me, but they kept my whereabouts a secret, so he never did. After I spent a couple of weeks there, they helped me find a job in another part of town and let me stay until I could earn enough to get out on my own.

"I dyed my hair blond and wore it differently. I gradually changed into the person you see now. I live one day at a time, hoping I'll never see him again. I find myself still looking over my shoulder, though. I bought a gun and registered it. I learned how to use it and if he ever comes at me again, I swear I'll blow his head off."

I was stunned after listening to her story. I couldn't find any words. She must have understood how I felt because she smiled and told me she was okay, that she had learned to live with it.

"I'm truly sorry after hearing your story, Tori. I really am."

"It's okay. I've come a long way since leaving him."

"I'm sure you have. You have a great job and you carry yourself well."

She smiled for the first time since I'd met her. When she did she lit up the room. There was a small emanation of warmth—but only a small one, then it vanished as quickly as it had first come.

It was time to get back on track about Rene, so I asked her if she had any other thoughts about what he was like.

"He was a self-seeker for sure. Self-confident. Shrewd. And I think he was secretive in a way."

"What makes you say that?"

"Just a feeling. He put up a wall, just like me when I don't want people to get too close. It was like that. I think that might have been the reason I was attracted to him, even though I didn't want to be. Guys like him seem to manufacture chemistry."

"Yes, I know what you mean." I thought about Vincent Fontaine asking me out to dinner and then sending those beautiful roses the next day.

"Tori, did Rene have a girlfriend, or date anyone that you knew about?"

"He never mentioned anyone. We tried to keep our

personal lives confidential around the office."

"I see. Well, this has been most informative. I really appreciate this little chat. I know it wasn't easy. I hope you'll let me know if you think of anything else that might be of help."

"I will, although I can't imagine what it would be."

"Something may jog your memory. You never know. Let's check out some shops, what do you say?"

"I'm ready. Sounds like a good diversion."

Scottsdale is famous for its specialty shops and it was fun looking into them. There were dress shops, accessory shops, western shops, art galleries, pottery shops, and soap and candle shops of every description.

Tori bought a cute purse made of soft brown leather trimmed with brass studs.

"Nice." I complimented her choice.

"I've always wanted a nice purse like this. I just never shopped for one."

"I hope you think of a pleasant day when you look at it, Tori."

She smiled. "I will. You've been nice to take me with you today, Jillian. I hope I wasn't too catty at the beginning."

"Not a problem. When people are on the defensive there's usually a reason."

"Well, you've been kind."

Before we arrived back and parted ways, I asked Tori to hook me up with Richard Sanchez at the earliest possible moment. It needed to be a casual encounter so he would be at ease. After we broke the ice a little, then she could find an excuse to leave us alone to talk.

In what seemed to be a spirit of mischievous enthusiasm, she agreed.

Chapter 8

Tori was true to her word. She sent a cryptic e-mail: *"Tonight. Ten o'clock. Jade Bar."*

I immediately thought of taking a nap, but there was no way I could sleep with everything going on. I checked in with Cecilia, who had finished an article for her paper while Teddy was at the vet.

"How did it go with Tori?" She looked up from her computer and stretched.

"It was interesting. I learned a few things about Rene Parker that gives me a little more insight into his personality."

"And that is…."

"Well, he perceived himself as a ladies man for one thing. He was cocky in Tori's opinion, and I think it could have contributed to someone killing him. She's setting me up with Richard Sanchez tonight so I can pick his brain like I picked hers."

"Do you think she could have killed Rene?"

"It's hard to say. She may have told me everything and then again, I felt like she was holding back in some way. I just can't put my finger on it, but there was something in the way she talked about Rene. It felt biased. Just a hunch."

"Your hunches are usually correct, Jillian. I'm sure it will surface, whatever it is."

"I'll have to wait until I can talk with her again. It looks like it's time to pick Teddy up. Cecilia, would you please call Dr. Morris and see if Teddy can go? I need to send a memo to my editor assuring him everything will be on time this week, even though I'm out of town."

"Sure thing. I'll call right now."

After I submitted my memo, I walked over to the fireplace and stared into the flames.

Cecilia made the call to Dr. Morris, then came and sat down in the chair next to where I stood.

"Teddy's ready. You look a little tired, Jillian. Would you like me to drive you over to pick him up? I'd be glad to."

"Thanks. I'd like to be able to hold him on the way back. I'm ready anytime you are."

"I'll get my purse."

It didn't take long to get to the vet clinic. It was nice having Cecilia drive. I hadn't realized how tired I was from all the stress. My mind wandered as we drove. Was I missing something? Could there be some detail that I hadn't noticed? Right now, my mind was too full of distractions. Maybe I would remember later.

Hearing barks...several dogs, including Teddy, was music to my ears. The receptionist gave me the bill and I happily pulled out my debit card, happy to pay. Out he came, leash on collar, tail wagging, and feet scurrying to get to me.

"I'm so glad to see you," he conveyed. "I missed you so much. Did you miss me? I'm hungry!"

He jumped into my arms, shaking, and began to lick my cheek. It felt so good to hold him again.

"Oh, Teddy, I've missed you. Are you okay?"

I didn't mention the play date with Lila for fear of riling him up too much, but just thinking about it made me smile.

"Come on, let's go home."

We both made over him after arriving back at our casita. Cecilia had called ahead for room service to have dinner delivered. Teddy hopped up on the sofa and made himself at home while we put our purses away and got ready for our meal. It arrived in five minutes. I had given Cecilia the liberty of ordering for both of us and she did a superb job. Heirloom tomato gazpacho and avocado cream for starters, farmer's market salads with snap peas, carrots, radishes and soy vinaigrette. The entrées were bacon-wrapped filets of beef, with Maytag blue cheese, roasted garlic mash, and a Merlot demi-glace. For dessert, she selected chocolate peanut butter decadence for herself and an almond tuile filled with homemade ice cream for me. And of course, she ordered a nice pot of tea for us both.

Cecilia took a small portion of the dishes and made a nice dinner for Teddy, who was most appreciative. He was so tired, that after a long sigh he fell asleep on the sofa. He was home. He was all right and I thanked the Lord once again.

It was only six o'clock. I had four hours until the meeting with Richard Sanchez so I made a call to Vincent's room.

"Jillian. Thanks for calling me back. Did you get Teddy home?"

"Yes, he's sleeping right beside me. The doctor says he'll be fine."

"Well, that's good news."

"I want to thank you for the beautiful roses you sent me this morning."

"I'm glad you got them okay. You seemed to need a little cheering up with Teddy and all and I really did enjoy your company last night."

"I had a fun time, too. Cecilia said you've invited me to lunch tomorrow."

"If you're free, I'd love it."

"I'm free. What did you have in mind?"

"That's a pretty loaded question, Jillian." He chuckled.

"You know what I mean. Where should we meet and when would you like to go?"

"Let's say eleven-thirty in the lobby. I promise not to have a drink so you can allow me to drive."

"I just don't take chances, Vincent."

"I'm hoping you'll give me a chance and I don't mean my driving."

"You are something else, Doctor Fontaine. Right now, I'll give you a chance to treat me to lunch tomorrow. That's all I can promise."

"That's a start. I'll see you tomorrow."

"Goodbye, Vincent."

***

I slipped off my shoes, turned on the TV, and stretched out on the sofa next to Teddy trying to relax a little. After several moments of channel surfing there didn't seem to be anything on of interest. All right then, time for a catnap. Soon I slipped beyond consciousness. The dark realm, my subconscious, took control. I started to dream.

Yvette sat near me, flipping through a yellowing album. She was showing me pictures of Rene. The pictures were recent ones as well as ones of him as a boy. She was so proud of him and smiled and laughed when she described what he was doing in each picture. Then, a picture of Rene holding the porcelain ghost orchid appeared. Yvette stopped laughing. Her face darkened and she took the photograph and tore it in half, then in half again, then tore it in half again until it was shredded to pieces. She threw the pieces in Rene's face and told him to get out of her house.

"Never come back," she yelled. "Never come back."

Then Rene disappeared from the scene and Yvette

was standing in the back room of her store crying, her hands covering her face. A man, whose face I couldn't make out was in the room with her. He put his arms around her and held her tightly. She screamed but no one heard her, no one at all.

"Jillian, wake up. You're having a bad dream. Wake up!"

Cecilia was gently shaking my shoulder. My eyes popped open.

"Are you okay?" She sat down next to me.

"I'm all right. Thanks. I just fell asleep for a second there. Cecilia, get me a pen and paper, would you please? I want to write down what I dreamed before I forget."

Cecilia got up immediately and brought a tablet and pen.

I wrote down sequentially what I could remember:

- Yvette shows me pictures of Rene.
- Yvette smiling and laughing.
- A picture of Rene holding a porcelain ghost orchid.
- Rene looking at the orchid.
- Yvette stops smiling and laughing; she turns dark.
- Yvette becomes angry and tears the picture into shreds.
- Yvette kicks Rene out of the house.
- Yvette is in the back room, crying, hands over her face.
- An unknown man puts his arms around her tightly.
- Yvette screams.
- No one hears.

"It was a horrible dream."

Cecilia brought me a drink of water.

"Cecilia, my mother used to always tell me to take my dreams backwards."

"Okay. If we were to take your dream facts in reverse, what would we have?"

I took up my pen again and began writing a new list:

- I've never seen pictures of Rene — maybe I should.
- When he bought the porcelain ghost orchid, something changed with Rene, not Yvette.
- The porcelain ghost orchid didn't upset Yvette, but it might have upset someone else.
- Yvette would never kick Rene out of the house and he always felt at home with her.
- Yvette doesn't fear any man in particular, but Rene might have.
- Yvette doesn't scream.
- Someone hears.

"That's quite a puzzle, Jillian. Do you have any idea what it means?"

"Well, one thing's for certain. There may be more evidence in this investigation than we're finding here in Scottsdale. I think a trip to Ocala is crucial if we're going to learn anything else, but I don't know if Detective Noble will go there or not. I think I'll give him a call."

"I wouldn't mention the dream to him, Jillian. You know how men are. Just tell him what you suspect."

"You're absolutely right. I'll call him now."

I punched in his number and waited for him to pick up. He answered on the second ring.

"Are you busy? I just wondered since you didn't pick up until the second ring."

"Hello, Jillian. Actually, I *was* busy. I'm sitting here at my computer looking up the profile on Ray Ackermann."

"Do you have anything?"

"He's pretty clean, no record, not even a parking ticket. He's worked for the same lumber mill for twenty years as their manager."

"What about his financial records? Let's say about six years ago—somewhere in that range. Something may surface there. I just have a hunch."

"A hunch, huh? I haven't checked those yet, but I'll be sure and do it. I'll tell you what though, after talking to Yvette, I sure would like to have a look at his room."

"I'd like to look at his camera in particular." I had another hunch.

"I was just going to say that."

"When do we leave?"

"Now wait a minute, Jillian. This is still my investigation. I don't want you to come with me. I want you to stay here and keep your ears open. Please understand that everyone must stay here until we've cleared alibis. I need you to help me get that proof."

"I suppose that's fair enough. What change are you going to hold them on?"

"We'll hold them on circumstantial evidence, of course. All of them were with the victim just before he was murdered. No one except Warren Burkett has an alibi and I can think of motives for each suspect."

"Can you, really? Just out of curiosity, like what?"

"Well, let's see. For starters, your friend Arthur Wingate could have some funny business going on with the grant. We found Mark Russell's key in the victim's pocket. Helen Morningstar locked up last, which means she could have easily done it...."

"You can't suspect Helen, Detective. She wouldn't

have a motive. She'd only met him that day."

"I'll give you that one. Then there's the old Floridians. Vincent Fontaine could have had a beef with Rene for some reason. Leah Fontaine could have been a jealous lover; Tori DeMarco could have been one, too. Richard Sanchez could have been a jealous lover as well, or maybe he wanted Rene out of the way, so he could get to Tori. You see, there are motives everywhere you look."

"Perhaps, but what evidence do you have, except for the key, of course, that would support any of them?"

"As far as I'm concerned, I'm keeping everyone right here where I can keep an eye on them. A detective is watching everyone round the clock, so if any of them decides to tip his or her hand, we'll be right there waiting for them."

"I'm impressed. I'll help in whatever way I can. At least poor Mark Russell isn't going anywhere. I'll stay in touch with him and let you know if there's anything new on that front. By the way, I've talked to Leah, Vincent, and Tori and so far—I've got nothing. Someone is hiding something. I just can't put my finger on it, but I will."

"Now I'm the one who's impressed. That just leaves Richard Sanchez."

"And I see him tonight. Tori set it up for me."

"And she cooperated?"

"She did, indeed."

"Jillian, you've earned my respect."

"Let's hope we can earn the respect of Yvette by finding her son's killer."

"I'm with you on that one, lady. I'll be in touch. Need to get some plane tickets to Florida. I'll escort Yvette back home after the funeral and check out Rene's belongings. The trail is getting cold. If we could just find the weapon, it would tell us a lot. "

"I think so, too. I've asked myself if I wanted to get

rid of a murder weapon and I was staying at this hotel where would I put it? I'm still thinking about it, but I have at least one idea."

"Tell me."

"I can't until I'm sure. I wouldn't want to let the cat out of the bag, so I have a gag order on my idea."

"Touché, Jillian. Hey, I've got another call. Good luck with Richard tonight. Call me if you learn anything. Talk to you tomorrow." There was another click on his end.

I felt invigorated after what little rest I'd had and looked forward to talking to Richard Sanchez.

***

Soft music played in the background as I entered the lobby. I walked toward the Jade Bar.

Richard and Tori sat in a booth with his back facing me. Although he was seated, I judged his height at about 5'10". His shoulders were broad. Tori motioned for me to join them.

Nonchalant, Jillian, nonchalant.

Richard stood as I approached and extended his hand in greeting. His grip was strong and warm and put me instantly at ease.

"Jillian, may I order you a drink?"

The server appeared and Richard ordered me a virgin lime Rickey. Richard had a low-pitched voice that held a slight accent I couldn't quite identify.

We made small talk until Tori excused herself, saying she was tired. The cover was that she had a few things to do for Leah before going to bed. We said goodnight and I offered to buy Richard another drink, hoping to loosen him up just a little. He graciously accepted and sat back in his seat in a relaxed way. His dark eyes met mine with confidence and I knew this was no ordinary man. Tori had probably warned him about me and he'd seen me with Detective Noble at ZuZu's the other day. I wasn't surprised when he spoke first.

"How come you're in on this murder, Mrs. Bradley?"

"I'm not in on this murder, as you put it. I had no motive, no means, and no opportunity. What if I asked you the same question? How come you're in on this murder, Mr. Sanchez?"

The server set out my drink and I took a long sip.

"So I'm a suspect?" He cocked an eyebrow. "On what grounds?"

"It's my understanding that everyone connected to Rene Parker who has no alibi is under suspicion." I smiled. "I didn't come here tonight to accuse you of murder, Mr. Sanchez."

He looked me straight in the eye and smiled. The smile was genuine and revealed imperfectly shaped but well-cared for teeth.

"Well, that's a relief. Why don't you call me Richard?"

"Sure and you may call me Jillian. You and Tori seem to get along well together I've noticed."

"She's a nice person. We do get along,"

I looked down at the table and spoke. "She told me about her marriage. I think she's done well, all things considered."

"That creep doesn't deserve to live as far as I'm concerned. Tori is distrustful of men because of him."

"You're making progress, then." I smiled at the allusion to something between them.

He nodded, pleased with the compliment.

"Why thank you, Mrs. Bradley. I'd like to think I've got a chance."

It was time to steer the conversation away from Tori back to the murder investigation.

"Richard, I will tell you that so far the police have little to go on to find Rene's killer. Collectively, everyone involved may have enough knowledge to give us some direction as to motive. You, for instance, worked closely with Rene. You saw him every day. You knew what he was like, who he hung out with."

"I will agree with most of what you're saying, Jillian. I did work closely with him. I thought I knew what he was like until he got murdered. He must have had a secret life, because I never had any reason to think he was having any trouble with anyone. No reason whatsoever. When I heard he'd been murdered I couldn't believe it. It didn't make sense."

"Did you like Rene, personally?"

"What do you mean, *personally*?"

"I mean just what I said—personally. Did you think he was a nice person? Would you have considered him a friend?"

"I suppose I considered him a friend. We worked together on projects all the time. I didn't *dis*like him."

"Did you hang out together at all?"

"Maybe once in a while but it was always with Tori. He and I never hung out together if that's what you're getting at."

"I'm sorry. I had to ask. Did he hang out with anyone else that you knew of?"

"Not to my knowledge. No, wait. Come to think of it, one time he did intimate that he had something going on with someone. It was just from a few things he said. I even suspected Tori, but she never said anything that made me think they had a relationship. It was odd but he never would give a name. I thought he wanted privacy so I respected that and didn't give it any more thought."

"What things did he say? They might be important."

"Let me think. I would ask him if he had any plans for the weekend—you know, just casual like. He would raise his eyebrows up and down and say nothing. If *I* did that, I'd want people to think I had a hot date."

"What else did he say?"

"I remember a time when we were working late on the grant project. We were pretty tired. I said something like I hoped it was worth all the trouble we were going to in order to win. He said, 'Everything is going to be just fine.'"

"Everything is going to be just fine," I repeated.

"Yeah, he said it like he was saying it to himself. It was as if I wasn't even in the room. It was weird."

"Thank you, Richard. It may fit into what I'm thinking happened. I just need some more pieces to the puzzle before I can be sure. How about another drink? It's on me."

"Thanks. I believe I will."

I motioned for the server. He was there in an instant and took our drink orders. I stayed with my virgin concoction, while Richard ordered another cocktail. He'd begun to relax, I noticed.

"Tell me about yourself, if you don't mind. How did you get to be Field Studies Director with Dr. Fontaine?"

I sat back and listened as he told me his story.

Richard Sanchez was a man of the swamp. At the age of thirty-eight he had spent most of his life navigating the Corkscrew Swamp in particular and had the bronzed skin to prove it. His arms bulged with muscles from lugging around research equipment and rowing canoes. His accent was Cuban.

"Our family emigrated when I was four. They only had enough money to support a small hut located on a tiny island, deep in the Corkscrew Swamp. My father ran a guide service for high paying tourists and scientists. Although our family was poor, my parents managed to earn enough money to pay for my citizenship and education. They sacrificed everything for me and I'm grateful."

"Your parents sound as if they're wonderful people." I sipped my drink savoring the lime goodness.

"They are. My father learned the botanical names of

every flora species to enhance his tour business and passed the knowledge to me. According to my mother, I have my grandfather to thank for a photographic memory. When I was old enough to carry equipment I was able to earn enough money helping my Dad to buy a used laptop and it opened up the world. What I saw and learned, I retained." He smiled.

"How fortunate to have such a gift. Not many do."

His expression turned serious. "Since I was so isolated growing up, owing to the fact that my mother was bi-polar and needed solitude, I didn't do sports or karate like most kids. I just helped my Dad and educated myself. I figured out how to get a degree online and did just that."

"Highly commendable. I'm impressed. So how did you come to work for Dr. Fontaine?"

"My Dad made sure I met all the important people who used his guide service. The clients were usually impressed with our family—we were friendly, polite, hardworking, and smart—qualities that eventually earned me a job working as a tech support in one of the clients' offices."

"And I'm sure it was all you needed. Am I right?"

He nodded and smiled. "I continued to meet all kinds of people and was so knowledgeable in the Everglades flora that Dr. Leah Fontaine hired me as her field study guide. I love my job and do conscientious work studying Florida's endangered species, their habitats, strengths and weaknesses, and document the progression of their demise."

"That's quite a background, Richard. How long have you worked for Leah?"

"It will be five years this coming January. Seems like only yesterday when I started there." He seemed lost in memory.

I decided it was time to take a chance and ask him.

"Did you ever remember meeting a man named Ray

Ackermann?"

"Ray Ackermann?" He shook his head. "Not off the bat, but I'm sure that's not the first time I've heard that name. Let me think about it and maybe it will come to me. Does he have something to do with Rene's murder, you think?"

"Maybe. It's just a possibility."

I downed the last bit of my drink and looked at my watch.

"It's late."

"Yeah, I'm calling it a night, too."

He stood, signaled for the server to bring the bill, then signed for it, insisting on paying.

"I'll be glad when this investigation is over so I can get back to work."

We started back to our rooms. "At least with the nice weather you can hang out by the pool." I smiled, thinking about him and Tori.

"True. That I've enjoyed." He seemed to catch my innuendo. "Jillian, you'll let me know if you learn anything, won't you? You're not officially with the investigation, are you?"

"No, I'm only helping with some leg work because I'm staying with all of the *suspects*." I smiled, teasing him.

He sighed and rolled his eyes.

"I'll have to run it by Detective Noble first before I can tell you anything, Richard. Let me know if you remember anything about Ray Ackermann as soon as possible. It might be important."

"Deal. Would you like me to escort you back to your room?"

"Oh, I think I'll be all right. Thanks for offering though. And thank you for the drink, it was kind of you."

We parted company. On the way back to my casita, about midway, I felt the hair on the back of my neck rise up. Was someone following me?

The night was dark and the path behind trailed off into the shadowy trees. I stopped and turned around to look back but saw no one. Maybe it was the same man that had been in the parking lot earlier.

"Detective?" I called. There was silence, so I assumed it wasn't him. I walked a little faster until I reached my front door. Whoever was following me had gone, but I was unnerved by the incident.

I slipped in quietly. Cecilia had already retired for the night. Teddy was sound asleep on his towel at the foot of my bed. He raised his head but after it registered that I'd returned, he immediately lowered it and fell back asleep. He probably still had some medication in his system. Poor thing. At least he was back safely.

I would take a bath in the morning. Cecilia needed some rest and I'd wake her with the water running.

In bed, my mind wandered into sleep. Why? Teddy was safely back with me…safely back with me…back with me. In my mind, I saw my precious husband in uniform trying to reach out to me from the fields in Vietnam but he slowly faded into the background and was gone. I wouldn't be able to say he was back safely with me until I joined him in Heaven. God was so good to me.

"Goodnight, Lord. Thank you for Teddy.

"And thank you for protecting me tonight."

Chapter 9

The pounds were creeping up on me with all of the food I'd been eating. No more avoiding the gym. I would leave a message for Cecilia and get it over with. I threw on my baby blue sweats and tennis shoes and left quietly.

The morning radiated with sunshine as I stepped onto the path. The flowerbeds were pristine and I enjoyed looking at all the amazing cacti and desert flora along the path to the fitness center. Many others apparently had the same idea because the gym was full and people were working the machines.

I placed my bag in a cubby, found a towel and looked around for a free treadmill. Only one left. Thirty minutes ought to do it. I began at a slow speed and after five minutes reset it higher. The man next to me was doing a grade six incline and moving fast. He had to use his towel frequently. I never used mine once. Oh well, at least I was working out.

I glanced around the room and saw Leah dressed in a pink and black tight fitting Capri sweat outfit lifting weights. So that was how she kept those skinny arms. She either ignored me, or perhaps didn't see me. I continued to do the treadmill until I saw her head to the bathroom. I turned the machine off, grabbed my towel and bag from the cubby, and followed her.

"Hello, Leah."

"Hi, Jillian." She began washing her hands, took a towel to dry them off, and reached into her bag for her hairbrush. "I didn't see you here yesterday."

"I only work out every other day. Keeping busy?"

"I'm trying to, but it's difficult not being in the office."

"I wouldn't know. I do my writing from home. All I need is a laptop."

"How nice for you. How is the investigation going?"

"It's going. We're getting some leads. Detective Noble is taking Yvette back at the same time they're flying Rene's body back home for burial."

"How nice of him. Is that standard?"

"Well, in this case it is. He's hoping to find out more by actually visiting Rene's home."

"You mean Rene was a secret agent and they hope to find a communications system? Something like that?"

"Something like that. Anyway, I'm sure we'll get to the bottom of it soon."

Leah placed her brush back into her bag and closed it quickly.

"Well, Jillian, happy hunting. I'm going back to my room to do some work. Have a nice day."

"You too, Leah." Something clicked in my mind but it didn't stay with me long.

I trudged back to my room and found Cecilia up and dressed. She stood at the kitchenette preparing Teddy's breakfast when I came in.

She smiled. "Jillian, there you are. I found your note. I'll order breakfast if you like while you get dressed."

"Thanks. That's a great idea. I'd like that grilled chicken Benedict again. And order me some orange juice, too."

"With a pot of coffee, of course."

"Of course!"

My cell rang just as I was about to step out of the shower.

"Jillian, it's Arthur." He sounded distraught.

"Hi. What happened? You sound awful."

"Bad news, I'm afraid."

"Is it Mark?"

"Yeah, he's going fast. The surgery couldn't help him. The injuries were too bad. Helen is with him now. Diana is with me in the waiting room. I thought I'd let you know. He asked for a pastor. Helen said he made peace with God."

"I'm coming down as soon as I get dressed, Arthur. I'll see you soon."

I whispered a prayer. "Oh, Lord God, thank you for making Mark one of Your own. Please give us all strength to get through this. And Lord, please help me find Rene's killer. I pray it wasn't Mark, but if it was, help us to know so it clears anyone else."

Breakfast arrived and I ate while I finished drying my hair and putting on my makeup. I was ready to go in forty-five minutes, a little longer than I'd hoped. At least it was only a short drive to the clinic.

"Cecilia, please call Elise and set up that play date for Teddy and Lila. He's getting awfully bored, I'm afraid. I think this afternoon would be fine if they're available."

"I'll call her. Remember you're having lunch with Vincent Fontaine at eleven-thirty today."

"Oh, yes. I remember. I hope he doesn't think I'm encouraging him, Cecilia."

"It's a woman's prerogative, Jillian, but a lunch date is nice under any circumstances."

"You're right, of course. I can tell it's going to be another one of those days. Well, I'm off. Thanks for all your help with Teddy. I should be back no later than two o'clock. Try to get the play date after Teddy's nap and mine! Three-thirty would be fine."

"I'll do my best. I'll see you this afternoon."

She scooped Teddy up in her arms so he couldn't follow me out the door. He barked two yips to let me know he'd miss me.

I couldn't help but smile.

I called Detective Noble on the way to see Mark. He said he would meet me there. I wondered if Mark had said anything about the key. I pulled up in front of the clinic to park with butterflies in my stomach. Not a good sign. Something was different today. It felt dramatic...and wrong.

The reception area was not as full as yesterday. I walked down the hall to the waiting room and stepped inside. Helen, Arthur, and Diana were all sitting together with downcast faces. Arthur stood when he saw me come in and gave me a hug.

"Glad you could come, Jillian. I'm afraid it's over. Mark passed away a few moments ago."

"I'm so sorry." Disappointment flooded me. I shouldn't have taken so long. But if I felt this way, Helen and the others would feel much worse. They'd known him longer.

"Arthur, you said he'd spoken to a pastor?"

"I'll let Helen tell you about it. She was there when Mark talked to him."

"Hi, Helen."

I sat down in the empty chair next to her and she reached for my hand.

"Jillian, it looks like God took him home."

She cried a little but then gained her composure.

"Mark asked me to call my pastor. He said he was ready to make peace with God. Pastor Richardson came over right away when I explained the situation to him. Anyway, the pastor did a wonderful job explaining to him how much God loved him. He asked Mark to confess his sins silently to God and he did. When he finished, he squeezed the pastor's hand.

"Mark told the pastor he believed Jesus was God's Son, and that he wanted to be with him when he died.

"Oh, Jillian, it was so hard to hear him talk about dying. Then, Mark smiled. He turned to me and said, 'I want everyone to know that I didn't kill Rene. I only gave him my key so he could alter our grant submission so his team could win. He was going to pay me....'

"I could tell Mark was in a lot of pain but he continued. He said, 'I want my insurance policy to go to the family I ruined.' He had taken care of that a few hours before the pastor got there.

"I bent down and hugged him as gently as I could and then I heard him breathe his last breath. He died with a smile on his face, Jillian, and I knew he was with the Lord. There was so much peace in the room — it was just unexplainable!"

"At least he's in no more pain, Helen, and we know where he is now."

Detective Noble arrived, hurrying as usual. After looking at us, he knew instinctively that Mark was gone.

"Looks like I'm too late."

"I don't think so, Detective." I shared what Helen had told me about the key and he seemed resigned that it was probably the truth.

"Jillian, could we have a word alone?"

I excused myself and we walked outside.

He looked at me with a dejected face. "I'm sorry about Mark. It looks like we're back to square one with him gone."

"Maybe not. At least we now know that Rene was up to no good on that computer and someone probably stopped him from going through with the alterations."

"So you think someone from the Arizona team stopped him from ruining their grant proposal?"

"It could well be. Nothing else makes sense right now."

"I'm glad I'm going to Ocala in the morning. I sure

hope I find something."

"I've been doing some thinking about Yvette. I know she's strapped for funds right now. I'd like to pay for Rene's funeral, anonymously, of course. She wanted to bury him next to her husband and I think that's fitting."

I handed him an envelope with Yvette's name typed on the front. "I had a cashier's check made out to her. I'd like for you to give it to her if you don't mind."

His face changed from concern to surprise.

"That's magnanimous of you, Jillian. I'll be sure and do that. You're really something."

I laughed just a little. "Oh, it's not me. I just believe that when we have an opportunity to help someone, God wants us to do it. I didn't have to bury my husband — the military did that and I'll never have to bury a child because the Lord never blessed me with any. Some sadness, but also, there are always reasons to be thankful.

"It's unfathomable to think what Yvette must be feeling right now, having lost her only son. God has blessed me so much financially in my life, I just want to share it with someone who I think would appreciate it."

He accepted the check and nodded with a smile. Then his face grew serious again. "Oh, by the way, I did some checking on Ray Ackermann's finances right around the time you said, and sure enough, bingo, I hit pay dirt!"

"Excellent. What did you find out?"

"I re-checked Mr. Ackermann's bio and ran across an outstanding warrant dated two years ago. He wasn't served because he left the country, probably for Cuba."

"What was the warrant for?"

"Are you ready for this? Poaching."

"Poaching? You mean like poaching game on private property?"

"Not game, Jillian. He was caught poaching a rare orchid which is totally against the law in Florida. Plus the financial records are pretty interesting, too."

"What did they show?"

"There were some large deposits made that look to me like payments of some sort. I still haven't checked them out entirely, but don't worry, I will. I need to leave. I have some work to do with some other cases I'm working on before I leave in the morning with Yvette. I'll be sure and give her the check."

"Before you go, Detective, you should know that someone followed me home from my meeting with Richard Sanchez last night."

"Do you have any idea who it was?"

"I really don't have a clue. Maybe they were trying to see what I was going to do with the information I got from Richard. Or, probably more likely, they were trying to scare me. They certainly succeeded."

"Now listen to me, Jillian. Things could get dicey now that we have some solid leads. I'll put an extra watch on you just in case. They'll be discreet, I promise."

"Thank you. That makes me feel a lot better."

"I don't want you to say anything to anybody because you could endanger yourself. I've seen it happen before and I don't want it happening to you, understand?"

"I understand. I do trust Cecilia, though. Couldn't I confide in her?"

"Are you sure she can keep her mouth shut?"

"I can trust her, Detective. Besides, she can be of great help when it comes to looking up information when I need it."

"Okay then, but no one else. I insist."

I wished him luck on his trip with Yvette and made him promise to stay in touch.

Emotionally exhausted from the visit, I got into my car. Poor Mark Russell. And the man who lost his wife and daughters in the accident had to be grief-stricken.

"Lord," I prayed, "please comfort the hearts of that family."

I felt a little better and started the car. I pulled out of the parking lot and onto the main road that took me back to the hotel. After a few minutes, I glanced in the rear view mirror just to check traffic and saw a car about six car lengths behind. It seemed to be following me. I switched lanes and slowly made a right turn. The car made the same right turn.

I maneuvered back to the main thoroughfare and checked my mirror again as unobtrusively as possible. There it was again! I was too far away to notice the license plate number but I did get the make and color. It was a dark gray, late model Mazda.

I raced home as fast as I could without going over the speed limit. By the time I turned into the resort entrance, it had disappeared. Did I imagine it? Somehow, I didn't think so. The car had immediately turned twice when I did. The road to the hotel was not a major one. They would have no reason to be going my way. This was no coincidence.

Then a thought occurred to me. What would a person who felt threatened, as I had felt just now, do to protect himself or herself? I always prayed for angels to protect me and on a few occasions they had, but not everyone believes in angels. Many people believe in alarm systems or weapons.

Had Rene been a threat to someone? Perhaps that person had a gun for protection. It was a possibility, anyway. Tori and Richard both had guns, but they couldn't have brought them through airport security without verification.

Did Vincent own a gun? He certainly looked capable of using one. I'm sure even Leah could own one for protection since I assumed she lived alone.

Finding myself lost in thought, I swiped the passkey and was home again. Safe. Teddy raced to greet me, barking until I picked him up. He gave me a few dog kisses. I put him down so I could rub his tummy and shower him with attention. I grabbed his favorite stuffed frog and we played fetch three times until he wore his little self out.

Cecilia asked if I'd like some coffee. After gratefully accepting the cup, we sat down to catch up.

"Mark Russell passed away this morning. It happened before I got there."

"I'm so sorry, Jillian. How sad for everyone. Did he have family?"

"It doesn't seem like he did. No one came to visit him, except his colleagues and he didn't mention anyone."

"Wow, I can't imagine being alone."

I bowed my head. Cecilia reached her hand toward me.

"It's all right, Cecilia. I'm not really alone, you know. I have the Lord. He's always with me. Besides, I have you and I have Teddy. That's all I really need."

"I'm sorry. But you're right. To have God, a friend, and a companion like Teddy is a lot for me to be grateful about, too. And don't forget, you had a husband that loved you with all his heart even if it was just for a short time."

"I know. So many people never really know what real love is. Speaking of love, my dear, you haven't mentioned Walter lately. What's going on with him?"

Cecilia chuckled, then blushed and looked a little embarrassed. "Well, things are happening."

"They are?"

"Yes, they are. He's been texting me twice a day. He doesn't really say anything, it's all small talk, but I think he really likes me, Jillian, and I sure like him. In fact, there's not a thing I don't like about him."

"It sounds like it's getting serious. Listen, before I meet Vincent for lunch, I need you to send in the

December Gardening Calendar for me. The stock one I always use for the Bay Area will work fine. Would you take care of it? I promised I'd get it in."

"Sure. I have plenty of time this morning. Oh, by the way, I set up the play date for Teddy and Lila. It's this afternoon at 3:30. Elise said to meet her on the dog lawn."

"Perfect. I also want you to Google Ray Ackermann for me. Get whatever you can on him."

"Sure."

"It's time I met Vincent for lunch. Teddy, behave. I'll see you later, boy. We're going to have a fun time with Lila this afternoon."

He started barking furiously and headed for the front door. Cecilia and I laughed and laughed as she scooped him up once again and I headed for the lobby for my lunch date.

There was no one in the lobby when I arrived. I looked at my watch and noted that it was 11:35 am — plenty of time to be fashionably late. I glanced around. Not seeing anyone I noticed the concierge seated at her desk in the small adjoining area of the lobby. There was a sitting area across from her. The chairs looked comfortable and I could wait there.

She typed furiously on her computer. Seeming to notice me for the first time, she took off her reading glasses and smiled politely. "May I help you?"

"I'm just waiting for a friend, thank you."

The artwork looked just as stunning as ever and I looked forward to hanging my new acquisitions when I got home. A group approached and their voices rang out in the lobby. I looked to where they were coming from. It was Vincent. Leah was with him. I stood and joined them.

"Leah, how nice you're joining us for lunch."

"I hope you don't mind the last minute change in plans, but Leah insisted." Vincent sounded apologetic.

Although I was a little disappointed at the threesome, I was glad to be able to observe the two of them together.

"I don't mind at all. I love getting acquainted with colleagues."

"Why don't we just eat here, then?" Vincent acted stiff and reserved.

I could tell he wasn't happy Leah had joined us.

Leah, on the other hand, looked pleased with herself.

"It's fine with me, if it's all right with you, Jillian."

"I'm sure we can find something delightful to eat." I turned my thoughts to what I would order.

Before we were seated, Richard and Tori came in. Vincent beckoned to them. "Why don't you join us? It seems we're having a party today."

Richard asked Tori if she'd mind. She graciously accepted the invitation.

"Would you like to be seated on the patio?" the young server asked Vincent. "The weather is beautiful outside."

Everyone agreed it would be nice to enjoy the view, so we procured a table overlooking Paradise Valley. Everyone ordered iced tea, or water with lemon, except for Vincent, who asked for a gin and tonic. Evidently, being around Leah made him up tight. I wondered why.

The server handed out the menus and we began perusing them.

Leah turned to Tori and asked, "Did you finish my reports on the new data?"

"They're almost complete. I just have a few more pages to input."

"I wanted them before noon today. I'm disappointed, Tori. You know we're behind because of the situation we're in."

Leah spoke harshly, disregarding the fact that someone outside of her office was present.

Tori sounded meek. "I apologize, Dr. Fontaine. If

you'll excuse me, I'll finish them right now."

She stood up to leave. Richard tried to stop her but she looked at him and shook her head. "It's okay. I should have finished them this morning. Enjoy your lunch, everyone."

After she left, Vincent looked at Leah.

"Was that really necessary?"

He waited for her to answer, took a sip of his drink, but never broke eye contact.

"Just because we're stuck here doesn't mean our work can't get done. She'll be all right. It's what I pay her for."

Vincent looked down at the table.

Richard looked as if he wanted to say something but sat back and kept quiet.

I mentally applauded his wisdom. We ordered and made polite conversation until the food arrived.

"Did everyone have a pleasant morning?" I hoped to find out if one of my lunch fellows was tailing me.

"I slept in, ordered breakfast, went to the gym, and stretched out by the pool, myself," Vincent said. "What about you, Leah?"

"I just stayed in my room and worked on some data I needed to integrate with a project. Not the most fun morning, but at least I got something accomplished."

"You'll be happy to know I did some work as well, Leah. In fact, I'll bring it over after lunch if you want." Richard made the offer quietly.

"At least *one* of my employees is earning their keep." Leah spoke under her breath.

My Southwest turkey club sandwich with fresh guacamole looked delicious. A pasta salad, with corn, peppers, and peas was a scrumptious side dish. I decided there really wasn't an ideal time to tell everyone about Mark so I said it as simply as I could.

"Mark Russell passed away this morning."

Everyone kept eating as if I hadn't said anything.

Then Richard spoke. "That's too bad. He seemed like a good guy."

Leah smiled. "It looks like both of our teams are down a player, doesn't it?"

Vincent suddenly glared at his daughter. "How can you be so cold, Leah?"

"I'm not being cold. I'm just stating a fact. Arthur has lost a colleague and so have we. Now we're both going to have to find replacements. I'm thinking about it because I'm the one who has to replace Rene. None of you do! No one seems to understand I'm under a terrible strain. I'm sure Arthur would understand if he were here."

I felt Leah might be heading for a meltdown, so I intervened. "I think I understand where you're coming from, Leah. This is stressful for everyone, but especially for you. I'm sure things will get back to normal when this is all over. We just have to be patient and take it one day at a time. Why don't we talk about something else? Richard, what did you do for fun when you lived on the island? I'm curious."

"When we weren't working, we were so tired, that just to eat a hot supper my mom made was fun for us. I guess fun isn't the right word really, but it was a pleasure after hiking around all day and canoeing through the swamp. After feeding us a breakfast of biscuits and gravy, my mom would pack us a cold lunch and send us out. We fished and hunted for our food; I guess you could call that fun. I always loved being with my father when I was growing up. I still do."

"I remember being with my boys on the weekends." Vincent looked reminiscent. "I'd take them fishing and boy, did they love it."

"You took me a couple of times I remember." Leah seemed calmer now.

"You weren't bad, either." He gave her an affectionate smile.

Leah beamed at the compliment. For a moment it seemed to transform her into a lovely young woman.

I thought of how much toll stress can take on a person.

"My family didn't have a lot of fun," I recalled. "My father thought the weekends were meant for cleaning the house and doing yard work. I used to think it was because he was in the military and had that sort of mentality. Looking back, I think it was more that he knew my mom needed the extra helping hands because she assisted him in his business all week. Funny the way you look at things differently when you get older."

"I remember teaching my boys how to shoot. We'd go to the shooting range about once a month to practice. When they each turned sixteen I bought them their own guns. I trained them how to respect a gun, how to keep it clean, how to store it unloaded, and how to keep it locked up." Vincent spoke with fatherly pride.

"By the way, Vincent, where are your boys working now? Leah said they worked overseas."

Leah stopped smiling and took a few bites of her Cobb salad.

"Vince Jr. works as head of HR for a large technology corporation based in Portland. He lives between New York and Beijing. I rarely see him. He spends most of his time working, but he says he loves what he does so I'm happy for him. I keep his room just as he left it. He'll come see me one of these days, but he hasn't yet."

"And your other son?"

"Robert is a bean counter for a large accounting firm in London."

"By 'bean counter' I assume you mean accountant?"

"Yes, he's a CPA. Robert's done well for himself. He says he loves London, everyone's more polite and there's always something to do. He hasn't come home either. A lot of their stuff is still in their rooms just sitting there. Vince's slippers are next to his chair where he left them years ago."

Leah spoke up. "I'd have thrown their stuff out a long time ago. At least dad keeps their rooms clean. He has hired a wonderful housekeeper since Mom's been gone."

Vincent nodded. "She cooks, too. It's a great arrangement. I should have done it sooner."

He sounded like he might still feel the pain of the divorce.

I ordered Key lime cheesecake and coffee for dessert. Never pass up Key lime anything. They topped it with nectarines, peaches, papaya, and toasted coconut— amazing! The sweetness was a perfect ending to lunch. I was ready for a nap.

Richard helped me out of my chair and Leah waited for her father to take the hint, which he did. Vincent signed the bill for all of us after insisting it was his idea for lunch.

If someone insists, I usually let him or her have their way.

Vincent looked at Leah sternly. "Jillian, please let us know when Mark's funeral is going to be. I'm sure we'll all want to attend."

"It will be on Friday. Detective Noble will be attending as well. I'll be sure and let you all know. Have a nice afternoon everyone."

I left them.

There was an hour-and-a-half before the play date, so I returned to the room and got ready to take a nap. Cecilia was busy on the computer.

She looked up for a moment and smiled. "How was lunch?"

"It turned into a foursome after Leah and Richard joined us. I don't think it's what Vincent had in mind, but it worked out okay."

"I'm glad. I have some information on Ray Ackermann ready when you have a chance to look at it."

"Excellent. I'll look at it after my nap. Wake me in an hour, all right?"

"Will do." Cecilia returned to her computer keyboard and started typing away.

***

Later, I put on my faded blue jeans, long-sleeved, black tee-shirt and donned a black hooded tee in case it turned chilly which the fall weather occasionally did in Scottsdale. Teddy bounced in excitement when I brought out his leash and told him we were going on a play date with Lila. He kept going in circles. I laughed trying to get him to be still enough for me to attach it. I combed his bangs into a ponytail, secured it with his special red bow, then brushed his hair one last time so he'd look impressive. We left for the dog lawn.

Teddy pranced ahead of me and communicated that I was to hurry up. I walked a tiny bit more briskly but I wasn't about to break into a sprint. I passed the pool once again and noticed the absence of Tori and Richard. I felt sorry for her being disciplined in public like that. What was Leah thinking? Maybe she was ill, like Arthur had mentioned. I hoped that she didn't have a brain tumor or something horrible. Perhaps she was just hormonal.

I quit thinking about lunch as soon as we came into view of the dog lawn.

Lila was sitting with Elise when they spotted us. Lila's long, fluffy white tail began wagging the moment she saw Teddy appear. He pricked up his ears and wagged his tail at the sight of her, then practically dragged me to where she was sitting. His uncontrolled behavior was a surprise and an embarrassment.

"Teddy, behave yourself. Calm down!"

Elise was smiling when we arrived. "Someone is

anxious to play, I see."

"Hello, Elise. Thanks for thinking of us. Teddy's ready to play. Should we let them loose?"

"We should, otherwise they'll get tangled up!"

We released the two dogs and what a sight! Teddy playfully jumped on Lila and then circled her until he almost fell over from getting dizzy. Lila barked her sweet little bark, saying what a fun dog he was. Teddy raced away beckoning Lila to follow him by returning for her again and again. Elise and I stayed nearby, in case either one decided to make a break for it.

Then it happened.

Teddy stopped cold in his tracks, turning away from Lila. He sniffed the air, barked twice, and took off running. I had to run after him. Elise scooped Lila up in her arms and followed close behind.

"I do not believe this!" I gasped. "He must really smell something. Look at him go!"

Teddy ran straight for the parking lot. Afraid he'd be hit by a car any moment, I panicked.

"Lord God, please stop him!"

A valet saw us coming. I shouted, "Catch him! Please!"

Teddy outran me. He raced through the valet's legs and headed right into the parking lot. Again, I pleaded for help to catch him. This time a man dressed in a sports coat and slacks joined the chase. A car pulled up to check in. I waved my arms trying to stop them before they reached the spot on the driveway where Teddy was. The driver didn't seem to understand because he kept driving forward.

I screamed.

"Teddy!"

Chapter 10

The man following Teddy put his hand on the hood of the car and deftly scooped him up, just before the car came to a screeching halt. Teddy shivered visibly in his arms and wiggled, trying to get free. I finally reached the scene, panting and out of breath.

The man handed Teddy to me.

"Here's your dog, ma'am." Teddy almost jumped into my arms.

"Thank you so much!" I said. I held on to Teddy as he whimpered and struggled to get down again.

"What's the matter with you, Teddy? You almost got killed running away like that."

The man continued to watch Teddy squirm.

"I don't know what's gotten into him. This is the third time he's headed for the parking lot. It's unusual for him to act this way, I can assure you."

"Well, that is one intent dog, I'm telling you. I had a hard time hanging on to him."

"I can't thank you enough, *Detective*, isn't it?" I surmised with a smile.

"Yes, ma'am. I'm Detective Ed Taylor, at your service."

I looked around for Elise and Lila but couldn't see

them anywhere. Elise might not want the attention of a crowd and I certainly couldn't blame her.

As people wandered away, I took Teddy back to the room and stroked him to settle him down. I was thinking hard about why he ran away like that.

"Teddy, there's something about that parking lot the police must have overlooked and you know it what it is don't you, boy?"

Teddy whined an affirmative "yes," and I knew I was on the right track.

"Don't you worry. We're going to find out what's bothering you, I promise."

Cecilia came in through the front door. When she saw me holding Teddy the way I was, she instantly knew something had happened.

"Back so soon from the play date?"

I told her what happened and she agreed Teddy could sense something.

"I'd call Detective Noble, but I know he's flying into Ocala right now and probably has his phone turned off," I said. "I think I'll just keep it under my hat until I put together more of the pieces to this murder. Where have you been, by the way?"

"I was out looking through some shops; there are so many exclusive ones here in Scottsdale. I had lunch in the hotel just for something different."

"I'm sorry you're so cooped up here in the room."

"I'm fine, really. Besides, it's what I'm paid for and I certainly don't mind."

She placed two shopping bags on the bed in her room and came back into the living room, sat down and put up her feet.

"I've been doing some thinking about Rene's killer, Cecilia. Whoever killed Rene must have had a reason. Why risk murder if you're Vincent, or Leah, or Richard, or Tori? They all have outstanding careers. It seems to me that every one of them has so much to lose if they did something like that."

"I think whoever killed him thought they had no other choice. Rene could have been trying to blackmail one of them for some reason."

"That's true and that would apply to Tori. Maybe Rene threatened to let her ex-husband know where she was if she didn't cooperate in some way, perhaps with the rigging of the grant proposal, for instance."

"That's a possible theory, Jillian. What about Richard Sanchez?"

"He seems, on the surface anyway, to be aboveboard in his work. I know he loves what he does. Now, what if Rene knew something that would jeopardize Richard's career in some way? It would certainly be a motive, but enough of one to kill for? From just being around him this week, I don't sense Richard's capable of killing anyone. He seems too intelligent. He also seems too gentle. That's why he's not married — he's a little shy."

"Jillian, you're always the matchmaker, aren't you?"

"I like to see everyone happy and loved, that's all. When I saw that Mark Russell wasn't married, I immediately thought of introducing him to you. Now he's dead and he may never have known love. I think it's sad."

"I know you mean well, Jillian. But times are different now. People are working on careers and...."

"And getting their ducks in a row. I know, Cecilia. But guess what? You never really get your ducks in a row. I also think men and women are different in their views of life now. Men don't want the responsibility. To them, families are a burden. Women don't want the responsibility of raising children all day — they think that it's burdensome. They think they have to sacrifice who they are for the sake of their husbands and children, and I suppose in a way they do, but it's for such a short time compared to their whole lives."

"You have a valid point."

"Frankly, I don't think enough marriages have held together to exhibit its rewards to their children. Instead, divorce has ruined marriage in the minds of many young people today. It's really a shame, too."

"I agree, especially for the children."

"When a marriage is made in heaven, like the saying goes, there's nothing more wonderful. When God blesses the marriage with children and grandchildren, it becomes even more wonderful. When you understand that marriage and a family are God's plan for you, it changes your outlook from being a burden to being an investment."

Cecilia smiled. "I suppose I've never looked at it that way, but I think you're right. My parents never divorced. They've been married for a long time, and even though they don't have a fancy house or an expensive car, they do have my brother and me. Come to think of it, they're always saying that we're their greatest blessings, besides each other, and they're happy."

"They're fortunate, Cecilia. Now take Vincent, for instance. I don't know what his marriage was like, but now they're divorced and their sons are totally out of their lives. Leah remains close to her father but she's estranged from her mother. Vincent seems happy. He has his work but he's lonely. At his age it's difficult to find companionship. I wonder if he had a reason to kill Rene. When I talked to him at dinner the other night he said he barely knew him. Still, you can never tell what's going on in a person's life."

Cecilia laughed. "That's not entirely true, Jillian. Have you ever been on Facebook or Twitter?"

"Okay, I get your point." I glanced down at Teddy who had jumped up on the sofa and found a spot to curl up and sleep. "He's got to be tuckered out after that chase! I think we could use a cup of tea. Cecilia, would you please put in a call? And let's order some of that chocolate cake. It might help us think."

"Great idea — I'm ready to relax and take a break."

She called in the order. "By the way, Jillian, there was a message from Arthur saying Mark's funeral will be Friday morning at ten o'clock. I left a message regarding the location for you. He said he would notify everyone."

"Thank you, Cecilia."

Soon there was a knock at the door. The tea and cake had arrived. "This is just what we needed." I switched on the fireplace, kicked off my shoes, and indulged in the glorious ritual of afternoon tea. I poured out, offering Cecilia milk first, then tea, and then sugar, gave the brew a small stir, and handed the cup to her. We ate the cake in small bites to savor the chocolaty goodness as we continued our discussion of the suspects.

Cecilia spoke first. "Jillian, what about Leah? Can you see her murdering Rene?"

"I really don't know. Leah is a dark horse. She acts aloof and isn't friendly at all. I've known people like her before. Sometimes, if you have a title it goes to your head, and in Leah's case, she definitely holds it over her employees. From what I've noticed she may also have an undiagnosed illness. I think she's definitely under some kind of stress but it could well be job-related."

Cecilia ate the last bite of cake. "But can you see Leah killing Rene?"

"I've tried to picture her doing so, but whenever I focus on seeing her, Tori comes into the picture and replaces her. I think that's because Tori actually told me she owns a gun and would blow her husband's head off if he ever tried to hurt her again.

"On the other hand I've only seen Leah upset once, and that was today at lunch when she berated Tori for not getting enough work done. It would be possible for Leah to kill Rene if she had reason enough, but there again, that applies to everyone and that's the problem. We have to get more evidence for a motive."

"I'm sure Detective Noble will find something in Ocala. They should have arrived by now, don't you think?"

It's more than likely."

I walked over to the desk to get my cell.

"I think I should leave a message about Teddy and the parking lot." I placed the call and was surprised at how quickly he picked up.

"Detective, it's Jillian. How was the trip?"

"We made it, but barely. There was all kinds of paperwork because of the body, but we managed to get through it. We just got to a restaurant for something to eat. You know they don't give you a whole lot on those flights."

"How is Yvette holding up?"

"She's actually doing pretty well, I'd say, under the circumstances. She handled the transporting of the body to the funeral home like a pro. By the way, she couldn't believe the check you gave her. She cried and said it was a miracle from God, which I happen to know it was."

"Well, she's an excellent business woman, so I'm not surprised she's handling everything efficiently. I'm glad I could help her."

"Jillian, you didn't call me just to see how the trip went, did you?"

"Actually, no. We've overlooked something around the hotel parking lot."

"I see. And you believe this because…?"

"Don't scoff now, but my dog, Teddy, has insisted on running to that parking lot ever since the murder of the guard and I trust his instincts."

"Your dog is now in on the investigation?"

"I told you. Don't scoff. Really, he senses something and I plan to check it out. However, I did want to talk with you first."

"Can you wait until I get back? What if someone is watching you and you discover something they don't want you to find? That could be dangerous."

"That's why I called. Okay, I'll wait until you get back. When will that be?"

"Rene's funeral is tomorrow afternoon. Yvette already made the plans and says there aren't that many people coming. I think by then I'll know if we have any evidence we can use in the case. I'm flying home after the funeral so I should be back late tomorrow afternoon."

"Oh...and I got word from Cecilia that Mark Russell's funeral will be Friday morning in case you want to attend."

"I do want to attend. I'm still keeping an eye on Arthur Wingate."

"Arthur didn't kill Rene, Detective. He didn't even know Mark and Rene were in collusion until Mark confessed it. What do you think his motive would have been?"

"You may have a point, Jillian, but I have to keep my options open. It's the way I do my job."

"And I respect that, but common sense tells me otherwise."

"That's why we're allowing you to help us out, in case you need to be reminded."

"Thank you for putting that kind Detective Taylor on duty as soon as you did. I have him to thank for saving Teddy's life."

"He saved your dog's life?"

"He did indeed. If it wasn't for him Teddy would have been an oil spot on the hotel parking lot."

"I'll be sure and make a note, Jillian. I can get him a special medal or something."

"Any recognition would be appreciated, I'm sure, but I think he was just glad to be doing his job. I need to tell you something else that happened."

"Go ahead."

"Someone followed me from the clinic to the hotel

this morning. I didn't get the license plate, but it was a late model dark gray Mazda."

"Late model dark gray Mazda. I'm writing it down. That means we're making someone uncomfortable. Stay on your toes, Jillian. Watch your back. You hear me?"

"Loud and clear. Don't worry. Detective Taylor is looking out for me."

"Listen, Jillian, I need to go. The server is here to take our orders. I'll call you when I've seen Rene's room, all right?"

"Enjoy your meal." I hung up before he could say goodbye. I smiled. "That will give him a bit of his own medicine."

Teddy came over to where I was sitting and put his little head in my lap.

"You want me to stay in tonight, don't you, boy? Okay, I will. You're such a good dog, Teddy. I love you." I gently kissed him on top of his head.

"Cecilia, would you please bring me my laptop? I want to check out a few things and Teddy needs me right now."

"Sure, Jillian. I'll get it for you."

She placed the laptop on my lap, gave Teddy a stroke, and excused herself. "I've got a text from Walter."

Cecilia disappeared into her bedroom.

I smiled and wondered what small talk Walter was making. When you're in love, any excuse will do. The signs were all there. No one else was in the picture for either one of them. Their hormonal and testosterone ages were just about right. There was constant communication for no reason at all (except to be close to one another) and there was a subtle melancholy I'd noticed lately in Cecilia.

Oh, yes. Things were progressing. Good for them. Yes, Jillian, you are indeed a matchmaker.

I checked my e-mails and saw one from Elise. She

was sorry the play date ended so abruptly and knew I'd understand her not running after me. I answered her back in the affirmative and apologized for Teddy's behavior. I was tempted to offer an explanation but thought better of it. Detective Noble said not to confide in anyone and I had to respect that. Arthur had sent a puzzling note asking me to call him. I did so immediately.

"Arthur, it's Jillian. You asked me to call you. I hope everything is all right."

"Hello, Jillian. Thanks for calling. I had to talk to someone other than Diana. I didn't want her worrying about my work."

"So it *is* your work. I knew it."

"The Hansens have decided to withdraw their grant if this murder case can't be resolved by the end of this week."

"That's not reasonable!"

"I thought the same thing, but they can do what they want. It's their money. I just wanted to find out from you if there's been any progress in the investigation."

"I can't disclose any details but it's safe to tell you we do have some leads."

"That's encouraging. What about that porcelain ghost orchid. Did they trace where it came from?"

"We do have a lead, but again, it's still a work in progress, I'm afraid."

"I understand, Jillian. I just want something to happen either way so I can get on with my work. It's difficult to focus on endangered species when I don't know if we're getting the grant or not. It seems like anything we want to do costs money and our funds are so limited."

"I understand, Arthur. If it were me, I'd go on working as if the grant wasn't going to materialize. That way you're not losing valuable time worrying about making plans that may never happen. Then, if by some miracle you do get the grant, you can begin planning in a new direction."

"You're right, Jillian. I agree with you. The stress is getting to all of us. You got my message about Mark's funeral on Friday, I hope."

"Yes, I did. Thanks. How are things at the office?"

"Oh, we're adjusting. Warren is trying to pick up the slack for Mark but I'm going to have to hire someone. The tech side is too much for him. Helen is doing a phenomenal job running the office. I don't know what I'd do without her."

"She's a gem all right. You need to treat her well, Arthur."

"Don't I know it? She gets her proper due at raise time, trust me. How about you Jillian, are you doing okay?"

"I am, but I'm with you. The sooner we find out who killed Rene the better.

"Arthur, can you think of anything at all that happened Friday afternoon that might be important?"

"I've wracked my brain and nothing comes to mind. Everything was going so well. Everyone seemed to be getting along...except...."

"What? Except what, Arthur?"

"You know, now that I think back, I remember Vincent and Leah seemed a little at odds with each other."

"What happened?"

"Well, Vincent was in a good mood, like he always is, and Leah seemed to criticize everything he said. I mean everything."

"Do you remember what she said?"

"It had something to do with his work, I remember. I think she said, 'You should stick to your real work, Dad.' Something like that. It didn't make sense at all."

"His *real* work? That would indicate to me he was involved in something else."

"Interesting."

"Arthur, there's an undercurrent going on between those two but short of being busybodies...wait a minute. I get the sense Tori knows something about Leah that she hasn't told me. It might answer some of the questions we're asking. I'm going to have a talk with her again and see if I can find out any more."

"You never know, Jillian. It might explain things a little better. Good luck. By the way, is there any chance of Diana and me treating you to lunch sometime while you're here? We'd love to."

"I appreciate the invitation. I don't have plans for tomorrow if you're free."

"Tomorrow sounds fine to me. I'll check with Diana and get back to you. Hey, thanks for listening to an old friend, Jillian. If anyone can figure this thing out, you can."

"Thanks for the vote of confidence and don't worry about the grant. Just do the best job you can and things will work out."

"Thanks, Jillian. I'll talk to you later."

"Goodbye, Arthur. Give Diana my love."

I perused the rest of my e-mails and deleted most of the ones that were ads. My bank balance indicated my paycheck had been deposited. It made me think of the financial records of Ray Ackermann. Yes, I would have to get them as soon as Detective Noble returned.

Now for Tori. I rang her room.

"Tori, it's Jillian."

"Hello, Jillian. What can I do for you?"

"I was wondering if I could treat you to dinner tonight, that is if you don't have plans."

"Actually, I was just going to order in. I still have a lot of work to catch up on."

"I see. I promise we could make it a short one if you'll join me. I don't want to eat in again and I don't enjoy eating alone in restaurants."

"Well, all right. I guess I could use a break. How about in an hour? I need to finish a report but that should be enough time."

"Thank you. I'll meet you in the lobby. We'll eat here to save time and remember, it's my treat!"

"All right, I'll see you in an hour."

Teddy stretched his little legs in front of him and then yawned and sat up. He jumped down, walked over to Cecilia's door and scratched on it. She opened it and looked down.

"Looks like someone wants his dinner." She picked him up. "Are you eating in or going out?"

"I'm going to have dinner with Tori tonight. You go ahead and order room service for the two of you."

"Okay. What sounds good, Teddy? How about a juicy turkey burger and some fries?"

Teddy barked as if he totally agreed with the menu choice.

We both laughed.

It was still light when I started walking toward the lobby. A few people lingered at the pool, reading books or napping. Must be nice, I thought. There were cirrus clouds in the dark blue sky that made another beautiful southwestern sunset a possibility for the evening. I looked forward to it.

The hotel grounds were enchanting at dusk. Lights were beginning to come on in the flowerbeds and walkways, spotlighting the beautiful plants. It was truly a feast for the eyes. I passed the business offices and turned into the main building entrance, keeping an eye out for Tori. Richard was in the bar sitting with someone. He turned around to glance my way and there was Leah sitting opposite him. She must have told him I'd come in. I nodded a hello and Richard did the same. Leah remained impassive.

Poor woman, I thought. She doesn't look well to me at all.

Tori entered, saw me, and walked my way. She noticed Richard sitting with Leah. I could tell both women were a little surprised. Tori nodded to Richard and he sheepishly nodded back.

"There's nothing wrong with trying to get on the good side of your employer." I tried to defend Richard.

Tori shrugged a little, then asked where I'd like to sit. It was still nice outside so I suggested the patio. It was so pleasant with potted plants everywhere and we would have a spectacular view of the sunset. She said it didn't matter to her, so the server seated us at a table for two at the edge of the patio overlooking Paradise Valley.

I looked over the menu. "The Chilean sea bass looks delicious."

Tori glanced over to where Richard and Leah were sitting at the bar. "I'm just going to have a grilled chicken Caesar salad. I'm not all that hungry."

"I think I understand." I tried to sound sympathetic. "I thought Leah was a little hard on you today at lunch. Does she get that way often?"

"She has on occasion, but it's usually my fault. She's quite a taskmaster but it's only because she's just as hard on herself. She's quite nice really."

"I'm wondering if she's well. Has she mentioned seeing a doctor?"

"Not that I know of, but I agree with you, she does seem preoccupied lately. It's probably this grant. We've all had to do extra work because of it. Leah has stayed late at the office many a night, I know."

"Working all alone? I think that would make me uncomfortable."

"I really don't know. I usually leave at 5:30, sometimes six o'clock at the latest. I can't work any longer than that. I don't have the stamina after...."

"I understand. You don't have to explain, Tori."

"Thank you and thanks for inviting me to dinner. It's

kind of you. I really needed to get out of the room. Sometimes Richard has offered to stay late and help. He really doesn't have anything else to do."

"And what about Rene, did he ever stay late?"

"He did on occasion."

The server brought our food and placed it before us. He then refreshed our drinks and replaced our breadbasket with a fresh one.

After he left, we resumed our conversation.

"Tori, I thought that maybe, when we spoke together yesterday afternoon, you wanted to tell me something. Am I right?"

"I don't know what you're referring to, Jillian. You must have misread me."

"I'm usually pretty keen at reading people but perhaps I was mistaken. Or, perhaps you won't tell me because you're afraid of losing your job." I was hoping to break through to her.

"You're reading me correctly on that one. I'm sure you can understand my reluctance to jeopardize my job in any way."

"Well, I do understand but I want you to understand that if you know something about Rene, or Richard, or Vincent, or even your boss, it may be an important piece of evidence. We might need it to find out who the killer is. If you don't tell me, you may be called to tell a jury what you know. I don't mean to be harsh with you Tori, but we have to find out the killer's identity as quickly as possible or they may kill again."

"I know what it's like to fear someone, Jillian. I don't think you do."

She thanked me for the dinner, even though she'd hardly touched it, and stood to leave.

She knew something. The killer might know too, unless Vincent was the killer. What if Tori was protecting herself? What if she had a relationship with Rene and wound up shooting him for some reason?

Then who would be in trouble? Me.

This was not good. I peered over the patio ledge and looked for Detective Taylor.

I couldn't see him anywhere.

Chapter 11

There I was, sitting alone on the patio, staring at the magnificent sunset unfolding before me. Instead of being able to enjoy one of my favorite spectacles, when Tori got up and left, I lost my appetite. I felt bad on one hand for pressuring her to give out information that she was not ready to give, but on the other hand, I felt uneasy at the possibility I had alerted a killer who was onto them.

Richard and Leah had witnessed our conversation. They both knew I was working on the investigation. I was losing ground fast. If Richard was the killer, he would know I was pumping Tori for something she knew that might be incriminating. If Leah was the killer, she would assume the same thing. If Tori was the killer, I had tipped my hand and there could be repercussions — repercussions I chose not to think about. Where was that detective anyway?

I looked around again after signing the tab and didn't see any sign of him. Oh, well, at least it was still light when I had to walk back. I prayed for God to protect me and believed He would. By the time I picked up my purse and started to leave, Richard and Leah had left. I wondered what that meant. My stomach had butterflies in it again as I made my way out the door.

There was no one around as I started on the winding path back to my room. Was I a fool to go home by myself? Maybe, but I wasn't going to show fear. I stepped up my pace and the gravel crackled under my feet. A late blooming yucca would have looked beautiful in the waning sunlight but because of the fear in my stomach, it had lost its allure. I decided to use a ploy for protection. I took out my cellphone and pretended to talk to someone. I talked, laughed, listened, and talked again. Finally, I slid my passkey across the lock on my front door. Safely home at last!

"Thank you, Lord, for giving me wisdom in that situation," I murmured.

"You're back early, Jillian." Cecilia looked somewhat surprised. "Did something happen?"

"Yes and no."

I put my purse away, changed into my comfy navy and red-trimmed sweats outfit, then went into the living room where I could vent to Cecilia. I switched on the fireplace and sat down on the sofa where Teddy happily joined me. I still felt upset over the whole evening.

Cecilia came in and sat on the chaise. "Care to tell me about it?"

"Cecilia, things are snowballing. Tonight I saw Richard and Leah sitting together having a drink. Tori is a closed book and I'm not sure if it's because she's scared of Leah firing her or if she's disenchanted with Richard. It's uncertain whether Tori was involved with Rene or not. If she was, it would have a huge bearing on the case."

"You're saying Tori would have a possible motive for killing him, say, if she was jealous or if he was ending their relationship."

"That's highly possible, and what if she's protecting Richard for some reason? It's just hard to know unless

Tori tells us what she knows. I blew it, Cecilia."

"You had to try, Jillian, and who knows, you may have stirred up the hornet's nest."

"I may have, but in this case, the hornets may come after me, and that's what worries me. I've had quite a day. I'll take a bubble bath and relax. I need to be ready for tomorrow when Detective Noble goes through Rene's room. It could be tedious waiting to hear about that."

"That sounds like a plan. Would you like a cup of decaf? I was going to make me some."

"That would be lovely. I'll start my bath while you make it."

Cecilia brought me the coffee, and I placed it on the side of the tub and slipped into the hot, sweet-scented bubble bath. The tension melted away as I soaked, taking sips of the deliciously satisfying coffee. What was Vincent doing this evening? I'm sure he didn't know anyone else in town to have dinner with. He was probably in his room having his meal delivered and watching something entertaining on television.

Would I be too forward if I called him to chat? We didn't get to talk much at lunch like we'd planned. Maybe I would. Perhaps he would tell me what was really bothering him about Leah. Where there's smoke there's fire. Arthur had seen the smoke. I was looking for the fire.

After my fingers wrinkled and I'd drained my coffee cup, I did the same with the bathwater and got out. I hadn't taken my makeup off, just in case of any eventuality. I was glad I hadn't. It was only seven o'clock after all. I dried off and put my sweats back on. Picking up my phone I sat on the sofa as Teddy hopped up in my lap and I made my room-to-room call.

Cecilia saw I was on the phone so she smiled, gave a small chuckled gesture of understanding, and went into her bedroom.

"Vincent, it's Jillian. Am I interrupting?"

"You're never an interruption for me, Jillian. Have you had dinner yet?"

"Not really. Did you order room service?"

"Not really." I laughed at our mutual deception.

"Let's go out and get something. It doesn't have to be fancy. What do you say?"

"I say great idea. How are you dressed? I'm in sweats."

"That I'd love to see. I'm just in jeans and a tee shirt. Hey, we could do barbecue. We're dressed for it and I heard about a place from Helen we could try. She said it was great!"

"Well, if Helen said it was great then I'm for it."

"Do you want to meet in the lobby or should I pick you up?"

"I'd like you to come by for me. I really don't like being out in the dark by myself."

"I understand. How about in ten minutes. Can you be ready by then?"

"I think so. I'll see you soon."

I told Cecilia about my plans and she smiled and laughed to herself. "Have fun but be careful. Remember what Walter said about suspects."

"Believe me, I'll be careful. Detective Noble promised to have me watched. Besides, I have my angels."

Vincent knocked at the door.

"See you later, Jillian."

We couldn't leave until Teddy had smelled Vincent and was satisfied that I would be safe with him.

Vincent picked him up and made over him. When he put him down Teddy rolled over on his back and Vincent rubbed his tummy much to Teddy's delight.

We walked down the path to the parking lot and a valet pulled up in Vincent's car. I was happy to see it wasn't the dark gray Mazda that followed me yesterday. The young man held the door open for me and helped me in. Vincent tipped the driver, closed the door, and looked at me with a boyish smile on his face.

"Where are we headed?" I asked.

"It's called 'The Big Apple Restaurant.' Helen said it's supposed to be a real *hoot*. She told me she and her sister go there quite often. Evidently, a man named Bill Johnson used to host a radio show right out of his restaurant. He was a real cowboy and quite a showman. Helen said he was what they called a true Arizona original.

"You get a lot of food for the money and it's authentic barbecue according to her. It's just over on Indian School Road which is not too far from here. She gave me the directions."

"I'll take notes just in case I'm the one driving home."

"Just for you, Jillian, and because it's the thing to order with barbecue I'm going to have iced tea. ' Sweet tea' in fact. Now that's authentic."

"That pleases me, Vincent. I'll order some, too."

We arrived at Bill Johnson's Big Apple Restaurant and went inside. It was definitely western décor. The server seated us and brought us two huge glasses of iced tea, sweet. We ordered the Wednesday night special, a 1 lb. T-bone steak dinner which happens to be my favorite steak. I asked that they bring me only half a portion and explained that I would pay the full price.

"So that's how you keep your nice figure." Vincent smiled.

We both ordered salads. The server brought them promptly.

"I'm glad you called me, Jillian, after lunch today. I was pretty embarrassed by Leah's behavior toward Tori."

"Leah must be under a great deal of pressure. Vincent, are you sure there's nothing wrong with Leah's health? She seems so paranoid. For someone as young as she is, the way she acts just doesn't seem normal unless there's something physically wrong."

"I've spoken to her about it but she clams up and changes the subject. She blames it on her work but I don't believe it. I've done her job. With all the help she has it can't be that demanding." He shrugged and looked down at the table. "I think we should change the subject. Since I have the floor, I'll start."

He studied his salad before he spoke.

"Jillian, I've wanted to say this ever since I met you at the dinner party. I think you're the most attractive woman I've ever met. I'd like to ask you something personal if you're willing to share. You don't have to, but I was wondering why you never remarried. You must have had tons of offers."

For a moment I was at a loss for words. Then I said, "Although you're right, it is personal with me, I don't mind sharing with you, Vincent. It's still painful when I think of my husband's death in Vietnam. Somehow, though, the pain becomes a tiny bit more bearable as time goes by because I've learned to think of a happy moment we shared instead of the fact that I still miss him so.

"He died shortly after we were married. So many young men died in that awful war. We had friends whose husbands never made it home as well. Our lives were never really the same. I chose to bury myself in my work and in my garden. The beauty of God's world was healing to me and I spent a lot of time outdoors. It was a salve for my pain. Of course, you don't meet many men in your garden except for maybe some hired help."

I smiled a little at my small joke.

Vincent smiled, too.

"Most people I knew were married already. Since most of the people killed in Vietnam were men, we woman outnumbered them. I guess you could say the odds of me marrying again were stacked. You know I'm a Christian."

"I think I've heard you talk about it before."

"It makes a difference in one's outlook on life. Christians believe that God is the One who directs our lives if we ask Him to. For whatever reason, and maybe it's because I've never asked Him for romance, I've never met anyone who's taken any sort of interest in me. And conversely, I've never been attracted to anyone since he died."

"Not even me, Jillian?"

"Now you're making me blush, Vincent."

I took a bite of salad and hoped my coloring would return to normal. "I'm still concerned about Leah. If she was my daughter, I would want to make sure there was nothing physically wrong with her."

"I can see you're not going to let go of that are you? Jillian, I'm going to confide in you with something I've never told anyone. I've carried the weight of this burden just about as long as I can stand it."

"I'm listening." I gave him my full attention.

"You'll understand Leah better if I tell you the truth. She has worked so hard to get where she is and I think she may have achieved what she has to please me. I know you think that sounds pompous, but hear me out.

"I've never been able to love Leah the way I've loved my boys. It's not her fault. I've never known how to handle it, but since I've talked to you, I realize she has to get help somehow.

"This is difficult to tell you, but unless I tell someone, it's going to eat me alive."

"I understand, Vincent. Please share whatever you're comfortable with."

"After our boys were born, I began working more and more with all the important research demands that kept coming my way. I would work late nights, weekends, and sometimes overnight at the office when I couldn't find a stopping point.

"My wife was understanding. She said she loved me and that she'd be okay doing without the time we usually spent together. We used to go for coffee on Saturday mornings and then do some shopping. We would watch TV together at night until we'd seen everything at least a dozen times.

"My work was so fascinating I couldn't get enough of it. It was my fault for choosing my work over my wife and family. Anyway, she made a life for herself doing charity work and spending time with her girlfriends.

"Then the situation changed dramatically, and the bomb dropped. She told me she was pregnant. I knew immediately I couldn't be the father. I yelled. She cried. She yelled and said it was my fault for ignoring her and causing her to yield to another man's attention. I cried and told her she hadn't been honest with me about how she really felt. Deep inside my gut though, I knew it had been my fault for taking her for granted.

"We made up and she promised to break off the relationship if I would claim the child as mine. She was concerned about her image in the community and wanted no scandal. I agreed. That was the first day I was truly miserable and I've been miserable ever since.

"We played out the role of happy expectant parents. Our boys acted as if they couldn't care less, probably because they already had each other for playmates. My wife's friends gave her showers and luncheons and she loved the attention. She figured out how to make a life for herself without me and all I had to do was pay for it.

"Boy, did I pay for it. I still spent most of my time at work and that drowned out the pain of her adultery. When I would get home, she usually wasn't there. She'd be off with her friends somewhere or doing charity work. We had a housekeeper who acted as a babysitter when my wife was gone. Some weekends when I was home, I found it easier to take the boys out shooting or fishing than to do something with the baby. Jillian, I couldn't even say 'my daughter' without thinking she really wasn't mine. It was horrible.

"When I look back, I'm sure my feelings had a negative impact on Leah and she's never understood. It's been very unfair to her. And yet, whenever I thought it would be best to tell her the truth, my wife would stop me and remind me of the ramifications of our social position, which of course meant her social position and what would happen to Leah if she knew I wasn't really her father."

I could only imagine how painful the situation was for everyone as Vincent continued.

"I couldn't disagree with her. Either way, Leah would be hurt. So, I did the best I could until she grew up. Unfortunately for Leah, by then my wife had no real reason to stay with me. Our relationship had completely died after Leah was born.

"Leah was only five years old when my wife divorced me. Because of her unfaithfulness, the judge ruled in my favor for custody of the kids. I proved I could be a loving father with enough financial support and I had my housekeeper who looked after them. That's my story. I hope it helps you understand why Leah may seem moody sometimes. I still don't know how to help her."

"I see. You never told Leah the truth about her parentage?"

He shook his head.

"Well, I guess there's really nothing you can do except support her in any way you can. Sometimes just being there to listen is all you can do."

"I think I've done that, Jillian. She sidesteps personal issues, especially hers. She never talks about romantic interests and that worries me. I mean, she should be seeing someone by now, don't you think?"

"I'm finding that things aren't the same as when you

and I were courting. In fact, I don't think they court anymore. If a couple does decide to get married it must be by osmosis!"

He laughed and agreed with me.

The server brought two platters each loaded with a large steak, a huge baked potato with all the fixings, old-fashioned green beans cooked with bacon, barbecue beans, a basket of rolls, and a saucer filled with fresh butter.

I cut off a bite of the tender, succulent steak, and dipped it into the rich barbecue sauce. "Boy, Helen was right about the serving sizes. One platter could feed four people!"

"I think I'll check with Helen for every meal from now on." He grinned. "This is amazing food."

"I wonder how many more meals we'll have before the investigation is over."

Vincent looked at me with kind eyes. "I wonder, too. I almost hate for it to end since I met you, Jillian. I love being with you, you know."

"The feeling is mutual, Vincent. I just wish we didn't live in different states."

"That is a problem."

I took a sip of iced tea, and Vincent changed the subject.

"How are things going with Detective Noble, by the way? Are you getting anywhere?"

"We're getting there, I think. Everyone is still a suspect except for poor Mark Russell and Warren Burkett who has an airtight alibi. I really don't think Arthur or Helen had any motive."

"So that leaves us, doesn't it?" He wiped a little barbecue sauce from his lips.

"I'm afraid so. It's funny. I think all of you are great people to know. I have a great deal of respect for each of you for the work you do. So, when I try picturing one of you killing Rene, it just doesn't seem possible."

"That's exactly how I feel, Jillian. Knowing these people the way I do, to me it's just impossible that one of them is a killer. You've got to believe me when I tell you it wasn't me. I had nothing against Rene."

"I do believe you, Vincent. But someone did, and we will find out who that person is. I hope for your sake it wasn't Leah."

"Leah? Why would she kill Rene? He was just her employee. I never saw her treat him any differently than anyone else."

"I hope you're right. It's pretty bizarre to think that any one of them could have done it. But someone did."

I was full, but when the server brought the dessert tray with choices of apple, peach, or cherry cobbler, the temptation was too great. My thoughts turned from suspects to dessert, and I was unable to resist.

"I'll have the peach with ice cream. And some decaf too, please."

"Make that two." Vincent smiled again.

After finishing the gargantuan bowls of cobbler and ice cream we sat back and moaned contentedly.

"Jillian, you may have to drive home because I have to tell you, I think I could fall asleep right here in this booth after that cobbler."

"You'll make it. Drink some coffee."

"But it's decaf!"

"Pretend it's regular. I do that all the time. It seems to work."

I paused to enjoy the moment just being with someone like Vincent and having a little fun. I knew, however, that I had to get on with my inquiries while I had the chance. After a moment I said, "Tell me Vincent, have you always worked for the State Department?"

"Why do you ask?"

"I'm just making small talk. I'm always interested in how people get where they are. You might say it's a hobby of mine."

"That's fair enough, I suppose. I've worked for the State of Florida since I graduated with my doctorate. They sought me out. Made me an offer I couldn't refuse!"

We both laughed at the godfather inference.

I took a sip of coffee. "And you've never done anything else?"

"You mean like waiting tables when things were slow?"

"No. You know, like starting a business. A lot of people do that so they'll have something when they retire. That sort of thing."

"I don't plan to retire, Jillian."

"You love your work that much?"

"I do."

"Well, that answers my question." I looked straight into his eyes.

He seemed just a little uncomfortable with my probing, but who wouldn't be, I reasoned.

I refused his offer of a third refill on the coffee.

"Are you ready to leave?"

"I suppose so. I need to get back and get a goodnight's sleep. Teddy's had me running more than I'm used to today. I'm pretty worn out."

"Let's go then."

Vincent took his time driving home. It was funny thinking of the hotel as home. We didn't speak. Both of us felt full and satisfied after such a great meal. I had to admit that the company was satisfying as well. I had feelings for this man and believed he felt the same way about me. It was really too early to tell if there was a possibility for a relationship. Maybe he treated all women this way. I would simply have to wait and see.

We took our time walking back to my casita. He held my hand for the last few steps. When we arrived, he squeezed it. "Thanks for having dinner with me, Jillian. It's been a long time since I've enjoyed such good company. And thanks for listening."

"That's what friends are for. Thanks for accepting my offer. And, Vincent, the feeling is mutual."

He leaned over and kissed me on the cheek.

We said goodnight.

Most of the lights were off when I stepped through the door. Cecilia must have gone to bed. Teddy greeted me as usual and was happy to see me. I prepared my bubble bath, running the water slowly so I wouldn't disturb Cecilia. The hot water was heavenly, and my whole body relaxed as I submerged underneath the sweet-smelling bubbles. Did a man just kiss me goodnight? A man who is a suspect in a murder investigation?

"Lord, I need wisdom. You're going to have to guide me, because I really like him."

After drying off and spraying myself with my favorite perfume, I turned off the lights and went to bed.

"Goodnight, Teddy. Goodnight, Lord."

I had only been asleep for a few minutes when Teddy began to whisper a growl. He always whispered when he knew I was sleeping; it was uncanny, but he did!

"What's the matter, boy?"

He continued to quietly growl and then sat up, his ears pricked up. I put on my robe and slippers and quietly walked into the living room. I could see nothing wrong. Teddy ran over to the front door and barked at what he saw. It was a single piece of paper, shoved under the door. I turned on a light and read the message. It had been typed and printed out from a computer.

Cecilia heard the commotion and came into the living room as I was turning on the light.

"Is something wrong, Jillian?"

"Teddy heard someone slipping this paper under the

front door so we had to get up and see what it was."

Cecilia took the paper I handed to her.

"This is a schedule of the hotel's weekend activities." She looked puzzled.

"Yes, I know. I'm sorry we woke you up for nothing."

"That's all right. I wasn't asleep. I've been talking to Walter all evening, texting of course. How did the dinner go?"

"We had an excellent time. We talked about some personal things that I'm not at liberty to share."

"I totally understand. That's one of the things I admire about you, Jillian, your ability to keep a confidence. It makes people trust you. Where did you go to eat?"

I told her about The Big Apple Restaurant and about the huge portions, then I looked at the clock.

"I think we'd better get to bed Cecilia, it's midnight!"

"Okay, but I don't think I can sleep."

"Walter?"

"Uh-huh."

"I'll tell you what I do when I can't sleep."

"Pray?" she asked.

"Yes, I pray, but I also fall asleep faster if I listen to some soft music. It's like a mother singing a lullaby to her child. Why don't you try it tonight and see if it works?"

"Okay. I'll see what I can find on the radio. I think I saw a CD somewhere from the hotel. Thanks, Jillian. I'll see you in the morning."

"Goodnight, Cecilia. Come on, Teddy. I think we can go to bed now."

With Teddy curled up on his towel at the foot of my bed again, I laid my head on the pillow and closed my eyes expecting to fall to sleep instantly.

I tried clearing my mind and turned on the radio, but instead, I thought about Leah's name. In the Old

Testament, Leah was the unloved wife of Jacob. Her father had tricked Jacob into marrying her because she was the older daughter and the custom was that the older daughter got married first. Her father had then given Rachel to Jacob as well, even though he had to work another seven years for the privilege. I'd heard a sermon on Leah one time, preached by a formidable woman preacher at a woman's meeting. I don't think I shall ever forget it.

The preacher said the name "Leah" meant "weak-eyed" one. Leah did seem weak to me, not physically, but emotionally. I now knew why. It was a self-perpetuating situation. The more Vincent ignored her, the harder she tried to gain his affection. The harder she tried to gain his affection, the more he ignored her. She had to be frustrated especially if she didn't know he wasn't her father.

I had learned something else tonight. According to Vincent, he didn't admit to having any other "work." Yet Arthur had overheard Leah mention it. Curious, either Leah was mistaken or Vincent was holding something back.

Not wanting to think ill of him, instead I thought about the delicious peach cobbler crowned with creamy vanilla ice cream, decaf coffee, barbecue beans, soft rolls and butter, home cooked green beans, huge baked potato with butter, sour cream, cheese, bacon, and chives, cool, crisp green salad, and that succulent, juicy, melt in your mouth, medium rare T-bone steak.

Sleep came at last.

Chapter 12

This morning wasn't my gym day. Thank heavens! I stretched a long moment before getting out of bed. Teddy stretched along with me and wagged his tail.

"Good morning sweetie." I cooed.

He licked my cheek.

"Thank you, sweet dog. Let's go see if Cecilia's made coffee."

Cecilia was dressed for the day in a smart casual outfit of baby blue dress jeans and a tan ribbed turtleneck sweater. She had pulled the outfit together with a brown leather belt decorated with a large turquoise and silver belt buckle. Brown leather boots completed the look.

"Cute outfit. Is that what you bought on your shopping trip yesterday?"

"Do you like it? I really wanted something with turquoise and the belt just begged me to buy it. Then I had to have the jeans and turtleneck. The boots are the same color as the belt and I couldn't pass them up."

"You look darling. You're beaming, Cecilia. Care to share with the class?"

"There's nothing to tell, really. I wish there was."

"Something will happen, just give it a little more time. When Walter sees you in that outfit, it may cut the time considerably!"

"I hope you're right, Jillian. I made coffee. Would you like some?"

"Thanks."

She handed me a cup, and I sipped it eagerly. "I wonder when I'll get a call from Detective Noble."

"It's two hours earlier in Florida, so it could be this morning." She sat down at her desk and reached for the phone. "Are you ready for me to call room service?"

"I saw a Southwestern omelet that looked scrumptious. It comes with potatoes fried with peppers and onions. I'll have wheat toast and ask if they have orange marmalade. I should buy me some to eat at home, but I never do."

"Do you want juice?"

"Yes, but this time I'll have tomato. I haven't had it in a long time. And order a pot of coffee, of course."

"Of course."

Cecilia dialed room service and breakfast was on the way.

It was time to get dressed, but I felt so lazy I decided to check my e-mails first. Everything was going well at the paper. Some ads for gardening paraphernalia I always received...click, delete; a comment from a reader saying they loved the last column on summer bulbs...enlightening; more solicitations for gardening tools...delete, and then I was finished. No personal messages, no family member in crisis, no one needing me in any way.

Maybe that was a good thing, but I couldn't fool myself. Being needed was what life was all about. Did Vincent need me? That remained to be seen. I shut down my computer and got dressed just in time for room service.

"This looks wonderful." The Southwestern omelet bulged with sautéed peppers, onions, and tomatoes. They'd smothered the top with jack cheese. The pan-fried potatoes were deliciously browned and studded with more peppers and onions. I spread some marmalade on a slice of wheat toast and began to eat.

"I can't believe I'm even hungry after what we ate last night."

"What *we* ate last night, Jillian?"

I noticed Cecilia's innuendo and couldn't let it pass.

"Now, Cecilia, think about it. He lives in Florida and I live in California. How could that ever work?"

"You could move to Florida."

"And give up my job? I don't know if I could do that. Besides, it's all conjecture. We like each other — that's all there is to it."

"He's nice-looking, don't you agree, Jillian?"

"Yes, he is nice-looking. But that probably means he has women after him all the time."

"Maybe. But he sent you roses and took you out to dinner twice already. *And*, he's asked you to lunch."

"But don't forget, I asked him out to dinner one of those times."

"True. Nature will just have to take its course like you're always telling me, Jillian."

I laughed and so did she.

I was glad to have Cecilia for a companion. I suppose it's what having a daughter might be like. I thought of Tori and felt empathy for her. I needed to call her and apologize. She'd suffered and didn't need more from me.

Cecilia was working at her desk so I would make the call from my bedroom.

"Front desk, may I help you?"

"I'd like to place a call to the room of Tori DeMarco please."

"One moment please. It's ringing, ma'am."

"Thank you." I tried to figure out what I was going to say when she answered.

"I'm sorry but there's no answer in the room. Would you care to leave a message?"

"Yes, if you don't mind. Ask her to call Jillian Bradley when she gets in. Thank you for trying."

I decided to take Teddy for a quick walk and see if I could find Tori anywhere. Maybe she was having breakfast at the restaurant. It was too early for the pool.

"Come on Teddy, let's go for a walk."

When he heard the word *walk,* he immediately headed for the front door. Reaching up with his front paws, he scratched to get out.

"Have a little patience, please. We need to put on your leash and collar so be still and let me get you ready. Cecilia, we'll be back shortly. I'll take my phone in case there's a call."

"See you in a little while."

"It's a fine day, Teddy. Let's go over to the restaurant and take a look, what do you say?"

He yipped and tried to run ahead of me.

"Now listen to me, Teddy. Sit."

He obeyed. I told him to forget the parking lot. It wasn't happening, not yet anyway.

He seemed to understand and calmed down.

We started on our way again. As we passed the pool, I noticed no one was there. We walked on until we came to the restaurant. I couldn't see inside because of the dark glass so I picked Teddy up and went in.

"Good morning, Mrs. Bradley," said the concierge. "How are you this morning?"

"I'm well, thank you."

"May I help you with something?"

"I was just trying to find a colleague of mine. She might be having breakfast."

"I could peruse the restaurant if you like. Who is it you're looking for?"

"Her name is Tori DeMarco."

"Tori DeMarco. As I recall, Ms. DeMarco and a Mr. Sanchez picked up some box lunches and went for a hike this morning."

She looked at her computer screen. "Yes, they were here about thirty minutes ago. I'm afraid you missed them. Would you like to leave a message in her room?"

"That would be fine. Please ask her to get in touch with me. I'll give you my cellphone number."

"Of course. Is there anything else I can do for you Mrs. Bradley?"

"That will be all for now, thank you."

"My pleasure. I hope you and your dog have a nice day." She smiled.

"Thank you. You, too."

I placed Teddy on the ground and we left the restaurant to return to our casita.

When we reached a fork in the path, Teddy whimpered, "Can't we please go to the dog lawn?"

"I suppose we have time. I wish I could let you off your leash but I can't afford to have you run away again."

We headed for the dog lawn and passed a young couple, arm in arm, looking into each other's eyes. They didn't even notice when we passed them.

"They're probably on their honeymoon," I told Teddy.

We continued walking until we finally came to the lawn strictly set aside for dogs. I sat down on the bench and let Teddy run as far as the expandable leash would let him. He barked at a bird and then rolled in the grass scratching his back. After relieving himself, he pawed the grass forcefully sending blades and dirt flying but only a little since he was so tiny. He panted and lay down with his back legs outstretched, totally enjoying himself.

The warm sun felt good on my face as I sat there contentedly. After Teddy had enough sitting, I knew we should get back so I could give him some water. "Come on boy, let's go home."

We started back but not before I checked to see if my

tail was watching. There he was. Behind a curved brick wall stood Detective Taylor. He stepped back and I couldn't see him anymore.

"At least I know you're there." I felt a sense of reassurance. "Let's go Teddy."

I pondered as we made the return trip. That was interesting. Richard and Tori on a picnic. What could that mean? The first thing I thought was, good for them. How would Leah react if she knew her employees were off having a good time instead of working?

Things were definitely getting interesting.

We soon reached the casita and after taking Teddy's leash off I put out a small bowl of fresh water which he lapped up thirstily. Cecilia was busy working on her articles for her paper.

I poured myself more coffee from the breakfast carafe and sat on the sofa. The walk had refreshed me. The air had bathed my face and my thoughts had grown lighter. Teddy hopped up next to me and curled up for a nap. What a life dogs had. I picked up a magazine and read a few articles on gardening in the desert. Then I remembered Arthur had said something about having lunch with him today.

"Cecilia, did Arthur call about having lunch?"

"Oh, I'm sorry, Jillian. He called while you and Teddy were out. He wants you to call him, I have his number right here. I apologize."

"That's okay. No harm done. I just remembered, myself."

Cecilia handed me the sticky note with Arthur's number on it.

"Hello, Arthur. It's me, Jillian."

"How are you, my friend?"

"I'm fine. And you?"

"I'm doing all right. Would you join Diana and me for lunch today?"

"Yes, lunch today would work."

"What are you in the mood for? We have just about anything you want here."

"I think I'm up for Italian. I've had so much Southwestern fare since I've been here, and I love it but it would be nice to have something different."

"Then we'll go to Il Terrazzo at the Phoenician. You'll like it. It's one of Diana's favorites, and mine, too."

"The Phoenician? I like it already. I'm glad she's joining us."

"Would you like for us to pick you up?"

"Yes, I would appreciate that."

"Let's say eleven-thirty in the lobby."

"Eleven-thirty it is. I'm looking forward to it."

I went into my bedroom to pick an outfit to wear. While I was trying to decide between my long skirt and sweater, or my dressy jeans and silk blouse, I heard a knock at the front door. Who in the world could that be?

Cecilia answered it and I heard her say, 'Please come in. I'll tell Jillian you're here. She'll just be a minute. Have a seat?'

Cecilia knocked on my door.

"Jillian, Dr. Leah Fontaine is here to see you. I told her you would be with her in a few minutes."

"Thank you, Cecilia." Since I was at least presentable I walked out immediately. "Leah, how nice to see you. How about some coffee?"

"No, thank you, Jillian. I can only stay a few minutes."

She looked at Cecilia. "I wonder if I could talk to you in private?"

Cecilia took the hint. She gently scooped Teddy up off the sofa, retreated with him into her bedroom and closed the door.

"Are you sure you wouldn't like some coffee? We have plenty." I tried to put her at ease.

"On second thought I will have some, Jillian. Thank

you. Black is fine. Jillian, I won't beat around the bush. I came to tell you that I've been spending quite a bit of time going over the projects that Richard was working on with Rene."

"So that's why you've been working so hard."

I handed her a cup of coffee and she took it. Her hands seemed steady.

"Yes. I started to notice some cost projections that seemed way out of line. I really didn't pay any attention at the time because I've seen similar bottom lines. But they were starting to become the norm and I felt something had to be in error."

"Could it be a mathematical error on someone's part?"

"That's what I thought at first but when I went over Rene's work I couldn't find any."

"What about Richard's work?" I asked.

"That's what I came to talk to you about. Jillian, I think he's been embezzling from the institute."

I tried to hold the coffee in my mouth. This was a surprise. I managed to swallow. "That's quite an accusation Leah."

"I know, Jillian. I'm upset about it. But if Richard is stealing from us, it has to stop."

"Have you confronted him?"

"Well, I think you saw us in the bar last night."

"What did he say when you told him you suspected him?"

"I wasn't able to confront him yet. It might be dangerous."

"I see. You think Rene might have discovered Richard's indiscretions and Richard killed him to keep him quiet."

"Jillian, I don't know what to think, but yes, it's definitely possible."

"Leah, do you want me to tell Detective Noble what you suspect?"

"If you would. I'd feel better about it. If I go to the police and Richard knows I did, I don't know what he'd do. Jillian, I'm scared."

"It's going to be all right, Leah, don't worry. I'm glad you talked to me. What you need to do is get the proof together showing where the withdrawals occurred. I wouldn't say anything to anyone else about this. I'll be talking to Detective Noble today, so try not to worry."

"Thank you, Jillian. My father was right about you. You are a true friend. I think I should get back to my room. I haven't seen Richard or Tori today but I know they'll be checking in with me soon."

She placed her cup on the coffee table untouched and stood to leave. "You'll let me know what Detective Noble says, won't you?"

"I'll come over to your room after I've talked to him. Try not to worry. Everything will turn out for the best. Leah, be careful. If you think Richard may be dangerous I wouldn't be alone with him to be on the safe side."

She nodded, ducked her head, and left.

I knocked on Cecilia's door.

"She's gone."

She and Teddy came out.

"What was that all about?" Teddy jumped up on the sofa to resume his morning nap.

"She thinks Richard Sanchez has embezzled funds from her institute and may have had a reason to kill Rene Parker."

"That's pretty incriminating if it's true." She sat back down at her desk. "What are you going to do, Jillian?"

"I'm not going to do anything until I've talked to Detective Noble. Her story makes sense if Rene was going to turn Richard in."

"Or if Rene was blackmailing him because he knew what Richard was doing."

"Anything is possible when a person gets greedy. It would also explain Leah's nervous behavior. I know I'd be nervous if I thought you were embezzling from me and might be a killer."

"At least you'll never have to worry about that with me, Jillian." She laughed. "But I see what you mean about Leah."

"What time is it, Cecilia? I don't want to be late for my lunch date."

"Then you'd better get going. You have about thirty minutes." She turned back to her computer keyboard and started pounding away.

Rene's funeral would be taking place right about now. I prayed for Yvette to have the strength to get through it. It would probably be a few more hours before I received a call from Detective Noble.

I selected the long rust and gold skirt and the black sweater set. My black suede boots and strand of pearls were perfect accessories. I retouched my makeup and combed through my long blond tresses finishing off my *do* with a light mist of hair spray.

"I'll be going now, Cecilia."

I stroked Teddy's fur. "I love you. Be a good dog,"

Teddy yawned, stretched out his legs and fell back asleep.

The temperature outside was balmy, with just enough cloud cover to promise another gorgeous sunset. I inhaled the fresh air as I walked the short distance to the lobby where I was to meet Arthur and Diana.

They were already there. We greeted each other with smiles and hugs. They were such fine people. The world would be a better place if it had more people like them instead of murderers and embezzlers.

"Jillian, I'm glad to see you again." Diana smiled. "How's Teddy doing since his scorpion episode?"

"Teddy's fine. He's a bit anxious to explore the hotel grounds but that comes with his breed."

"I'm glad he's all right. You'll like Il Terrazzo. The

food is amazing and the Phoenician is always fun to see."

"I heartily agree. I've only been there once but I'll never forget it. My sister and I went with her family one summer. The kids counted seven waterslides on the property. We all had such a good time."

"All set, ladies?" Arthur waved us ahead of him.

We self-parked and walked through the sumptuously beautiful golden lobby of the Phoenician Hotel. It was just as spectacular as I had remembered it. A massive crystal chandelier hung from the ceiling over a tiered fountain. A stunning tile star mosaic adorned the center of the floor. A few servers were setting up afternoon tea in the Lobby Tea Court. I would love to return for that!

We walked across a black floral carpet to the inside of Il Terrazzo. The server seated us in a high-backed brown velvet upholstered booth. Arthur sat in a plush gray chair across from us. Sparkling crystal and silverware adorned the white-linen covered table. A small bouquet of fresh flowers stood in the middle.

We studied the menu and made our selections although there were so many incredible choices it was difficult making up my mind. I decided on the tempting veal chop, pounded and crusted with wild arugula and served with a confit of cherry tomatoes, Parmigiano-Reggiano, and lemon. I also decided to order one of my favorite beverages, a vanilla pear Bellini. I glanced briefly at the dessert menu where I would be certain to order an espresso to go with my selection.

We kept the conversation light at first, listening to a few of Diana's concierge experiences with quirky guests.

"Jillian, I've been trying to get Arthur to take a break and get away for a week or two. I wish you would help me convince him."

"Good luck getting a scientist like Arthur to take a

break from work. His work is like a vacation, I'm afraid. It's just too interesting to leave, right, Arthur?"

He laughed a little.

"You're right, Jillian, but Diana has a point. Just because I'm happy working all the time doesn't mean she and I don't need to get away together for a day or two."

"Why don't you both come to Clover Hills? I'll take you to Filoli, and we could do the Japanese Gardens and Golden Gate Park. They're all close. We could day trip. All you would need is a couple of plane tickets. I can personally recommend the 'Bradley Hotel' and since I know the manager, I could book you a great room!"

Diana looked hopefully at Arthur. He couldn't seem to help smiling back.

"All right you two, it looks like you have me cornered. I'll check with Helen to see when the next possible few days I can take off are and we'll do it. How about that?"

"Really, Arthur? I love you." Diana pecked him on the cheek.

"Of course, it will have to be after the investigation is over. We're not free to leave just yet." I sadly brought us back to reality.

"Is there anything we can do to help speed up the process?" Diana asked.

"I think all we can do is watch and pray. And think."

"I wish I could have foreseen Mark and Rene trying to rig the grant award. This might not have happened if I had." Arthur shook his head. "I should have paid more attention."

"You shouldn't blame yourself." I tried to reassure him. "It's curious that the actual transaction never took place. Someone killed Rene before he could follow through on the deception. I'm wondering if that's why he might have been killed."

"But that would point to someone on our team,

Jillian." Arthur sounded stunned. "After all, how could it not benefit the Florida team?"

"I know. But I also know you are incapable of doing anything as heinous as murder and you and I could both vouch for Helen that she had nothing to do with it."

"That just leaves Warren and Mark. After Mark's confession, I really don't believe he killed Rene. He had nothing to lose if he did, so why lie?"

"The police said Warren had a perfect alibi the night Rene was murdered. It was validated by his wife. Besides, why would Warren want to kill Rene? Do you think he knew about the plan to discredit his team? That would be a motive, but not a strong one. All he had to do was to tell you, Arthur, and you would have handled it."

"True, Jillian, but you must remember there was no proof of any kind that we could find. Someone had to have deleted the file."

"And that someone probably deleted the file after they shot Rene. They didn't want the unfair advantage to win the grant. That leads me to believe that whoever killed him must have been a decent person at one time."

I didn't say aloud what I was thinking. But whoever placed the porcelain ghost orchid over the bullet wound may have been making a statement of some kind relating to the subject of the Florida grant proposal. I'd have to find out if their endangered species was, in fact, the ghost orchid.

We also discussed Arthur's progress on the Arizona agaves. He seemed discouraged as he explained how the wildlife kept destroying the new pups by eating them as food.

I agreed that the plants needed protection soon or they would die out eventually. I sliced off a tender bite of veal chop and slipped it into my mouth.

Arthur hung his head just a little and put his fork

down on his plate.

"How is Helen these days?" I asked.

"She's a little down right now due to Mark's death. I'm afraid she took it hard. We had such hopes that he would pull through. She insisted on handling all the funeral arrangements. I offered to help but she wouldn't hear of it."

"I know she regarded him almost as a son. She had no children of her own, like me. The service tomorrow won't be easy for any of us, I'm afraid. They buried Rene today in Ocala."

Diana spoke quietly, "I didn't get a chance to meet Rene's mother when she came here. I'm sure this is like a nightmare...surreal."

I laid down my fork and took a sip of my Bellini. "Actually, she's doing quite well under the circumstances. I had her over for tea the other day just to talk. She seemed squared away considering she was widowed so young and now she had to deal with her son's murder. Yvette is a strong Christian and told me her faith was getting her through. I really admire her courage."

"I've heard before that a person's faith can overcome just about anything. I suppose it's really true in a case like this."

"Yvette has faith that the killer will be caught. Somewhere, at some time, they'll make a mistake and we'll catch them when they do. I believe it won't be long either."

"What do you know, Jillian?" Arthur leaned in.

"I'm not at liberty to tell you everything, but I'm forming a picture of what happened. Arthur, you know that a chair was knocked over at some point indicating a possible struggle."

"I remember."

"That means it was probably someone defending themselves. Whoever killed Rene isn't happy I'm poking around. I've been followed at least twice"

"Jillian." Diana looked concerned. "This is getting dangerous for you."

"Probably, but I have my guardian angels protecting me. One of them is actually a body guard, a real body guard who follows me around!"

Diana smiled and the concern left her face.

After Diana and Arthur split a dessert of tiramisu, and I had the Torta di Ricotta, accompanied by my espresso, Arthur paid the bill and we stood to leave. Although we had enjoyed our lunch together no one spoke after we got into the car.

The talk and weight of finding the killer had us all stewing in our own private thoughts.

Chapter 13

I felt a nap coming on after eating all that wonderful Italian food. It didn't take Teddy much convincing to join me. I placed him on the bed, kicked my shoes off, and crawled into the soft cloud-like covers for a quick thirty minutes.

The door to Cecilia's room was closed when I had arrived home, so I figured she was taking a nap as well. I decided not to disturb her. She had not been eating a whole lot lately I noticed. At least not as much as she did before we came to Arizona. Perhaps it was the change in climate but I didn't think so. She was young and vibrant and I had watched her consume huge meals with never an extra pound to show for it.

I admired Cecilia because she exercised regularly. When she wasn't working out at home she took walks and hiked in her spare time, something I shunned. I suppose it's because I like to exercise my mind instead of my body. To each his own. Hopefully she was feeling better.

I finally dozed off. When I awoke it was two o'clock. I had slept for an extra hour. I probably needed it. My cellphone vibrated and I flipped it open.

"Jillian, it's Tori. I had a message saying you'd called this morning."

I rattled my brain to recall the apology speech I had prepared but it wouldn't come.

"Thanks for getting back to me Tori. How was your hike and picnic with Richard?"

At first there was silence on the other end but then she spoke.

"I didn't realize our hike was public knowledge, Jillian."

"Tori, let's not get off on the wrong foot. I wanted to apologize for lunch the other day. I was getting way too personal and I'm sorry. Please forgive me. I really do want to be friends."

"It's all right. I probably took offense too easily. It's just the stress of all this mess that's getting to me."

"I'm stressed, too. It makes me tired and yet at the same time any new twist in the case gets me the biggest adrenaline rush."

"Has there been a development?"

"I'm not at liberty to reveal what I know, but things are happening."

"Well, I'm glad. I can't wait to go home. It's not much, but it's mine and I'm comfortable there."

"I know what you mean. I just hope my plants are doing all right. I'm glad this happened in November and not July!"

"The weather in Florida is pretty much the same all year. I think that's why I like it. Jillian, I know you're wondering about Richard and me. Your curiosity is pressing me even over the phone!"

"You've got me, Tori. I'm an old matchmaker at heart. I just can't help wanting to see people get together and enjoy married life. I'm sorry. I hope you don't take offense at what I just said...."

"It's really all right, Jillian. No offense taken."

"Thanks, Tori, but since you brought it up...."

She laughed. "Richard and I are just friends. We both needed to get away from the hotel for a break. We thought a picnic and a hike would be perfect. He's quite the outdoorsman, you know."

"I gathered that from talking to him the other night. Tori, how has Richard been taking this whole thing? Has he changed in any way since it happened?"

"Not any more that any of the rest of us have. He just talks about the future and things he wants to accomplish in his field. He's passionate about the Everglades. It's been his home for most of his life."

"I see." I remembered how fondly he talked about growing up on the small island. "Do you think he has a chance of moving up in the Society?"

"There's not a lot of room at the top. But he believes he could do more if he had the opportunity."

Embezzled funds could do a lot to create such an opportunity.

"You must be tired after your hike, Tori. I'll let you go. But before I do, I need to tell you that you can tell me anything. I promise I won't reveal the source unless you give me permission."

"Jillian, you think I'm holding something back?"

"Maybe, maybe not. Something seems wrong or perhaps just hidden beneath the surface."

"You have a sixth sense?" she asked. "That's fair enough. I'll tell you something about me. I'm not about to say a word about anything if it will jeopardize my job or my safety in any way. Do you understand?"

"I read you loud and clear, Tori. Just remember that I'm ready to listen to anything you have to tell me."

"I'll remember that, Jillian. Now, I'd better go. There's another call coming in. Have a good afternoon. 'Bye."

"Goodbye, Tori."

I hoped she would tell me before something happened to her, too.

Cecilia came out of her room stretching her arms over her head. "I missed you coming in. I was talking to

Walter and dozed off after he hung up."

"I just got through talking to Tori. Something is bothering her but she won't tell me what it is."

Cecilia stifled a yawn as she shuffled over to the kitchenette to make a fresh pot of coffee.

"We need some coffee." She poured the water into the back of the machine.

"How's Walter doing with his new detective job?"

"He loves it. He said he wishes he was here with you though so he could learn your techniques."

"Are you sure he wishes he was here with me instead of you?" I smiled.

"He probably wishes both from the way he's talking. Things are happening, Jillian. He's starting to talk to me about *our* future instead of just his."

"Well, that's a good sign. Have you talked about how many children you want yet?"

She laughed. "We're getting close. He talks a lot about his Dad and Mom and how he wants a marriage and family like theirs."

"That's a very good sign, Cecilia!"

"I think so, too. Say, not to change the subject, but you received another invitation from *you know who* for dinner this evening. I said I'd have you call him."

My heart skipped a beat. "Where's his number?"

Before I had a chance to dial Vincent's room my cellphone rang. I recognized Detective Noble's number. Finally.

"Detective, how are you doing?"

Cecilia handed me a cup of steaming hot coffee. I put the cup on the coffee table and sat down on the sofa. Teddy immediately hopped up in my lap.

"Hey, Jillian, things are progressing here. We just got back from Rene's funeral and we're going to have some food the church people brought in. There must be enough food here to last a week!"

"That's what church friends do for each other when

one of their members loses someone. How did the funeral go?"

"It was long. Yvette told me she wanted people to remember the positive things about Rene's life not the fact that he was murdered. I learned a lot about him. He was actually a pretty nice fellow considering he lost his dad during his teens."

"It's probably due to Yvette's influence on him. She tried her best to raise him right. Well, I'm glad it's over for her."

"Jillian, I have to tell you that it was a nice funeral thanks to you. She was appreciative and told me to thank whoever was responsible for being so generous."

"I'm glad I could make it easier for her. Have you had a chance to look at Rene's things?"

"I'll do that this afternoon after the well-wishers leave. Yvette wants to be with me when we go through them. The forensics people are coming later this afternoon, too. I'll probably call you when I get back if it's not too late, or if it is, I'll call you first thing in the morning."

"Don't forget the funeral for Mark is at ten o'clock tomorrow morning."

"Listen, Jillian, people are arriving, and it's getting noisy. Take care and I'll talk to you soon."

"I almost forgot to tell you. There's been a development regarding Richard Sanchez."

"I can't hear you, Jillian. Sorry, it'll have to wait. 'Bye."

What would I tell Leah? Well, all things in good time.

I called Vincent.

He picked up on the first ring.

"It's Jillian. Cecilia said you called while I was out this morning."

"Hello, lovely lady. I called to see if you wanted to have dinner with me tonight. Although The Big Apple might be hard to top, I've found a quaint little place you'd like."

"How nice. Can we make it later? Say about eight?"

"Eight's fine. I'll pick you up at your casita."

"See you then. ' Bye."

With dinner plans made, I decided to take Teddy for a walk before it was time for his dinner. At the mere mention of the word "walk" he was off my lap and barked twice in the affirmative that he was indeed ready to go outside.

"We'll be back after a while, Cecilia. I'm taking Teddy for a walk. I have my cellphone if anyone needs to get in touch with me."

"Enjoy!"

***

Teddy and I embraced the fresh fall air. We walked in a different direction than the path leading to the main entrance. I hoped to see more desert flora along the way. Everything was quiet and peaceful. A few wispy clouds floated overhead against a bright blue sky. How so much turmoil could exist in peoples' lives was truly sad.

A young man dead leaving a mourning mother. Another man dead from being in the wrong place at the wrong time leaving a wife, children, and grandchildren. Then there was the man who lost his wife and daughter in the car accident with Mark Russell. I had to ask myself why God would allow things like this to happen. The answer came in the realization that God allows us free choice. Sometimes those choices lead to death.

We were, every one of us, going to die sometime. If everyone died of old age, the dynamics might change in our society and probably not for the better. It reminded me of *Soylent Green*, a movie where people of a certain age were recycled as food for the younger masses. The old cliché came to mind, "Ours is not to reason why, ours is but to do and die."

So much for my philosophical musings.

Teddy caught wind of a fresh new scent and started to scramble toward the parking lot again. I really should go and see what was bothering him so much.

"All right, Teddy, let's see what's so interesting in the parking lot."

I let out the expandable leash as far as it would go and ran behind him giving him as much leeway as possible. Sure enough, he headed straight to the parking lot toward the end where the carts were stored.

"This has something to do with Simon's murder, doesn't it, boy?"

Teddy yipped and led me to the spot where the pavement met the desert.

"I see, boy. Yes, I see. I'm afraid we're going to need Detective Noble's help on this one and the groundskeeper's, too."

Then...there was something. An image tried surfacing, something important, some clue. Something about those carts. Jillian, try to remember!

"Lord, please help me to remember."

The image would come. I could depend on God to reveal it to me at just the right moment.

Teddy seemed pleased with himself at directing my attention to what had bothered him in the parking lot.

When we returned home he drank long tiny laps of water. Cecilia was busy at her computer working on an article for her paper. I was getting hungry for a snack and a cup of tea and asked her to join me.

"I'm ready for a break, too. Would you like me to order tea for us?"

"I'll order it. You're busy right now and I have time. I just want to catch my breath before my dinner date tonight."

Cecilia looked briefly away from her computer and gave me a conspiratorial look.

"All right, it's nice to be asked to dinner." I picked up the phone and ordered tea for two and some small sandwiches and cookies.

Cecilia smiled and bent her head to work again. I sat down on the sofa and put my feet up. Teddy jumped up with me and snuggled down for a nap.

There was a quick knock at the door. We heard the word, "housekeeping."

Teddy barked his warning bark. As he jumped off the sofa ready to defend us Cecilia motioned for me to keep my seat and rose to answer. She scooped Teddy up in her arms and cracked opened the door.

"Just a moment please," she said to the young woman standing in front of the cleaning supplies cart. "Jillian, is it all right for her to make up the room now?"

"Of course." I picked up a magazine and perused it.

"Please come in," Cecilia said. "I'm putting Teddy in his crate so you can work in peace."

"Thank you, ma'am. Do you need anything?" She looked directly at me.

"I'm okay for the moment. Cecilia, do you need anything?"

"No, I'm fine."

The housekeeper seemed to watch us as she began emptying the trash. I felt there was something on her mind. Of course, it could be my imagination but I was not often wrong. I kept making eye contact with her and finally, she felt comfortable enough to approach me.

"Excuse me ma'am, but aren't you the lady working with the police?" She held a trash can in her arms.

"Yes, I'm working with Detective Noble. I'm Jillian Bradley and this is my assistant, Cecilia Chastain."

"I'm Maria Vargas. It's nice to meet you. I just wanted to make sure. You see, the workers here at the hotel are scared about what happened to Simon. I told them I would talk to you and ask if they had any suspects yet. Some of us are afraid it might be one of us and we're uneasy. I hope you understand, ma'am."

I sat up and put both of my feet on the floor. "I do understand, Maria. All I can tell you is that the police are working hard to find any information that will lead us to Simon's killer. No one has been arrested yet, but it's still early in the investigation."

She lowered her eyes and looked uncomfortable.

"I see. I must get back to your room, ma'am. Thank you for taking a few minutes to talk to me."

She started to take the trash out the front door and I let her get on with her work.

After stripping the beds, she replaced the linens and towels and filled the bathroom tray next to the sink with designer toiletries. A quick dusting of the furniture, polishing the mirrors, and vacuuming completed the cleaning. She started to leave.

Just as she was about to close the door, I called, "Maria?"

"Yes, ma'am?"

"We would appreciate it if you can think of anything unusual that happened the night Simon was killed to report it. Please ask your co-workers to do the same. Sometimes a small piece of information can be just the clue we need to help solve a case like this."

She finally gave a lovely wide smile. "We will help in any way we can. Thank you, Mrs. Bradley. I'll tell everyone. It was nice to meet you, Miss Chastain. Enjoy your evening."

Maria closed the door. We could hear her push her cart to the next casita.

Eventually room service arrived. The server placed an appealing tea tray down on the coffee table. Plates of dainty tea sandwiches, cookies, and petit fours were set out for us to enjoy with our blackberry sage tea.

"Come take a break, Cecilia. The tea will perk you up."

"Thanks, Jillian. My back is a bundle of knots and the

food looks delicious!"

"I can vouch that it tastes as delightful as it looks. Everything is so fresh. They must do their own baking here at the hotel. Here, try one of these curried chicken salad sandwiches. They're yummy!"

She helped herself and before long we had devoured every morsel, sipping our steaming hot tea as we enjoyed the feast.

I watched some of the local news. After hearing the weather report, I stood up to stretch.

"It looks like we might have a little rain tomorrow. I hope it won't rain during Mark's funeral. That would be awful."

I placed the tea tray outside the front door for housekeeping to pick up. It was time to check my e-mails.

The first one was from Herbert Jamison confirming he would be the representative for the Hansens at the funeral. He wanted a moment to talk afterwards.

It sounded too personal to discuss over the computer so I made a mental note to catch his eye tomorrow. The second one was from my paper. It didn't look good. News publications were going through a paradigm shift with so many readers using online services instead of home-delivered papers. I had hoped it wouldn't affect me but knew it probably would. Was this the moment of truth? I opened the message.

Dear Jillian,

As you know, The San Francisco Enterprise *has been going through a period of downsizing due to the reduction of the number of our readers. In an effort to reduce expenses, we are trying to make the transition to online publication and are meeting with some success. Our readers are gaining in that arena as they dwindle in the paper rag format.*

Therefore we are announcing a mandatory 10 percent reduction of pay for all employees until we become profitable again. Most of you would rather take the cut in pay than have some of your fellow workers lose their jobs altogether.

The pay cut will begin next month on the 15th. If you have any questions or concerns, please contact me and I'll be happy to address them.

Fred Beckworth, Editor-in-Chief

Lovely. Oh well, it had to happen eventually. I felt sorry for breadwinners with families who got this notice. I prayed for the Lord to help all the families at our paper find a way to meet their obligations. I also prayed for all the families in America who were going through the same thing or losing their jobs entirely.

"What time is it, Cecilia?"

Teddy barked to let me know he thought it was dinnertime. I laughed as he stretched out his front paws. He sprawled out flat and rested his little head, looking up at me as if to say, "I'm hungry, would you please tell Cecilia to feed me?"

"Teddy wants you to feed him. He's looking at me with his *please feed me* look."

"I'll get it for him. It's about six-thirty. When's your date?"

"Not until eight o'clock. He's picking me up here."

I glanced at her computer which had piles of papers on either side.

"Why don't you order room service? You look totally caught up in your work."

"Great idea. I think I'll have that roasted chicken you had the first night you were here. I need some comfort food and I imagine they'll do mashed potatoes for me, don't you think?"

"They aim to please. Well, I'm off to the tub. Thanks for feeding Teddy for me."

I scooped him up in my arms and hugged him gently. "Enjoy your dinner, sweet dog."

The soak in the bubble bath was rejuvenating. I dried off and applied my makeup. Then I slipped into my special black jersey dress with the cowl neck. After adding black and silver accessories and smart black pumps, I took one last look in the mirror, pleased with the result, and was ready to go. It was nice to look pretty for someone again.... *Could an older woman look pretty, hot, attractive?*

Maybe *somewhat attractive* would be more appropriate. Oh, who cared? I was just going to have dinner with a respectable man who happened to be quite charming.

Careful, Jillian, he might just charm you! Ha! As if he hasn't already.

It was eight o'clock before I knew it. Teddy "yipped" excitedly and ran to the door at Vincent's knock. I picked Teddy up and told him to behave before I could open the door.

Vincent stood in the doorway looking handsome in his dark brown and tan Ralph Lauren houndstooth sports coat, black mock turtleneck, and chocolate brown slacks.

"You look beautiful, Jillian." He took my hand and kissed it. I couldn't help but blush as I set Teddy down.

"Are you ready to go?"

"Indeed I am. I'm curious as to where you're taking me tonight."

***

The Sanctuary was lit with garden lights. They created a striking effect on the landscape. The lighting seemed to showcase each individual plant and they again mesmerized me by their unique beauty. What amazing creations the Lord had made.

Vincent sensed my lack of attention and asked what I was thinking. When I told him, he seemed a little disappointed I hadn't been thinking of him.

"I can't help it." I smiled. "I love beauty. I have ever since I was a little girl. I would spend countless hours straightening up our house just to make it look nice. I'd rearrange my room every other week, sometimes in the wee hours of the morning."

Vincent chuckled. "I can see you doing that. I really can."

"Whenever I'd earn babysitting money I'd spend it on decorating my room. One time I took a bus downtown to shop for a mirror. Struggling to bring it home was a huge chore, but once I hung it over my dresser it was worth the effort. Kids don't do that today, do they?"

"I really wouldn't know. That's one thing I regret. Not really knowing where my kids were or what they were doing most of the time. It was a real failing on my part.

"When they were little, I just assumed my wife was taking care of everything for them. Now I know that wasn't the case. My kids raised themselves for the most part with a lot of help from the housekeeper." He looked regretful.

"But you said you spent time on the weekends with them, teaching them to shoot and hunting skills."

"True, but those times were few and far between. I hardly know my boys anymore. And Leah is all grown up and seems to be doing well in her job."

I thought about her latest accusation against Richard Sanchez.

"Do you ever discuss her job with her?"

"It's curious, but we haven't actually spent any time talking about her job since this all happened."

"I think we're all in a state of flux right now. It's hard to focus on anything with the investigation still going on. I'm sure there'll be times you can enjoy being with her as soon as this is over."

"I hope so, Jillian. I just hope she can hold up under the strain."

We arrived at our destination at last and I was suitably impressed with what I saw. A line had formed for people waiting to get into the "Metro Brasserie" in the SouthBridge district of Scottsdale.

Vincent helped me out of the car.

"It must be good if there's a line outside."

He laughed. "I heard it was superb from *the source.*"

"Helen Morningstar?" We pushed past the line.

"Who else?"

He gave the front desk his name for the reservation he had made for 8:15 pm

The server seated us on a patio facing the town square of SouthBridge. It was the most charming patio I'd seen since Paris, decorated to look exactly like the sidewalk cafés I'd been to. Rattan chairs, so indicative of Paris, framed tables covered with cream-colored linen cloths. Candles flickered as centerpieces. It was so romantic and Vincent must see in my face that I was pleased.

"If the food is as good as the décor, we're in for a nice evening, Jillian."

The server brought the menus and took our drink orders, pointing out that the *Dinner for Deux* included the white or red house wine, and beignets. It was a hard choice between the rainbow trout served with the almond vinaigrette, haricots verts, and Beluga lentils, and the beef burgundy dinner for two. Vincent was trying to decide between the steak frites, a prime hanger steak, beurre maître d' and pomme frites, or the beef burgundy dinner for two. When I read aloud the description of the beignets served with Nutella, vanilla cream and raspberry coulis, it was no contest. The beef burgundy won hands-down. Vincent asked if I would join him in an appetizer of country pate, pickled vegetables, cornichons and mustard.

Except for the cornichons, which I had never heard of and neither had he, I liked everything else, so I agreed to share it with him. We would act as if we were sophisticated and pretend we knew what they were when they arrived. It turns out they were small pickles, so we had a laugh and enjoyed the delicious starter to our meal.

Helen had indeed given Vincent a good lead when she told him about this restaurant. We had a pleasant evening together and almost completely forgot about the investigation.

Almost. Until my cell vibrated and I excused myself to take it.

"Hello, Jillian."

"Hello, Detective Noble."

"I know it's late but I just got in. I wanted to talk just briefly about our findings in Ocala. Can you talk now?"

"I'm having dinner with Vincent Fontaine, but we're almost finished."

Vincent's face clouded over in concern.

"Can I call you early tomorrow, before the funeral?"

"Sure, but make it early. I'm afraid it's going to be a long day with what we've found. And Jillian, I'd get home as soon as possible if I were you. Be careful. My tail is there for you if you need him. Don't let on I'm talking to you this way if you get my drift."

"Of course I will, Detective. I'll see you at the funeral tomorrow."

Vincent nodded toward my cellphone. "Is there anything wrong?"

I did my best to act nonchalant about my conversation which was disconcerting to say the least.

"Nothing's wrong. He only wanted to touch base."

I was glad Detective Taylor was in the wings as we drove home in silence.

Chapter 14

The evening did not end as well as I had wished. After Detective Noble's call, the romantic atmosphere cooled considerably. There was no handholding, no goodnight kiss, and no 'I'll see you tomorrow' from Vincent when he walked me to my door. I simply thanked him for a wonderful meal and said I'd see him tomorrow at the funeral. He looked as unhappy as I felt, which for me, was little compensation.

Cecilia had gone to bed.

Teddy greeted me with two tiny whispered "yips" and followed me into my bedroom.

I closed the door quietly and then placed him on the bed. My thoughts were going in two directions at once. First to the ominous conversation with Detective Noble. I wondered why he thought I might be in danger. Second to my attraction for Vincent.

The thoughts were definitely conflicting. I felt Detective Noble was warning me about Vincent and yet I hadn't met a man as charming as he since my precious husband many years ago. After lighting a candle and taking a soothing bubble bath, I slipped beneath the covers and began to pray.

"Lord, you know how I feel. I really like Vincent and I think he likes me, too. He certainly has shown enough attention to me. Please guide me in this relationship. I don't want either of us to be hurt. Please help me keep my feelings in check. Help me to focus on the facts and not on my fears or hopes. And Lord, I pray that if it's in Your will, things will work out for the best for us both."

The burden left my shoulders as I transferred the problem to Him. I was finally able to fall peacefully asleep.

***

The phone rang and I looked at the clock. It was 7:00 am. After two rings, I grabbed my cell and gave a groggy, "hello."

It had to be Detective Noble.

It was. I could almost picture him up and dressed for the day. Truly a man of no nonsense.

"Good morning, Jillian. Are you awake yet?"

"Good morning, Detective. Yes, go ahead. I'm listening."

"You were right having us check Rene's room at his home."

"What did you find?"

"Some interesting magazines and instruction manuals for starters. It seems Rene was into spying equipment and recording devices. We found his camera but the memory card is missing."

I placed my feet in my slippers and eased out of bed. "Hmm. That suggests to me he wanted to gather information to blackmail someone."

"That's what I thought. I talked to Yvette again but she never thought Rene had any reason to film someone. I questioned her again about Ray Ackerman. She agreed he was a remote possibility, but Rene had never talked about it."

"Did Yvette say anything else while you were with her?"

"Let's see. She said the whole thing was still a mystery to her. She couldn't believe Rene would be mixed up in anything like that. She talked about what a devoted son he was and then she'd reminisce about how smart he was, how much he helped her in the store, and how sweet he was to her. She showed me a music box that Rene had given her. She said it stopped working right after Rene left home."

I was wide-awake now and thought that sounded interesting.

"That's almost an ominous foreshadowing of what happened, isn't it? Yvette's life has music when Rene is with her and then the music stops when he leaves and is murdered."

"Jillian, I'm sorry to have to cut this short but I've got another call from my boss and I have to take it. See you at the funeral."

The call ended and then it dawned on me I had forgotten to tell him about Richard Sanchez. I guess I would just have to wait until after the funeral.

Teddy barked for me to let him out so I put on my robe and walked over to the door. There was a light knock, then Cecilia's voice came through. "Are you awake, Jillian? I have coffee made."

I opened the door and Teddy ran out, ready to go outside.

"Good morning, Jillian. I'll take Teddy out if you like while you get dressed."

It was so nice to have Cecilia with me. She was already dressed in cute jeans, boots, and a long-sleeved black turtleneck.

"We'll be right back. And we need to talk when you get back from the funeral."

That sounded interesting. My first reaction was that it had to be about her and Walter.

I poured myself a cup of coffee, and sat down on the sofa to watch the news for a minute. The weather report confirmed a couple of showers were headed our way. I had better take an umbrella with me.

My hair was going to frizz, regardless. Oh, well, there was nothing I could do about it. Besides, today was about Mark Russell, not about me.

Lord, thank you for being with me today. Please bless the services this morning. Thank you so much for the blessing of Your sacrifice. Mark is now with You and not in that coffin.

Cecilia and Teddy returned and I finished my coffee.

"I'm going to get dressed. Be a sweetheart and order me some fruit and cottage cheese for breakfast, will you?"

Cecilia smiled. "Done."

The morning's overcast skies threatened to pour. I hoped I would be home sitting in front of my fireplace sipping a nice hot cup of tea and munching on a delectable slice of cake when the rain started falling.

Helen had invited everyone to her house after the service. Detective Noble would probably join us. I had to speak to him about Richard and Teddy's discovery.

I felt a little low but it was normal. I was, after all, attending a funeral. I wish I had known Mark better. Maybe we would learn more about him from the obituary.

I pulled into the funeral home parking lot which was almost empty. Luckily, the Mazda that had followed me was not among the cars I could see. That meant whoever owned it was wasn't here yet. I would certainly take note.

A few people gathered in the chapel of the funeral home. The chapel was small, intimate. Soft music played as people respectfully filed past Mark's casket. There were a few bouquets of flowers, but not many. A split leaf philodendron sat alone on the floor at the foot of the casket.

I walked past and paid my respects. The makeup people had done an outstanding job in making Mark look as natural as possible considering he'd been in a car accident.

Returning to the pews, I saw Helen seated toward the middle and decided to join her. She looked up and smiled when she saw me, and moved over to let me sit down.

"I couldn't wear black, Jillian," she whispered. "Mark's in Heaven so I chose something appropriate to wear for his sake. He's looking down and telling us that everything's okay now."

"I agree with you, Helen. Wearing black makes me think of people who have no hope of ever seeing their loved ones again. That's certainly not the case for Christians, is it?"

"I knew you'd understand, Jillian."

I was reminded of a funeral I'd attended years ago for an older gentleman whose wife wore a red dress and gave his obituary. She said that this was a glorious day for her husband, not a sad one. I had always remembered that funeral. I smiled as I sat there next to Helen in her turquoise print dress.

I glanced around and noted the attendees. Tori and Richard sat next to each other toward the back on the opposite side. Arthur and Diana sat in front of them. They both smiled when I looked their way. Warren Burkett sat next to Diana. He was alone.

In front of Helen and I sat Herbert Jamison. He turned and acknowledged we'd arrived. He, no doubt, was representing the Hansens. A young man that I hadn't seen before sat next to him. Could be a relative or friend of Mark's.

A few moments later, Leah and Vincent walked in and passed our row. They didn't stop to say hello but went straight to pay their respects, walking past Mark's casket.

It looked as if Vincent was trying to get Leah to come and sit with us, but I saw Leah shake her head and lead him to sit on the opposite side a few rows back.

An attractive red-haired young woman wearing a short black dress walked to the platform and picked up a cordless microphone. She waited a moment for the audience's attention, then began to sing a beautiful a cappella rendition of *Amazing Grace*.

Detective Noble came in and sat in the row behind Helen and me. I turned and smiled, truly glad he could make it.

The music stopped as Pastor Richardson, dressed in a dark blue suit and red print tie, stepped behind the pulpit.

"Welcome, everyone. Thank you for coming to honor Mark Russell's home going. Although I didn't know Mark for long, I had the privilege of talking to Mark on several occasions before he passed away. Mark suffered a lot of pain due to the accident but now he is in pain no more."

Pastor Richardson pulled a white envelope out of his pocket. "I have a letter here that I was given. It shows the condition of Mark's heart before he passed. It reads:

To the friends and family of Mark Russell,

I needed to write this letter to all of you regarding Mark Russell, who has since passed away. I am the husband and father of the victims in the car accident Mark was involved in. We buried my beloved wife and daughter together two days ago. I know the pain first hand that all of you must be feeling right now. That was the hardest day of my life. And yet, I have to tell you that God has given me great peace through all of these past few horrific days and I pray He will give you peace as well.

Mark asked me to come see him in the hospital two days before he died. He told me he had no recollection of the accident but the police told him he was at fault. He told me he was sorry beyond any words he had to offer. He asked me to forgive him for taking away my wife and daughter. I could barely speak because my grief was so great. I told him that I forgave him and he was so grateful that I did.

He told me that he had repented of his sins and asked Christ to be his Lord and Savior. I told him Christ was my Savior, too. That made us brothers. That was hard for me but Mark needed to know that truth.

I received a call from Mark's lawyer the next day telling me that Mark had made me his beneficiary upon his death. The lawyer said it was Mark's way of offering some small restitution for what he'd done.

I write you this because you need to know what this means to the rest of my family. That money paid for the funerals for my wife and daughter. It paid for a leave of absence which allowed me to go through the grieving process with my other two children. It provides for the services of a housekeeper and sitter when I return to work and most importantly, it provides the means to pay for the ongoing doctors and hospital bills for my youngest daughter. She suffers from a rare blood disorder and this extra income will save her life.

This letter is a testimony to me and to you about God's goodness and faithfulness to his children — the ones taken home at too early an age like my wife Susan and my daughter Amy, and the one who had just come to know him, Mark Russell. I wanted to tell all of you that God is the only One who can give anyone peace. He is the only one who could have possibly given it to me in the loss of my precious wife and daughter.

Thank you for letting me share my heart with you today. May God bless each one of you.

Sincerely,
Steven A. Dowdle

Someone cried softly but I didn't want to turn around and look.

The pastor refolded the letter and put it back in his jacket pocket. Before he could go on there was an interruption at the back of the room. Everyone turned to see who had come in.

An attractive woman who looked to be in her early thirties walked self-consciously down the aisle and took a seat in the front row. She wore a dark black business suit and looked exceptionally well-tailored. I observed the expensive jewelry she wore and the designer bag she carried.

The pastor smiled at the newcomer and nodded as if he knew exactly who she was.

"We're glad Mark's sister could join us. She was out of the country when Mark had his accident. She only found out the day before yesterday that he'd passed away. Welcome, Karen."

Karen smiled back weakly at Pastor Richardson. She looked straight ahead.

As the pastor resumed his eulogy, everyone tried to refocus on what he was saying.

The eulogy was brief. There was not much to say about Mark since he had no family around to talk about his upbringing. I was happy when the pastor told of Mark's conversion and the peace that he felt when he accepted Christ as his Savior and Lord.

After the pastor finished, he asked if anyone wanted to say anything in remembrance. At first no one came forward, but then Helen stood and walked to the pulpit.

She held a crumpled handkerchief in her right hand as she adjusted the microphone with her left. Bowing her head briefly, she began to speak.

"As most of you know, I worked with Mark for three years. He was always a nice young man and easy to work with. He came to work on time and would stay late if a project required him to. He didn't complain about anything and was happy to have the job he did working with Dr. Wingate and Mr. Burkett. I know he loved sports. He always talked about the games he was going to watch on TV or a good round of some sort or other outside with a buddy.

"There really wasn't anything I didn't like about him. He was one of those people who gets along with everybody. He was an excellent worker and always had a smile for me when he came into work every day. I will miss that the most about him."

Helen looked up. "Mark, I know you're in Heaven now and you do not have to suffer pain anymore. I look forward to seeing you again one day."

She broke down, said a tearful thank you, and found her way back to her seat.

The pastor waited a few moments and after no one else made any movement toward the front, he got up and invited everyone to a luncheon at the home of Helen Morningstar at the conclusion of the services. He then asked the pallbearers to come forward. Arthur and Warren stood along with two young men who must have been friends of Mark.

Everyone drove slowly to the gravesite. A clap of thunder boomed overhead and a few dark clouds began to roll in from the west.

I was glad I had my umbrella with me.

We sat in folding chairs placed in front of the gravesite. The pallbearers sat the coffin on supports placed across the opening. After everyone was seated, Pastor Richardson read the passage where Jesus spoke to comfort his disciples.

"Do not let your hearts be troubled. Trust in God, trust also in me. In my Father's house are many rooms. If it were not so, I would have told you. I am going there to prepare a place for you. And if I go and prepare a place for you, I will come back and take you to be with me that you also may be where I am."

Thomas said to him, "Lord, we don't know where you are going, so how can we know the way?"

Jesus answered, "I am the way and the truth and the life. No one comes to the Father except through me (John 14:1-6)."

"Lord God, we commend our brother, Mark Russell, to his final resting place. It is not in this cold dark grave, which we are gazing upon, but it is with You in Heaven which You promised to those who believe. Your word says in John 3:16 'For God so loved the world that he gave us his one and only Son, that whoever believes in him shall not perish but have eternal life.' Verse 36 says, 'Whoever believes in the Son has eternal life, but whoever rejects the Son will not see life, for God's wrath remains on him.' Thank you Lord. Mark believed in Your Son, Jesus, and he is with You. Amen."

The pastor again announced that after the service lunch would be served at the home of Helen Morningstar.

A few mourners paid final respects to Mark's sister. The rest mingled for a while before returning to their cars. Detective Noble stood apart from the group. As we finished, he motioned for me to come over.

I signaled that I would be there shortly, but first, I wanted to speak with Helen.

She was composed and smiled a half-smile as I approached her.

"It was a nice funeral, wasn't it, Jillian? I think I did all right."

I gave her a small hug of reassurance. "It couldn't have been any better, Helen. Tell me, who were the two pallbearers besides Arthur and Warren?"

Helen paused and refocused her thoughts to what I was asking.

"They were friends of Mark who called the office when the obituary appeared in the paper. They asked if there was anything they could do and I told them we needed pallbearers."

"I'm glad it worked out."

"I'll see you back at the house. Did you get the directions I e-mailed?"

"Yes, and thank you. Do you need help setting up? I can assist."

"Thanks, but I have everything ready. My sister is going to help me. She's setting things out right now so there really isn't anything to do before we get there."

"How nice of her. I'll look forward to meeting her. See you in a few minutes."

The rain began to come down, a few sprinkles at first, then a deluge.

The detective was still waiting but I shook my head. I would talk to him later at Helen's. There was no way I was going to stand outside in this storm.

Chapter 15

The rain ended as quickly as it began. By the time I reached Helen's house, the storm had completely cleared except for a few lingering gray clouds. The air smelled fresh and clean. I inhaled deeply. Refreshing.

There was a parking spot a few doors down from Helen's house. I pulled over. Detective Noble was right behind me. After parking his car behind mine, got out and walked over.

"I'm not going in, Jillian. I have to get back. This will have to be short. You said you needed to tell me something?"

"Yes. Leah Fontaine came to me and said she believed Richard Sanchez was embezzling from her society and she wanted you to know."

He looked surprised and taken back a bit with the news. "Boy, now that's what I call a development. Does she have proof?"

"She told me she was gathering the evidence, but she was sure. She said to ask you what she should do next. She's afraid of what Richard will do if he knows she suspects him."

"Could it have given Richard a motive to kill Rene?"

"That's what we both thought. Either he might have killed Rene to keep him quiet if he knew about the stolen funds...."

"Or Richard killed him because Rene might have been blackmailing him."

"What should I tell Leah?"

"Tell her to give you the evidence and that you'll give it to me. If she came straight to me, it might alert Richard and he might retaliate. That's the safest way to go."

"Got it."

He started to get back into his car but stopped and turned to me again.

"You said something about your dog finding a clue, Jillian?"

Hesitating at first simply because I knew he might take it wrong, I walked toward him and looked at him as straight-faced as possible.

"This may be hard for you to believe, but I think Teddy has found the murder weapon."

"What? Where? When did this happen? Why didn't you tell me before now? For crying out loud!"

"I haven't had a chance! Things kept coming up, but that doesn't matter now. What we need to do is get some of your people to check it out. But I must warn you, I would have the groundskeeper help you retrieve it."

"Why do we need him? We're professionals, Jillian."

"Do you trust me, Detective?"

"I suppose so. You've been right about everything so far. Okay, I'll get hold of the groundskeeper and I'll let you know when we've retrieved the weapon, all right?"

"All right." We were finally going to get some answers. Not only were we making progress on the case, but I had also won him over.

"By the way, before you go inside, Jillian...we found some interesting receipts in Rene's possession."

"Receipts? For what?"

"Let's just say they were made out to Vincent

Fontaine."

I felt a weakness in my knees and stomach and leaned against the wet car. Jarred by the dampness, I stood erect. "What do you think they mean?"

"I don't know. The receipts were for gas and sundry items purchased at Yvette's store. In and of themselves they don't mean anything, but they'll fit into the overall scheme of things, I'm sure. I know you've been seeing him, Jillian, and I'm sorry. Maybe he'll tell you what he was doing there, but I wouldn't ask him yet.

"We're still interested in Ray Ackerman. Who knows? They may fit in together somehow. For now, don't say anything. Just keep up what you're doing and I'll keep you informed as this thing works itself out, agreed?"

"I agree. It's funny, but Vincent doesn't strike me as the kind of person who would shoot someone. It seems impossible to me."

"Believe me, Jillian. If we could typecast all murderers our job would be easy. All we can do is find motive, means and opportunity. It looks like we're getting close to finding the motive. I'll call you as soon as I get a team together. Remember to be careful."

A call came in for him on his cellphone. He nodded to me, got into his car, continued with his call, and drove off.

I'll be careful all right. Careful to keep myself from falling in love.

"Get hold of yourself, Jillian! Get your head back into this investigation. Vincent could be innocent and he could be guilty. Use your brain, not your heart."

I took another deep breath and knocked on Helen's door.

A woman who favored Helen a little opened the door. She smiled and welcomed me into the small living room where I saw a few familiar faces, including Vincent and Leah. She introduced herself as Helen's sister and led me to the kitchen where Helen was busy putting more sandwiches on a tray.

"I see you made it. Come into the dining room and get yourself some food."

I followed her into the tiny dining room where I found a table laden with food. It all looked succulent and I was famished, as usual.

Helen pointed to a particularly delicious looking dish. "You must try some of this. It's an old Indian family recipe handed down from my grandfather who used to make it in an outdoor oven."

I placed a spoonful of the stuffed pepper on my plate and took a bite. "This is wonderful, Helen. What is it?"

"I thought you'd like it. It's a Poblano pepper stuffed with chicken and jack cheese and special spices."

I helped myself to a few finger sandwiches, some pasta salad, a spoonful of marinated bean salad, a scoop of a delicious looking chicken casserole, some raw crudités and dip and finished off my selections with a spoonful of marinated olives.

Arthur and Diana were getting some food as well and I took the opportunity to ask why Warren's wife wasn't at the funeral.

"She had a prior engagement she couldn't wiggle out of. Diana said her son was getting his wisdom teeth pulled. She had to drive him home."

"I see. There were so few people there. Mark's sister didn't stop by?"

Arthur shook his head. "She had a plane to catch. I did speak with her briefly though and found out a little about their relationship. Her family life left a lot to be desired, so when she was old enough to go out on her own, that's what she did. She said she never looked back and unfortunately lost contact with Mark until she read about his death."

"That's so sad. Poor Mark, it sounds like he had it tough himself. I'll talk to you both later. I need to find a seat."

I looked for a place. Richard Sanchez sat alone on the sofa.

"Mind if I sit here?"

He scooted over a bit to make room for me and smiled.

"Have a seat. There's room."

I sat down and began to eat, waiting for him to begin a conversation. It didn't take long. As soon as my mouth was full, he started to make small talk.

"What did you think of Mark's funeral, Jillian?"

I nodded a positive affirmation and reached for the cup of punch Helen had brought me. When I could talk without choking at the same time, I answered him.

"All in all, I thought it went well. Helen did a marvelous job of coordinating everything, don't you think?"

I took a few more bites as he chatted. I was hungry.

He sat back after placing his empty plate on the small coffee table and wiped his mouth with a napkin.

"I'll tell you what I was most impressed with."

"What was that?"

"It was that letter from the man who lost his wife and daughter in the wreck. Boy, that was something else. I mean, for a guy to be going through a loss like that and then to find time to show his gratitude to a man who would never even listen to what he had to say. Well, I was impressed."

"I know. I believe Mark's heart had changed to a point where he wasn't thinking about himself anymore. He was thinking of how he could help the man whose loss of his family was Mark's fault. I wonder Mark never spoke of having a sister."

"I don't know. I really didn't know Mark that well, but if I had a sister like that I would at least acknowledge the fact."

"That's right. You were an only child, weren't you,

Richard?"

"Yeah, it got lonely at times with only my parents to talk to, but we worked so hard during the day we usually went to bed early."

When my plate was empty, Helen's sister immediately took it away. I smiled at her. "Thanks."

"Richard, have you been able to recollect anything about Ray Ackermann since we talked last?"

He furrowed his brow and pursed his lips.

"When you mentioned him at first, I had a brief flash of recognition. The more I rack my brain the more I'm sure I've actually seen him somewhere."

"Perhaps when you worked with your father? Maybe you came across him at some point."

"That's probably where I remember him from. I'll tell you what. If it's really that important to you I'll give my dad a call and see if he knows him."

"That would be great, Richard. Thank you."

Tori sat on a dining room chair brought in for extra seating. She didn't seem to notice me. She was staring at Richard.

"Tori is looking at you, Richard."

He turned and glanced around the room as if searching for her, but he couldn't fool me. He'd been looking at her the whole time. "Would you excuse me, Jillian? I think Tori wants to talk. I'll call you later."

"Of course. Thanks for the offer to talk to your dad for me. I'll hold you to it."

He chuckled. "I know."

Vincent's eyes bored into me from across the room after Richard went to speak to Tori. Tori's face lit up when Richard headed her way. They certainly were more than friends, even if they didn't know it.

Vincent came over to me.

I braced myself to focus on fact, not fiction.

"Mind if I sit down?"

"Be my guest," I said as nonchalantly as I could.

He sat down and folded his hands. I supposed he did it to prevent him from putting his arm around me.

He looked at me straight in the eye.

"Is anything wrong?"

From his tone I believed he was referring to our relationship. I avoided the question.

"I have the investigation weighing on my mind is all."

He nodded as if he accepted the explanation, then glanced at Leah who had not taken her eyes off us since he got up to sit with me.

"How is Leah doing? I know the funeral wasn't easy for any of us."

"I really can't explain what's eating her, Jillian. When I mention calling you or taking you out to dinner, she tells me I shouldn't get involved with someone who lives in California."

"Does she resent me, Vincent?"

"She must or she wouldn't be steering me away from you every chance she gets."

"It's normal for an adult child to be wary of their parents becoming involved with someone other than their own parent, I suppose. But, after all, we're not involved, are we Vincent?"

He looked down briefly and took a breath.

"I guess I know how you feel, now. I was hoping we might be getting to be more than just friends, Jillian."

"Do you realize how difficult a relationship would be for us, Vincent? Leah's right. You live in one state and I live in another. You have your work and I have mine. You already have a family and …."

"Stop it, Jillian! If two people love each other all those things can be worked out."

"I'm sorry, Vincent, but until this investigation is over, I can't encourage you in any way."

"And why not, I'd like to know?"

Helen must have seen the sparks start to fly because

she came to my rescue.

"Jillian, could I see you alone for a moment? Pastor Richardson is waiting. Would you excuse us, Dr. Fontaine?"

I followed Helen into the kitchen where Pastor Richardson stood, holding a plate of food in his hands. He smiled at me we came in.

"Hello, Pastor. I'm glad I have a chance to tell you what a wonderful job you did on the service today. The Lord was surely honored by everything you said."

He chuckled and flushed a little at the compliment.

People began to leave after paying their respects to Helen and her sister for having everyone over. They complimented the delicious food and reiterated how nice the services were, then they were gone.

I offered to help clean up but Helen wouldn't hear of it.

"You get back to the hotel and rest a little. I'm sure Teddy misses you and until everyone is gone, I won't get to rest myself!"

***

"Cecilia, Teddy, anybody home?" I called as I walked in the front door of my casita. I put my purse down on the entryway table and looked around for a note. Not finding one, I decided they had probably gone for a walk not knowing when I'd be back, so I didn't worry. I checked for messages on my room phone and saw none. I kicked off my shoes and changed into my sweats. With my laptop and cellphone I sat down on the chaise end of the sofa and put up my feet.

There were no messages on my cell so I decided to check e-mails while I had some peace and quiet. Most were just ads and then I came to one from Vincent. He'd sent it before we talked at Helen's. It might explain something, but it would probably be rather awkward. I clicked the message open.

"Well, here goes."

> *Dear Jillian,*
>
> *I know there's something wrong between us. I felt it after you talked to Detective Noble last night. I don't know what I've done to push you away, but I wish you'd let me know so I can fix it.*
>
> *Whatever happens during this murder investigation, I have to let you know how I feel about you, even if it comes to nothing, so here goes.*
>
> *First, I think you're attractive, Jillian, and I admire your amazing knowledge about flora, which I find attractive as well. You also have an incredible gift for helping people with their gardening issues and I admit I've been a fan of yours for years. I wasn't trying to flatter you at dinner the first night we met. I meant the compliment sincerely, so you know I have a great deal of respect for who you are. However, I have to tell you I like you for so much more than just what you look like or what you know.*
>
> *I've watched you around other people and I've seen how much you really care about their personal lives. Few people I know are like that. That quality drew me to you instantly. I felt like you just might care for me.*
>
> *I think you're witty and I love being with you. These past few days have been the most fun I've had in years in spite of the circumstances.*
>
> *I hope I'm making sense. I care about you and I want to be with you as much as I can. What I like most about you is that you're whole — nothing is missing. I think what's missing in me is you. I just wanted to tell you how I felt.*
>
> *Vincent*

I couldn't answer back. I felt flattered. I felt honored. I felt like a young woman again and that was dangerous. No. I wasn't a young woman anymore. I had to think about what my answer would be.

"Lord, help my thinking process in this matter with Vincent. You know I like his attention. I just want it to be right if it's going to happen at all."

Cecilia and Teddy came in just as I finished my prayer.

"Hi, Jillian. Sorry we weren't here. I thought we might get home before you did. How was the funeral?"

"It went fine. Mark's sister attended."

She undid Teddy's leash collar so he could come and jump up in my lap. He was happy to see me and started licking my cheek and wagging his tail. I gave him a hug and stroked his fur to calm him down as he curled up next to me.

Cecilia sat down in the armless chair next to the fireplace and slipped off her shoes.

"So, where were you off to while I was gone? Teddy looks all tuckered out."

"We ran into L-i-l-a and her walker so we joined up and let the little love birds enjoy their walk together."

Teddy didn't even twitch when Cecilia spelled out Lila's name.

We both had to smile.

Cecilia walked over to the phone. "The walker is really polite but he hardly says a word. I can't figure him out. Is he Elise's personal trainer or something?"

"You never know with wealthy people. They can afford anything or anyone they want. You know just to talk to Elise you would never guess she's as wealthy as she is. I find that refreshing."

"You do want me to order tea, don't you, Jillian?"

"By all means. It sounds lovely. I wonder what kind of special dessert they're featuring today?"

"I'll ask."

She gave her full attention to the room service operator and ordered for us.

"Twenty minutes. Just enough time to check my e-mails."

Her cellphone vibrated and she answered it immediately. Her thumbs began pounding out responses to what I was sure must be texts from Walter. I thought about the appropriateness of their love as young people. Was it appropriate for mature people to be as caught up in love as they were?

Somehow, I didn't see it as the same at all. Maybe it was because subconsciously we would always be comparing our present relationship to our past ones. It would take a great deal of determination to overcome that, but if happiness and companionship was the goal, I believed anything was possible.

But now? No, my belief was shaken. Detective Noble's call had changed everything. Who was Vincent? What was he trying to do? Seduce me? Sully my mind, my intelligence? Draw me off the path of this investigation?

I didn't know for sure, but I needed to be careful. My heart didn't want to see it, but in my mind, I knew he had more hold on me than he should have.

The phone rang again. Detective Noble's number popped up on the screen.

"Jillian, I'm glad you're home. I just got back from a horrific crime scene. Trying to shift gears to the Parker murder may take me a minute. Did anything of interest happen at Helen's I need to know?"

"Well, a few romantic glances exchanged between Tori DeMarco and Richard Sanchez. My relationship with Vincent Fontaine capsized so I suppose there were a few notes of interest."

"Sounds like I missed a lot!"

"Have you put together anyone to check out the

parking lot at The Sanctuary?"

"Yes, they're coming over in about an hour. I didn't want to waste any time if there is some evidence for this case. I'll bring those receipts we found so you can take a look at them and see what you think."

"I would be interested in the dates. It might be something. Do you have the financial records on Ray Ackermann ready?"

"As a matter of fact, I do. I'll bring them over when I come today. Hopefully, something will crack this case. So far, a bunch of comic books isn't what I'd call hard evidence, Jillian."

"Detective, have you ever played Sudoku?"

"Yeah, I work a few before I go to bed at night. It helps clear my mind from the day and I seem to sleep better. Why do you ask?"

"Finding Rene's killer is like finding all the numbers in the boxes in Sudoku. One by one, you find all the missing numbers. However, sometimes I get stuck. My mind wanders or I'll be trying too hard. Then, unless I've led myself astray with a wrong answer, I'll find a clue. That clue is usually the key that unlocks the rest of the puzzle and then it's easy after that."

"I'm stuck right now, Jillian. It's like nothing adds up."

"I know, but it's just because we don't have that one clue. You and I are going to keep digging until we find it."

"You wouldn't believe all the unsolved cases we have just because we never find the one key. Well, I'll call you when my team is here."

"Goodbye, Detective. I'll see you later."

Room service arrived and the cheerful server set the tea tray down on the coffee table for Cecilia and me. The pimento cheese sandwiches and fresh banana cake with rum frosting looked delicious. I was ready for something pleasant to enjoy. I poured out and we sat and enjoyed the afternoon tea for what it was, pure pleasure.

Cecilia seemed distracted, her mind far away. Like most young people, she kept her phone with her at all times. While I was pouring a second cup of tea for us, the phone vibrated. I didn't have to ask who was calling. Her face said it all. Before she typed an answer back, I saw her eyes grow wide as saucers. The next thing I knew, she let out a scream that sounded like someone had just scared her to death!

"What on earth is wrong, Cecilia?"

"Jillian, Walter just told me he loved me. It's the first time he's ever said it."

"You mean *texted* it?"

"It's the way we talk nowadays. It means the same thing."

"I see. Well, what are you going to text back?"

"I'm going to tell him I love him too, of course, and Jillian, I really do. Walter is perfect for me. I've known all along that he's the right one. He just now told me the same thing. Oh, Jillian, I'm so happy. That's why I screamed. I'm sorry if I startled you but I couldn't help it."

"I know, Cecilia. It's the most wonderful thing in the world to know you've finally met the right one. Your story is ending happily ever after, isn't it?"

"It may not end happily ever after, but right now it's happy, and I want to tell the world."

"Cecilia, go right ahead. I'll watch Teddy and feed him his supper. I've missed being with him, so this will give us a chance to catch up on some companion time. You go ahead and text away. I'm sure you and Walter have a lot to talk about."

"Thank you, Jillian, you are so understanding. Oh, I'm so happy!"

She left the room and went to lie down on her bed, phone in hand, texting away.

I was happy for her and yet somehow it made me sad as I remembered when my husband and I had fallen in love. Our love didn't end happily ever after. It was only happy for a short time, and then it was gone.

I gathered up the tea service and placed the tray outside the door.

"Shake it off, Jillian. Things happen. Just be glad that two people you're fond of have found each other. Be glad for them."

I prepared Teddy's dinner and gave him a teeny cup of milk and a bowl of fresh water. He ate and drank heartily, thankful I remembered him. I rinsed out his dishes and freshened up so I'd be ready when Detective Noble called.

"Teddy, you're coming with me when I go. I think you'll rest better if you see what's been bothering you all this time."

I had butterflies in my stomach when Noble called for me to come and meet him. Was it a good omen or a bad one? I would soon know as I put the collar and leash on Teddy and said goodbye to Cecilia.

I really don't think she heard me at all.

Chapter 16

Detective Noble took one look at Teddy, then his eyes moved back to me. "You brought your dog, Jillian?"

"Detective, this is Teddy's discovery. He needs to be here for closure."

"Closure, for a dog? But he's so small."

"You know what I mean. He'll rest easier knowing that whatever has been bothering him is taken care of. Dogs are like that, don't you know?"

"Sorry, I'm allergic to dogs, so no, I wouldn't know. Well, come on, let's get this over with."

There were two other police officers waiting in the parking lot as we approached. They also took one look at Teddy and then back at each other. That's okay, I thought. Just wait until they find whatever Teddy knows is out there. They'll have a little respect then.

Teddy pricked up his ears and began to growl.

"That means he's picked up on something that's not quite right, Detective."

The groundskeeper was heading our way from the hotel entrance.

"Looks like we have everything we need now. Jeff's coming."

Jeff Gorman sauntered up to where we were standing and Teddy started to wag his tail as he remembered him from the tour.

"Hello, Teddy." He stooped down to give him a pat.

Teddy barked as if to say, "Let's go you guys; I really want to show you something!"

"We'd better let him show us what he's found," I said.

Teddy tugged at his leash and wanted us to follow him into the parking lot. He led us to the base of the jumping cholla and barked at something up in the spiny limbs.

Jeff looked to where Teddy was looking and realized it was the Cactus Wren's nest.

"Okay. It's that nest up there. There's really nothing else here except for the cholla itself. I'd better get some gloves and a ladder to reach it so I won't have to brush up next to it. I'd wind up covered in spines."

He didn't take long to retrieve a ladder from the cart shed. I glanced toward the carts, and had a strange feeling of déja vu. Those two things, the cart and the plant went together somehow. Jeff continued his search and interrupted my thought altogether when he reached carefully into the nest. What he pulled out astonished us all. The handle came first, then the barrel of a handgun.

"Here you go, Detective." He carefully handed the gun over. Detective Noble reached for it with a plastic bag. After placing the gun inside, he zipped it shut and looked at me with a satisfied smile on his face.

"It looks like a .22 to me, Jillian."

He handed the weapon to one of his men and ordered a report as soon as possible. Detective Noble bent down to Teddy's level.

"You're the smartest dog I've ever seen, Teddy. Your mistress is right. You have my respect. My apologies, Jillian, for having any doubt about this animal. It's...he's really something. You ought to call him *Sleuth*

Dog."

I couldn't help but laugh. "Thank you. Maybe I will. He's pretty special."

I thanked Jeff for his help.

He parted with a word of caution.

"I would be pretty certain that whoever put that gun there will have a spine or two somewhere on their belongings. That cholla is pretty sticky. It's just a thought. You'll excuse me, won't you? I have one last tour to give before I go home."

Detective Noble thanked him again and offered to walk me back to my casita.

"I'm still flabbergasted at Teddy finding that gun, Jillian. This might be that key to solving this case, finally. Ballistics won't take long. I'll bet we'll know whose gun it is by tomorrow morning."

We had reached my casita. I slid my passkey through the lock once again and opened the door. Cecilia had not moved from the bedroom the whole time I was gone.

"Won't you sit down, Detective?" I motioned to the sofa or chairs.

"Thanks." He took a seat in the large overstuffed club chair.

He reached inside his coat pocket and withdrew a long white envelope. "Here are the receipts and some records I want you to take a look at." He handed me the envelope.

"Is it okay to look inside?" I asked, kidding about the protocol.

"Sure, look away, it's the financial statements for Ray Ackermann for the last six years but only the sections that stood out as irregular entries. We disregarded the everyday stuff."

"Would you mind if I held onto them, just for a day, so I can have Cecilia check out a couple of things I've been thinking about?"

"Of course. Those are just copies. You can keep them as long as you like, but please give them back when you're finished. And I would appreciate it if you didn't make any copies."

"Why would I do that?"

"I guess it's just the criminal mind I come into contact with so much that makes me suspect everyone has an ulterior motive. For instance, I thought you might use that information in some way to your advantage."

"Do you know how ridiculous that sounds? However, I guess I can see how dealing with criminals can cause you to be a little crazy. I forgive you, Detective. Now let's get on with this investigation and stop chasing rabbits."

How could he think so ill of me? I tried to refocus.

The envelope wasn't sealed. I opened it and carefully took out two receipts, sitting them on the table. The date on the first receipt was in March. The second one April. Two visits by Vincent, each one month apart. I calculated from the year on the receipts that Rene was a senior in high school. That same year Ray Ackermann had accosted Rene's mother.

Detective Noble rose and said he'd better be going home. I thanked him for listening to Teddy.

At the sound of his name, Teddy raised his head and jumped down off the sofa to see him off.

"Thanks again, boy, for helping us find the gun. You're all right in my book." Detective Noble gave him a pat goodbye, and sneezed.

We laughed.

"I'll call you when we find out who owned the gun."

My spirit dreaded to know. After all she'd been through in her life, what if the gun was Tori's? What if it was Richard's because he found out Leah was coming after him for embezzlement? What if the gun belonged to Leah? Why would she kill Rene? Then the worst thought of all, what if it was Vincent's?

"Lord, please don't let that gun be Vincent's!" It was selfish, but I couldn't help praying it.

Cecilia finally emerged from her room and smiled dreamily. "Has Detective Noble gone? I heard you two talking."

She finally refocused on me instead of Walter. "Did Teddy find anything?"

"Teddy found what we believe is the murder weapon used to kill Rene Parker."

"Incredible! How do you know it's the same gun?"

"It just stands to reason. We found it near Simon's cart that had blood on it. Simon was murdered after Rene was killed. There doesn't seem to be any reason for it other than Simon probably interfered with whoever was trying to hide the gun."

"I see what you mean. It's like one thing leads to another."

"Just like in Sudoku."

"Not to change the subject, Jillian, but my life is just beginning since Walter told me he loved me."

"I understand, Cecilia, believe me I do. Life begins, and life ends. What was it Yvette said about the music box Rene gave her? I must think. Something about when Rene left home and the music stopped. No. The music box stopped working right when Rene *left*.

Cecilia! I know where the disc is! I've got to call Detective Noble right now. Cecilia, this is the real clue, the real key. I know it!"

I quickly placed the call. "Hello? Detective? Listen carefully. I know where the missing disc of Rene's is. Get hold of Yvette and have her look inside that music box Rene gave her before he left home — the one she said stopped working when he left. He hid the memory card inside, in case someone found out he videotaped them."

"Okay, Jillian. We turned that house upside down and didn't find anything. I'll call now. We may solve this case yet!"

Hopefully, I was right. We needed that disc if we were going to learn anything about Vincent's involvement with Rene or Ray Ackermann.

"Cecilia, I need you to look up something for me. Meanwhile, I'm going to check out these financial records of Ray Ackermann's and note the dates. If I'm right, we can begin to see the big picture."

"Does this mean I should order cheeseburgers and fries for dinner tonight?"

"That would be perfect."

"I'll call now."

"Don't forget the chocolate shakes."

We worked for a few hours until we couldn't keep awake any longer. Our findings yielded some pretty damaging evidence, although inconclusive without further proof.

A jury could construe corresponding dates as coincidental. I had Cecilia look up the conference on plant propagation that Vincent told me he attended a few years ago in Chicago.

After diligently searching for forty minutes, she finally came up with one in February that corresponded with the year matching the dates of the receipts Rene had kept.

As far as Ray Ackermann's financial records went, someone had deposited a check for $1,000 in his account in May of that same year. An identical check in May for the next three years had also been deposited. That would mean that up until two years ago, Ray Ackermann was poaching for ghost orchids for which someone paid him a total of $4,000. It wasn't adding up too well for Vincent in my mind. I would have to look at Vincent's financial records, both personal and work-related, to determine if the figures and dates matched. I hoped they wouldn't, but I was going to find out either way.

"I'm going to bed, Cecilia. Can't stay awake any longer."

"I'm with you." She yawned. "It's midnight already. Goodnight. I'll see you in the morning, but not too early, please."

Teddy had been asleep on my foot for at least an hour. Every hour or so he would open one eye and look at me as if to say, 'Don't you know it's bedtime?'

I chuckled and had to agree. I got ready for bed and was almost asleep when I remembered to pray.

"Dear Lord, I don't know what's going to happen tomorrow but You do. I pray that You'll give me wisdom and discernment as I try to help Detective Noble find out who killed Rene. At first, I wanted to help for Arthur's sake because he's my friend. Now, Lord, I want to know for Yvette's sake, so she can be at peace.

"Why do I feel this way? It's as though if I help her find peace, mine will be taken. I do care for Vincent. I know I shouldn't, but I do. Lord, help me to do what's right and just, and not what is wrong and selfish.

"And Lord, I pray again with all of my heart that Vincent didn't kill Rene, even though at this point, he may have had more of a motive that anyone else. If it's Richard, I pray he'll be caught before anyone else is hurt, especially Tori. Please help me to sleep and give me clear thinking in the morning. I'm relying on Your strength, Lord. I love you. Amen."

Sleep had almost won when my cellphone rang. Groggily, I picked it up and answered it.

"Sorry to call so late, Jillian, but I had to let you know."

"Oh, hello, Detective. You had to let me know what?" I hoped I would remember what he told me later.

"Jillian, you were right on the money about the memory card. I had one of our men go over to Yvette's and check it out with her. It looks like Rene stuck it inside the gears to hide it."

I was wide-awake by now. "Have they taken a look to see what was on it yet?"

Teddy whimpered as if to say, 'Why don't you go back to sleep?'

"Yeah, they brought Rene's camera with them just in case, so they played it right away. You're not going to like this, Jillian."

I felt a wave of fear, and my stomach fell to my knees. "It's Vincent, isn't it?"

"I'm afraid so. It's a video showing Vincent meeting with Ray Ackermann at the lumberyard and discussing the payment for procuring the ghost orchids."

"So that's why Rene had those catalogues and comic books. He wanted to get evidence against Ray."

"What I can't understand is what motivated a teenaged boy like that to videotape an illegal transaction. I mean, that was pretty daring of him, don't you think?"

As I pictured Rene setting up the camera in Ray Ackermann's office ready to capture any wrongdoing on his part I finally realized why he did it.

"Detective, I think Rene made that video as an insurance policy against Ray Ackermann."

"An insurance policy? How do you mean?"

"He was trying to protect Yvette against Ray's unwanted advances. Rene probably thought if he had something on Ray, he could use it to make him stay away from his mother. It was like an insurance policy. By stuffing it in Yvette's music box, he made sure no one but he alone would be able to find it and use it against Ray Ackermann."

"That makes sense. But here's the deal. Ray Ackermann hasn't been seen for over two years, so how do you figure Vincent Fontaine fits into all of this, Jillian?"

"I'm still working that out, but it fits together in some way. Listen, I'm really tired and my brain is pretty muddled from all this. How about we talk in the morning?"

"That suits me fine, except for one thing."

"What's that?"

"We'll be arresting Vincent Fontaine sometime tomorrow for probable cause. Blackmail is a motive, Jillian. If ballistics pan out like I think they will that gun will belong to Vincent. And if it does, it's the nail in the coffin."

"I understand, Detective. Goodnight."

I flipped my phone shut and wished I could flip my relationship with Vincent shut. I was hurt. It was as if Vincent had used me to curry favor and keep me from learning the awful truth. He might be a murderer and probably a liar as well.

I cried softly into my pillow and vowed never to be taken in again...by anyone.

Chapter 17

Sleep was difficult after Detective Noble's phone call. Through prayer and tears, I struggled my way through the night. Eventually, a peace did come over me. Everything would turn out for the best. I merely had to be patient and focus on finding the truth.

Someone knocked softly on my door.

"Jillian? It's six o'clock. You wanted a wakeup call for the gym this morning. Are you awake?"

I stretched to get some blood flowing.

"Thanks, Cecilia. Yes, I'm awake."

I threw on my robe and followed Teddy to my door.

Cecilia stood smiling on the other side.

"Good morning. I'd appreciate it if you'd take Teddy out for me this morning. It's going to be a tough day."

"Come on, Teddy. Let's go outside for a walk."

She put the collar and leash on him but he hesitated.

"What's the matter, boy?"

Teddy looked back at me and whimpered.

"I think he senses something's wrong, Jillian."

"He's right. I don't think anything good is going to happen today. We'll just have to wait and see. I've prayed, but that's all I can do at this point. Have a nice walk."

"We'll see you later. I ordered breakfast to be sent over after you get back from the gym."

"You're the best, Cecilia. Thank you."

I dressed for working out and headed to the fitness center. I would need a clear head and lots of energy today.

The gym was full. I would have to wait on the bench inside the door until a treadmill was free. My bag fit nicely in the storage space along the wall. Perhaps not everyone brought one.

I took my seat. There were the typical go-getters here, young, thin women, with sprayed on tans, hair pulled back in ponytails and sweat pouring off their faces as they did running uphill treadmill workouts.

The men were just the opposite. Overweight, panting, and walking at a slow pace. They watched the news on the TVs attached to the machines.

I didn't see Leah anywhere. Perhaps she had come in earlier. A young woman finally finished her treadmill workout and I took my turn. Before I stepped on the machine the front door opened and who should walk in but Leah. She saw me and waved hello. Hopefully, I'd be able to talk to her before I left. After putting her workout bag inside the shelving unit she went to the weights and started her routine with knee lunges. I knew she'd be here awhile so I continued with my treadmill for thirty minutes.

Leah finished her workout and motioned for me to join her in the women's shower area. I turned off my machine, blotted my forehead with my towel, and got a wipe to clean off the handles. Gym courtesy.

"Good morning, Leah," I greeted as I came into the shower room.

After washing her face, she looked up from the sink. "Good morning, Jillian. It's a beautiful day outside, isn't it?"

This was different. I hadn't seen this side of Leah before. It was a nice change.

"I haven't been awake long enough to notice, but I'll take your word for it."

She took a guest towel to dry off her face. Opening her bag, she found her hairbrush and began to fix her ponytail into the up do she usually wore.

Being the snoop I am, I couldn't help glancing inside and took note of the contents. It was quite a conglomeration of paraphernalia some of which would not be needed in a gym.

To each his own.

As for me, organization was paramount. All I had in my bag was my passkey, my cellphone, and a windbreaker in case of rain. Leah's looked like a proverbial tool chest with all kinds of makeup, a pair of sunglasses, workout gloves, hair clips, rubber bands, flashlight, a Sudoku puzzle book and several pens. I noticed her passkey and cellphone stuck in an outside pocket. She wore her windbreaker tied around her waist and I could certainly see why. There was no room for it in her bag!

She packed up everything she had used and looked at me face to face. "Did you speak to Detective Noble for me?"

"Yes I did, although we didn't have much time to discuss it."

"What did he say? What should I do?"

"He said the best thing was to give me copies of the evidence showing Richard's embezzlement. It wouldn't be as obvious that way and might protect you from Richard."

"I see. Well, I have the copies ready. May I come to your room?" She zipped her bag and placed the strap on her shoulder.

"That would be fine. Let me shower and eat my breakfast and then come on over. How about in an hour?"

"An hour then. Thanks, Jillian. I really appreciate you helping me with this. It's been most stressful."

I followed her out the door. We parted ways as she

went to her room and I to mine.

I was hungry by the time I got back to my casita and couldn't wait to eat the breakfast Cecilia had ordered for me. I hoped it was something substantial.

Teddy came running as I opened the door with the passkey. He flew into my arms, and I welcomed him with hugs and kisses.

"Did you have an exciting walk, sweet doggie? I hope there were lots of interesting smells for you to find."

Without changing, I sat down on the sofa and lifted the lids off the waiting breakfast dishes. Cecilia had ordered a fresh fruit plate of pineapple, cantaloupe, honeydew, strawberries, and blueberries for a starter which I devoured quickly. After consuming a deliciously rich cup of French roast coffee and taking a sip of freshly squeezed orange juice, I started on the fluffy orange French toast with hot cinnamon syrup. I gave Teddy some tiny bites to remind him of how much I loved him. He was most appreciative.

"Cecilia, I'm going to hop into the shower and get dressed. Please listen for any calls if you would. My cellphone is on the coffee table."

"I've got you covered, Jillian."

Teddy lay on his towel at the foot of my bed while I showered so he could feel like he was with me. With his little brown face resting on his front paws and his back paws outstretched, he closed his eyes and took a nap.

The shower revived me but there was still no call from Detective Noble. Well, I could check in with my editor.

The computer glowed on the work desk. My column was already prepared for publication. My boss was pleased with the number of inquiries I'd received and so was I, though I felt a bit indignant that they'd cut my salary.

No, it wasn't personal. Still, I was a little tired of

working for *The Enterprise*. I had, after all, worked there for many years and wondered if it was time for a change. I had several offers of writing for other rags, but up until now, I hadn't taken any of the offers seriously. It would probably mean a move. That was not a pleasant idea. The offers were standing ones though. Did I need a change?

Cecilia knocked on my door.

"You have a visitor."

Had it been an hour already? I scooped Teddy up in my arms. Cecilia was sitting on the sofa with Leah when I came into the living room. Teddy jumped down out of my arms and ran to say hello to the guest.

"Teddy, stay!" I commanded before he jumped up on Leah's lap. Teddy obeyed and stopped just short of Leah's feet.

"Oh, it's okay, Jillian. I like dogs but I'm allergic to them."

"I'll take him into my room, Jillian."

Cecilia picked him up and carried him away.

"Thanks, Cecilia. Leah, I'm sorry I'm not ready yet. My mind wanders these days and I lose track of time."

"That's quite all right."

Leah took some papers out of a large manila envelope and handed them to me. "I've highlighted the discrepancies for you showing where I found the numbers not adding up. If you'll look at this first page, you'll see that the expenditure I noted was for $4,567.73."

I looked at the first page and saw that she had highlighted three entries. Leah continued her explanation. "I added them up and reached a total that was significantly less than what Richard came up with. It happens over and over again as you can see where I've highlighted the entries."

I looked at each of the six pages she handed me. "How much are we talking about, Leah?"

"I calculated an average of $500 per page, so for six pages, that's $3,000. And that's for just one month, Jillian. I don't know how long he's been doing it. It could be in the tens of thousands for all I know."

"This is serious. I'll get these to Detective Noble as soon as I see him. I think it will be sometime this morning, but I'm not sure. He's busy with other cases."

She handed me the envelope and I put the papers back inside. She rose and thanked me again for helping her unburden herself with the evidence. I walked her to the door.

"I'll call you as soon as I have instructions from Detective Noble regarding the next step."

Leah nodded curtly, which was warm for her, and left.

I needed to dress. Cecilia said she was going to be on the phone with Walter. She would watch Teddy for me in her room. She threw me a coy little look, cuddled Teddy to her nose and left.

Ah, love—a wonderful sickness that takes over your mind, body, and soul! It's a good thing that eventually it only affects your soul or people would never get anything done.

Done. I needed to get stuff done. I had the information from Leah. I'd call Detective Noble. I dialed and he answered right away. He must have been busy from the terseness of his answers.

"What's going on, Jillian?"

"Leah just left. The evidence against Richard Sanchez is here. Should I bring it to you or are you out and about today?"

"Actually, I'm waiting for the ballistics report, but I guess they can call me on my cell when they have the information. What are you doing for lunch?"

"I have no plans. Where would you like to meet?"

"I don't have a lot of time. Why don't we just meet at ZuZu's again, say one o'clock? I can't get away before."

"I'll see you then."

Since I was dressed and ready to go, I had enough time to check my e-mails before heading to ZuZu's. There was not a word from Vincent. Evidently, I'd succeeded in discouraging him by my ignoring his messages.

I wanted another cup of coffee, so I poured me one and sat down on the sofa to relax. It would be good to get home. I was looking forward to hanging my new paintings in the conservatory. They would complete the room.

Actually, the whole house would be completed once I had these additions. I had simply run out of walls. My yard had reached its zenith as well. Everything was either evergreen, blooming trees or shrubs, and perennials that only needed to be pruned and fertilized.

With annuals growing in pots on the front porch and on the back terrace for touches of color, I could honestly say that my house was perfect. I had all the furnishings, inside and out, for my personal needs and for my visual needs, beautiful paintings and accessories wherever I looked.

If it weren't for Teddy, though, my home would seem like a mausoleum. When I got back, I would throw a spectacular dinner party and invite a ton of people over. That would keep me busy. Yes, busy. Must stay busy. I subconsciously began planning a holiday menu when my cell rang.

"Hello?"

"Jillian, it's Richard Sanchez."

My stomach did a flip-flop in fear.

"Hi, Richard." I decided to let him speak first so I would know what he was up to.

"I wanted to let you know I talked to my dad last night. You know, about Ray Ackermann?"

"Yes, thank you for calling him. What did he say?"

"It turns out he remembers him from a few years

ago. He told me Ackerman wasn't a pleasant fellow. It seems he was a little on the wrong side of the law."

"I see. Did he take a tour with your dad by any chance?"

"As a matter of fact, he did. My dad called him a 'swamp creature.' He said Ray Ackermann always took an empty leather backpack with him when he went into the swamp and when he came out, it was full."

"Your dad didn't suspect him of poaching?"

"Oh, he suspected him of poaching all right, but he didn't believe it was his job to inspect his clients' belongings. He told me he left that to the authorities."

"So Ray Ackermann got away with it."

"Jillian, you have to understand that in Florida, even though poaching is illegal, it's difficult to prove anything. The authorities just look the other way most of the time. When someone is convicted, they usually receive a fine or maybe a short sentence."

"Then I wonder why Ray Ackermann hasn't been seen for two years, if poaching wasn't that serious."

"I couldn't tell you. Maybe the gators got him on one of his trips into the swamps. He didn't always take a tour, I'm sure."

"You have a point. What did he poach, do you have any idea?"

"It was probably rare orchids. Orchids are a hot item in the floral business and they're hard to grow. I've heard of a few people trying to clone them, but so far, no one has had success, at least not to my knowledge. Listen, I have to go. I promised Leah I'd get a report out on a field study I did before all this mess happened."

"I understand. I appreciate you finding out about Ray for me. There's just one more thing. How is Tori? Is Leah working her hard again?"

"Tori's fine. Leah has always been a taskmaster. She hovers over us as if we were children. I just ignore her most of the time and do my work."

"I see. Well, thanks again, Richard. Goodbye."

So poaching wasn't that big a deal in Florida, according to Richard. If that were true, why would Vincent kill Rene over something so non-threatening? It didn't add up. It must have been deeper than that.

It was time to meet Detective Noble for lunch so I told Cecilia goodbye and gave Teddy a hug before I left. As I walked to the front entrance, I thought hard about the things Richard had told me. Before I knew it I was there. The valet brought my car to me. I tipped him with cash and a smile.

He thanked me, helped me into the driver's seat, and closed my door.

"Have a good afternoon, Mrs. Bradley."

***

The day was beautiful on the main thoroughfare. The sky was a deep clear blue with no sign of smog, which was unusual for the Phoenix area. The storm from yesterday had cleared the air; it smelled sweet and fresh. I looked forward to another stellar meal from Café ZuZu's.

Detective Noble sat waiting for me by the white quartz fireplace. He stood and we walked to the reservation podium at the end of the long bar.

"Table for two?" The hostess smiled. "Right this way, please."

She sat us in a high booth that provided us with the necessary privacy and gave us menus to look over.

A server appeared immediately. "May I offer you a selection from our drink menu?"

"Detective, lunch is on me today. I insist. Please order whatever you want. I'm always hungry when I'm trying to solve a problem and I can't be responsible for running up a large bill for your department."

"Well, thank you, Jillian. If you insist!"

"I'll have a virgin raspberry mojito please," I said.

"And I'll have a guava momma, please."

"It's nice to be able to have soft cocktails in the middle of the day, don't you think, Detective?"

The server left to get our drinks.

"With me, it's absolutely imperative!"

We looked over our menus. I saw what I wanted immediately.

"I'm going to have the giant shrimp cocktail and the iceberg wedge salad with bacon. What would you like?"

"I'm having the beef stroganoff. I've heard it's really good here."

I took the manila envelope from the seat beside me and discreetly pushed it over to Detective Noble.

The server set our drinks out, smiled, and left.

"Is this the evidence from Leah?"

"According to her, yes."

"You don't sound convinced, Jillian. Why not?"

"If you talked to Richard, I think you'd know why I have a hard time believing he's an embezzler."

"Explain, Jillian."

"It's a feeling I have. When a piece of fruit has rotten spots visible from the skin, you tend to throw it away, knowing instinctively it's rotten. With Richard there have been no visible rotten spots."

"Except for the one Leah's produced."

"Exactly. You can tell from talking to a person if they're hiding something. They will avoid making eye contact and pull away from the conversation when you try to engage them. I never got that from Richard. He deserves a chance to explain himself and I'd like to be there when he does."

"Well, you're going to get your chance. I have to bring him in as a person of interest now."

Detective Noble's cellphone vibrated. He answered it immediately as the server brought our drinks.

He listened intently. "Thanks, officer."

He closed the phone and put it back in his pocket. Taking a sip of his drink, he looked across the table directly into my eyes. I could tell whatever he was told didn't bode well for Vincent.

"What happened?" My appetite left me momentarily.

"Bad news I'm afraid. That was ballistics. The gun Teddy found was registered to Dr. Vincent Fontaine."

No, Lord! Tears sprang to my eyes and I took a sip of my drink to regain composure.

"Does that mean…."

"I'm afraid so. I'm going to have to arrest Vincent Fontaine on suspicion of first-degree murder. I'm also going to have to arrest Richard Sanchez."

I wasn't hungry but I ordered anyway. I had to keep up my strength. Detective Noble seemed to take it in stride that he was about to arrest two people. For him it was all in a day's work. For me it was traumatic to watch two people's lives ruined.

After eating what we could, he spoke again. "I'll save the lemon meringue pie for another time, Jillian. Are you ready to get going?"

"I'm *not* ready but I know we have to get this over with. You're going to let me come with you, aren't you?"

"I don't see why not. I've ordered my men to make sure neither suspect has left the hotel. My guys won't move a muscle until they hear from me. I'll call them now and let them know we're on our way."

It felt like I was in a dream driving back to the hotel behind Detective Noble. So, it was true. Vincent killed Rene. He probably killed Simon as well. How terrible. And I was dating him after he committed such heinous crimes! It made me nauseated.

Come on, Jillian. Get a grip! You were working for justice and it's here. Keep that in mind, no matter how he reacts to being arrested.

Two police cars were parked in front of the lobby

and guests were starting to congregate around them, no doubt wondering what was going on.

A film crew from a local news station arrived in a van. They had received a tip of the pending arrest from some source. Several other people from the press arrived and had microphones ready to record the event.

Detective Noble took my arm and together, with two officers, we pressed through the crowd to Vincent's room, the press following behind.

Chapter 18

Detective Noble arrested Vincent first. He was read his rights and handcuffed, hands behind his back. The whole time it was happening, he kept looking into my eyes, bewildered. He went peacefully and never said a word.

Cameras flashed, the press fired questions all at once and our strange entourage walked slowly to the arrest of Richard Sanchez.

Richard reacted differently. He was outraged and demanded to know who had accused him of such a crime.

Detective Noble had to handcuff him as well for the trip to the police station.

I watched as Vincent and Richard were led away and placed in the police cars, officers pressing my friends' heads down to avoid injury as they entered the back seats.

A newscaster began to ask Detective Noble questions about the arrests. He gave them the answer they wanted.

"We've arrested Dr. Vincent Fontaine for suspicion of murder in the death of Rene Parker. Richard Sanchez has been arrested for suspected embezzlement in the Research and Preservation Society for the Florida

Everglades. That's all I have for now. Thank you."

He gave no other information but it was enough to create the sensational news the press and TV stations hungered for.

Then the camera crews turned to ask me questions. "What was it like to be close to a murder suspect and someone accused of embezzlement?"

I literally ran back to my casita in order to avoid what would have been a painful confrontation.

I made it back safely and banged on the door for Cecilia to let me in.

"Jillian, what is going on?"

Teddy started yipping. I picked him up and hugged him tightly to my chest.

"They've arrested Vincent and Richard. It was horrible to watch, Cecilia. It's probably on TV already. Turn it on would you, please?"

Cecilia picked up the remote and found the local news station as we sat down.

The news was on every station announcing the arrest of Rene Parker's alleged killer and his possible accomplice. It was like a dream that couldn't be happening and yet I knew it was real. Was this my answer from the Lord, I wondered?

"Please give me strength," I prayed, "and please be with Vincent and Richard as they go through this...even if they're guilty."

"This is shocking, Jillian. I can't believe it's finally over."

"I can't either. Detective Noble said I could listen in at the inquiry this afternoon. I have just enough time to have a cup of tea and eat something. I wasn't hungry due to the impending arrest, but it's hitting me now and if I don't eat, I'm going to faint!"

"Let me order something. You lie down and put your feet up. That should help get the blood flowing to your head."

I lay on the sofa and Cecilia ordered tea.

"Please bring it as soon as possible."

She came back and sat on the chaise end of the sofa. "Those reporters said the police found out Vincent owned the gun they believe is the murder weapon. That's pretty hard evidence, Jillian, don't you think?"

"It is. But just because it's your gun doesn't prove you pulled the trigger."

"I agree, although it's pretty suspicious, I'd say. How did Vincent get a gun through airport security?"

"You're assuming he brought a gun with him from home. What if he purchased it here?"

"It's possible I suppose, but why purchase a gun in one state when you know you have to get it back to another one? It doesn't make sense because of all of the security checks they do.

"When did the Florida group arrive, Jillian, do you know?"

"Arthur said everyone came in Thursday the day before Rene was killed. Why?"

"Either Vincent was planning to kill Rene here, maybe to make it look like a random crime, or he just likes to carry a firearm wherever he goes. It seems unlikely he shot Rene because of an altercation they may have had. What do you think?"

"You're starting to sound like a detective, Cecilia. I've asked myself those same questions. I'm sure the police are checking on the gun registration. If he purchased it here it might mean pre-meditation. If he just liked to have it with him, it could be it was for protection. Why do people own guns? They either just enjoy shooting as a sport or they buy one for protection. I can't think of any other reason, can you?"

"No, you're right. Didn't you tell me that Vincent took his sons shooting?"

"Yes."

"Well, that could mean he used it for sport. He made

no secret about that, did he?"

"No, in fact he was proud that he taught his boys how to shoot. Even Leah learned to shoot by watching her brothers. Vincent thought he was equipping his children to protect themselves if they ever needed to. He really tried to be a responsible dad."

"So why bring a gun with you to a grant presentation? It doesn't make sense at all."

The tea from room service arrived with a small knock at the door. The server brought in the lovely tea tray laden with finger sandwiches and pastries. He smiled as I signed the check and then spoke.

"It looks like they caught the murderer. Everyone here is relieved, I can tell you!"

My heart sank at the realization that now everyone believed in Vincent's guilt. Did I believe he was guilty, too? I had to talk to Detective Noble and find out when they were going to question Vincent. I had to be there to see his face when he answered those questions, even if it was from behind a two-way mirror.

After the server left, and before I could make my call, someone knocked on the door. It was probably reporters, so I took a deep breath to prepare myself and walked over to answer it. I was surprised to see Tori standing there looking distraught. I'd seen her like this once before when Richard and Leah were together in the bar.

"Come in, Tori." I scooted Teddy off the sofa. "Let me pour you a cup of tea. Sit down. Cecilia, why don't you take Teddy outside for a stretch?"

"Sure, Jillian."

She knew I needed to talk to Tori privately.

Tori sat down where I motioned, taking a seat facing the fireplace. I waited for her to speak, knowing she had something on her mind.

Tori glared at me. "I don't care for any tea, Jillian. You know they've arrested Richard for embezzlement, don't you? Please tell me you had nothing to do with it."

Tears started to form in her eyes and I felt terrible having to tell her the truth.

"I'm afraid I was the one who had to give the evidence to the police, Tori."

"But why? Have you been after Richard all along and were just using me? I can't believe you'd be so evil!"

I understood her being upset because I knew she was in love with Richard. I remained calm as I tried to explain.

"Tori, Leah asked me to give the evidence to the police in case Richard might retaliate."

"Retaliate? You mean as in hurt her in some way? I'm sorry, Jillian, but you obviously don't know Richard like I do. He'd never hurt anyone!"

"Maybe not, Tori, but Leah had a viable concern and needed to report it. This could even be related to Rene's murder, don't you see?"

"No I don't see, Jillian. Richard is the most sincere person I know. All he cares about is protecting plants. He's not a criminal. I won't believe it! I won't!"

"Tori, if you want to help Richard, you'd better tell me all you know or he could be indicted for murder. You're holding something back. Why don't you tell me what it is, please, for Richard's sake?"

She stopped crying and said she'd changed her mind about the tea. I poured her a cup and offered her a sandwich.

"That's better, Tori. Take your time. Tell me the truth, that's all I ask."

"I really don't know where to start. First of all, I love Richard. But I think you already know that, don't you?"

"Since that night we had dinner together. I could tell you were upset that he was with Leah."

"Well, I think Richard loves me, too. It's just that he's so shy he hasn't had the courage to tell me so."

"I hope you're right, Tori."

"Oh, I know what you're thinking—if I made a bad choice with my first husband, why wouldn't I make one with Richard? But I know Richard isn't a criminal, Jillian. All he talks about is the swamp and the flora. Would a criminal talk like that?"

"I have to agree. A criminal would talk about money instead. Did Richard ever talk about money to you, Tori?"

"No, never, I swear to you! As I've told you before, he only has dreams for preserving the Corkscrew Swamp."

"All right, we've established the facts that you two are in love and that Richard loves his work. What else do you know?"

I took a sip of my tea and ate a cucumber sandwich, then sat back and waited for her to finish.

"What I haven't told you before is about Leah. Jillian, she can be formidable at times and she'd fire me on the spot if I said anything against her."

"I understand, Tori. But if you don't tell me what you know, the police will accuse you of withholding evidence, and you don't want to go there."

"If you put it that way I guess I have to tell you. Besides, it makes me furious that she would accuse Richard of embezzlement. If anyone embezzled funds, it would have to have been Rene."

"Why do you say that?"

"Rene was the one who talked about money all the time. He drove an expensive car and wore expensive clothes."

"Do you know if he lived in an expensive apartment?"

"I never saw his apartment, so I don't know, but he always bragged about where he shopped and where he ate."

"Go on. Tell me what you know about Leah."

"You asked me before if I knew about any relationships Leah might have had. The only person I ever saw her being even remotely friendly with was Rene Parker."

"What? Why didn't you tell me this before?"

"I was afraid what would happen if she knew I had said anything."

"How do you know she was friendly with him, Tori?"

"Do you remember I said we all would hang out at Starbucks© sometimes?"

I racked my brain trying to remember our first conversation.

"Vaguely."

"Well, it was one of those times I saw her. Richard saw them, too."

"By 'them' you mean Leah and Rene?"

"Yes."

"What happened?"

"Leah walked into Starbucks© with Rene right behind her. She didn't see Richard and me. We were sitting around the corner from where they take orders. It was a large Starbucks© and always busy at that time of day."

"Go on." I took a pink petit fours and placed it slowly in my mouth.

"Rene had his arm around Leah's waist and he was standing close to her. After she ordered, she just smiled at him. Richard and I couldn't believe it. As soon as we saw them, we hid as best we could hoping they wouldn't see us. I don't think they did because they kept up the affection until they got their order and sat down at a table on the other side of the room. We decided to wait until after they left before we did, so they wouldn't know we saw them."

"You believe they were seeing each other secretly?"

"Yes, I do. Richard thinks so, too."

I offered to pour her another cup of tea, but she declined.

"Jillian, I need to get back to see what I can do to help Richard."

"Has Richard posted bail?"

Tori stood to leave. "The District Attorney declined bail because of the possibility he could be involved in the murder somehow."

"Tori, I'm going to ask Detective Noble to check Rene and Richard's financial records and see if there is money unaccounted for. It may tell us which one was the embezzler."

"I wish you would, Jillian. You'll find Richard is aboveboard in his. Thank you for doing whatever you can. We both appreciate it."

Cecilia came back after she saw Tori leave and gave Teddy a fresh bowl of water. He lapped it up thirstily. She placed the leash in the hall closet, then came and sat down on the sofa next to me.

I got a mug from the coffee service on the side table. "How about a cup of tea?"

"I'd love some, thank you. What happened with Tori? Can you tell me?"

I poured her a cup, draining the pot, and picked up my own cup to finish it.

"Tori told me she saw Leah and Rene together in what looked like a romantic relationship when they were at a Starbucks©."

"Do you think she was telling the truth, Jillian?"

"I think she was. She's fighting for Richard. I know that. I don't think she would risk lying if it would hurt him somehow."

"That means if Leah and Rene were in a relationship then they could have had a lover's quarrel…."

"And she could have shot him. It's a good possibility, but how would we go about proving it? We would need strong evidence for sure. I've got to call Detective Noble and find out when they're going to question Vincent. I can't miss it."

"I understand, Jillian. You go on ahead. I promised I'd call Walter as soon as I got back from taking Teddy out."

I discovered Vincent would be questioned in the morning. He was getting an attorney and they were holding him in jail overnight.

My mind wandered to Leah. I had to ask myself some hard questions. What if Vincent killed Rene to protect Leah somehow? But if he did, why place the porcelain ghost orchid over the bullet wound? What did that mean? What was he doing with that porcelain orchid anyway?

I couldn't be still. I paced the room, and racked my brain. I didn't know much at all. But Detective Noble did.

My cell rang and I answered it as I walked into the living room and sat down on the armless chair next to the warm fire.

"Hello, Detective. What's going on?"

"We've had an interesting new development."

Suddenly, I felt a wave of discomfort wash over me. I hoped it wasn't more bad news about Vincent.

"I'm listening."

"A maid at the Sanctuary, by the name of Maria Vargas, just came in with her husband."

"Maria came in? Did she have some evidence?"

"Boy, did she! It seems that her husband insisted she come forward after the news came out about the arrests. He told me that his wife had brought something home that she found in one of the hotel rooms trash cans when she was cleaning. She hadn't thought about it until the news reported Vincent Fontaine had been arrested. She said you had told her to tell her friends working at the hotel to come forward with anything out of the ordinary."

"Yes, I remember telling her that, and it turns out..."

"It turns out she had something out of the ordinary that she thought might be a clue. She wasn't sure until her husband insisted she come down and show it to us."

"You're killing me, Detective. What was it?"

"A box."

"A box?"

"Not just any box, Jillian. It was a fabric box that held a piece of porcelain at one time."

"And she found it in a trash can in one of the hotel rooms?"

"That's right. When she heard that Vincent Fontaine had been arrested, she told her husband it might not be *that* Fontaine. That's when he brought her in. Jillian, the box was from Leah's room."

"Can you hold them there until I come down? I'd really like to talk to them."

"Sure, I'll give them something to drink and make sure they stay put until you get here. It looks like Vincent might be innocent after all."

"I'm on my way right now."

I grabbed my purse. I gave my *sleuth dog* a love pat and headed out the door, walking fast. But I wasn't fast enough.

My cellphone rang.

"Jillian, it's Leah. I really need to talk to you about my dad. Can I come over?"

My mind froze in midstream. I didn't think Leah knew Maria had gone to the police and therefore couldn't be suspicious of me knowing the truth. I had to play along.

"I was just on my way to the parking lot."

"That's fine. I'll meet you in the lobby and then we can go somewhere to talk. I really need a friend right now. I hope you don't mind."

"Not at all, Leah, I'm glad you called me. I'll see you in a few minutes."

What was I going to do? I knew Detective Taylor was lurking in the background so I really wasn't worried about my safety, but how to get Leah to confess would be the trick.

I dialed my cell stealthily. "Detective Noble, there's been a new development...."

***

Leah was waiting for me as promised. I acted happy to see her, giving her a hug and a friendly, sympathetic hello. She told me her car was waiting, and we proceeded to walk out from the main entrance. There it was. The dark gray Mazda, the one that had followed me home the other day.

I pretended not to recognize it and got in the passenger side as the valet held my door open for me. Leah and I drove out the hotel driveway in silence. Being the usual talkative one and not wanting her to suspect I knew the truth, I began the conversation.

"Leah, I'm so sorry about your father."

"You and me both." She sounded calm. "Of course, this will really dampen his career and that's most unfortunate. Don't you think so?"

"I'm afraid you're right. But Leah, the gun we found belonged to him. The police have proven that."

"So that means he killed Rene? I don't think so. And what about Richard? He could have killed Rene just as easily to keep him quiet about the embezzlement. The police have more proof on him than they could possibly have on my father."

"You may be right. But what if it was Rene who was embezzling funds and not Richard? He was very computer literate and could have made Richard look like the culprit."

"Rene was smart, Jillian. Oh, he was smart all right."

"What do you mean by that, Leah?"

"You know, Jillian, I think you've poked your nose into our affairs just a little too much. In fact, if it hadn't been for you my father wouldn't be in jail right now."

Fear rose in my throat as Leah pushed down on the accelerator. I decided to play my cards and throw her off guard.

"Why did you follow me the other day, Leah? What were you afraid I was going to find?"

"I don't really know. I just wanted to watch you and see where you went. I followed you whenever you went to dinner with him, did you know that?"

"No, I didn't know."

"He really fell for you. And look where it got him — in jail!"

She laughed in a voice I'd never heard before.

"Daddy's in jail and mommy's gone away with her boyfriend, and I'm all alone again...I'm all alone again," she said in a strange childlike voice.

"Leah...!"

"Shut up Jillian!" She didn't sound so childlike anymore. "You've ruined everything you know. Daddy wasn't supposed to get arrested."

Calmly, she continued to press down on the accelerator until it approached 80 miles an hour. I looked around and realized we had turned off the main thoroughfare and were heading up Camelback Mountain on a back road. The sun had already set. Since there were no streetlights anywhere we had no way to see where we were going and Leah didn't seem to be on the same planet!

I held onto the armrest for dear life.

"Leah, you've got to slow down!"

Leah stared straight ahead. I only knew to do one thing: Pray!

"Lord, please give me Your angels to protect me."

Suddenly a car came out of nowhere and pulled right in front of us, forcing Leah off the road. The last thing I remember was Leah swerving.

Then came the hard unforgiving face of the mountain.

Chapter 19

The voices were muffled.

"Hang on Jillian, we'll get you out—just hang on!"

Something was under me. Hot...and soft. The air bag. My torso was on the dash. The airbag must have spared me from going through the windshield. Broken glass littered me. I kept very still for fear I might cut myself. The smell of gas was everywhere. Leah was pinned between the seat and the airbag. She wasn't moving. Was she dead?

"Dear God, please don't let Leah die. Please, Lord for Vincent's sake."

The voices rang clearer now. I heard one of them say, "We've got her, she's alive!"

Detective Taylor smiled at me as he and two other officers I recognized as Sergent Niemi and Sergent Bryers helped me out of the crumpled car. They laid me gently down on the ground and went back to get Leah out.

My head was spinning as I watched them pry the door off with the Jaws of Life and then slowly pull her from the wreckage. Officer Niemi ran to the unmarked patrol car, grabbed a fire extinguisher from the trunk, and used it to put out a small fire that had erupted. Someone moaned beside me. It was Leah. She was alive!

"Oh God, thank you! Thank you so much for saving us."

Detective Taylor spoke to me as two paramedics arrived and checked her vitals.

"What happened, Jillian? We saw your car flip over. Did you grab the wheel to try and stop her?"

"No. That car pulled in front of us and Leah swerved to miss it."

"What car? We were behind you but stayed out of sight until she started speeding up. We knew you were in danger, but there was nothing we could do. Then your car flipped and crashed into the side of the mountain."

The ambulance arrived and took Leah and me to the hospital. I didn't have any pain and except for a small cut on my arm from the flying glass, I was unscathed.

The paramedics insisted on transporting us on gurneys. I capitulated even though I felt fine. I was worried about Leah. There was that moment when I thought she had really gone over the edge. Talking like a child, telling me to shut up, and speeding like that as if she were trying to kill us both. She had to be bordering on insanity. I knew now that she had probably killed both Rene and Simon, but I still hadn't been able to get her to confess like Detective Noble and I had planned.

After I called him and told him I was meeting Leah, he'd had one of his officers pose as a valet and place a recording/tracking device in Leah's waiting car. Detective Taylor would follow us until I could get the confession. The plan was working until we crashed.

Detective Noble came into the examining room where the doctor was checking me out.

"Boy, am I glad to see you, Jillian! For a minute there I thought you were a goner."

"I'm happy to see you, too. I've never been so scared in all my life! That car swerved in front of us and my whole life started to flash before my eyes. I thought I'd be seeing the Lord Himself."

"Jillian, you keep talking about *that car,* but we can't find any evidence there was another car involved."

"Maybe it just drove on ahead and didn't stop when we flipped over."

"I don't think so, Jillian. My men drove a little ahead of the crash site and had to stop."

"Had to stop for what?"

"There was a barrier set up where the road ended. The only thing on the other side of it was a rock slide completely covering the road."

I was stunned. There was only one possible explanation and if I told Detective Noble what it was he would probably have me hospitalized for a head injury. It was too important for me to get back to the investigation to risk it so I just shrugged my shoulders and smiled. I would tell him later when he was sitting down and could take it in better.

"How is Leah doing?" I slipped my shoes back on.

"She's going to be all right. The doctor is with her now. I'm going to have to bring her in for questioning since we got the evidence from Maria Vargas. I plan to leave Leah here overnight under police protection so she won't spend the night in jail. After listening to the recording we made, I'm also ordering a psychiatric examination before we question her. If she's dangerous, I want to know."

"That's wise, Detective. She sounded strange at several points when she talked to me in the car. I don't suppose the Vargas's are still at the station, are they?"

"No. After you called I told them to go home but not to leave town in case we needed to talk to them. They laughed and said it wouldn't be a problem. They said they were always in town."

"Maria was sincere when I talked to her. What did she say about finding the box?"

"According to her, she was starting to empty the trash and noticed the red fabric box on top of some paper trash. She said this all happened the morning after the murders took place. She asked Leah if she was sure she wanted to throw the box away and Leah said, and I quote, 'I never want to see that box again. Take it!' So Maria put it in her cart and proceeded to finish cleaning the room."

"So did Maria know that the murders had taken place when she found it?"

"She says she didn't know about either one of them until after she found the box, because she started work early that morning and hadn't had her break yet. When she got home that day, she showed the box to her husband and he said he thought she should use it to keep rings in.

"It wasn't until they saw on the news that Vincent Fontaine had been arrested that Maria remembered what you'd said about finding anything unusual around the time of the murders. She realized the box could mean something, especially because it had been upsetting to Leah."

"Yvette told me that each porcelain piece had an identification number stamped on the bottom of the box that corresponded with a number on the piece itself for authentication. If the number on the orchid covering Rene's wound matches the one on that box, it has to be one and the same."

"Listen, Detective, this accident was a blessing for one reason. When I was talking to Leah she told me that her daddy wasn't supposed to get arrested. Vincent wasn't the killer. It was Leah. Everything fell into place. Leah was the one who took Vincent's gun from her brother's room. She probably had it sent to the hotel. We can check on that with the concierge. Leah also took the garden tour because she mentioned it when we had lunch together, so she would have known about the jumping cholla and she would have known about the nest. The thing that had bothered me the most was Simon's flashlight."

"The one we *didn't* find in his cart."

"That's right. We didn't find it because, somehow, it accidentally wound up in Leah's gym bag. I remember a valet was taking me home one night and he used his flashlight to help me get into the cart because it was dark. I had a flicker of remembering I'd seen one like it before, but it wasn't clear at the time where. I finally remembered seeing a flashlight on two different occasions but never put two and two together until I started to suspect Leah. It would prove she was at the scene of Simon's murder."

"Jillian, I just had a thought. What if Vincent and Leah were in on this together? They are, after all, father and daughter."

"But what was their motive? We have to find that out before we'll ever know the truth."

"I agree."

"I would like to talk to Leah but now is not the best time."

"Don't worry, I promise I won't start without you, Jillian. I wouldn't dare!"

"Thank you. Now, how about a ride back to the hotel?"

Detective Taylor escorted me back to my casita through a line of press anxious to get the story on the crash since it involved another Fontaine. We made it to my door without having to make any comments. He swiped my passkey for me and ushered me inside.

"I have to get back, but stay put until Detective Noble gives you a call. And get some rest. You've had a tough night!"

"Thank you, Detective. And thank you so much for being there for me this whole time."

"Just doing my job, ma'am. It was my pleasure, I

assure you."

Teddy began yipping at my feet the moment I stepped through the door. If I could have yipped, I would have. I was so glad to see him.

"Come here, you sweet doggie!"

I picked him up and gave him a hug and several kisses on top of his little head.

He licked my cheek as if to say, "I'm so glad you're home safe, I was worried!"

Cecilia joined us and turned on the TV so we could catch the news.

"Jillian, are you all right? The news said you were in a car crash with Leah and taken to the hospital!"

"Boy, I can't believe how fast they get their stories. They must really be good! Listen, here it is."

The report said, *"Another suspect in the murder investigation, Dr. Leah Fontaine, and gardening columnist Jillian Bradley were involved in a bizarre car crash that totaled the car but left both passengers virtually unhurt. An unidentified vehicle was purported to have been involved in the crash, but has not yet been found. Dr. Leah Fontaine is the daughter of Dr. Vincent Fontaine whom authorities detained earlier today in connection with the murders of Rene Parker and Simon Collier. Police say Dr. Leah Fontaine is being held for questioning in the two deaths as well."*

"So they're holding Leah now," Cecilia said. "What exactly happened, Jillian?"

"Let's just say Detective Noble and I concocted a plan to get Leah to confess to the murders and it went horribly wrong. It's a miracle we're even alive."

"What about that car they said was involved?"

It was quite a story, but Cecilia would believe me if anyone would. I explained the ordeal and the mystery car's actions.

"That's the only explanation I can come up with, Cecilia. Whether anyone will believe me or not, I know what I saw. The question is, did Leah see it, too?"

"I think you'd better get to bed Jillian. I've fed Teddy

and taken him out numerous times, so just rest. You've had a shock, whether you realize it or not. I'll make you a cup of decaf tea."

"I'm going, Cecilia. I need a bubble bath first, though. I probably have dirt all over me."

After my bath, my mind reeled from the violence of the day. What drama! I lay there in the darkness staring at the ceiling trying to piece everything together.

Tori said Rene and Leah were romantically involved, but why keep it such a secret? Was Richard telling the truth about not being an embezzler? Could Rene have been taking the money and altering the books on Richard's side of the business? And how did Vincent's orchid cloning scheme fit in to all of this?

What was Leah doing with the fabric box? Did it really belong to Vincent? I didn't think that made sense. Men don't give other men porcelain flowers. So, if Rene gave the porcelain ghost orchid to Leah, that must have meant he told Leah her father was buying them illegally. Was that it? Rene's hold over Leah? She was the only one now who could give us the answer.

"Thank you again, Lord, for protecting me today. Thank you for letting Leah live. The truth will come out now I'm sure. Please continue to give me wisdom and discernment as we question Vincent, Leah, and Richard. Amen."

Chapter 20

I felt sore all over. Slamming your body against the side of a mountain will do that. Thankfully, nothing was sprained or broken. I fractured my right foot once as a young person and had to sit in a chair for eight weeks. Talk about boredom!

Teddy stretched out his front paws and yawned. I gently rubbed his ears and patted his back. He jumped off the bed and rolled around on the carpet to scratch all his itches.

I opened the door for him to go find Cecilia so she could take him out while I readied my aches and pains for the day, offering a small prayer for God to get me through it and find the truth

I still fretted over what to wear to the questioning. Strangely enough, even after all that had happened I was still attracted to Vincent. He had spent the night in jail and my heart went out to him. Soon he would receive the news about his daughter's involvement in the case. If he wasn't involved also, it would be a bitter pill to swallow. At least Leah was still in the hospital. At least she hadn't died.

Cecilia knocked lightly on my door and greeted me

with a smile. "How about some breakfast? What would you like me to order?"

I hobbled behind her into the main room and perched on the sofa. "This morning I need something sustaining. The stone cut oatmeal with the five-spice raisin compote and fresh bananas might do the trick."

"Any juice?"

"The freshly squeezed orange juice sounds marvelous and a pot of coffee."

In my inbox, there was a message from *The San Jose Herald.* It asked to add my column in the weekend supplement. I scrolled down and saw another one from *The Sacramento Daily Times* asking to bring me on board as well.

"Cecilia, look at this." I showed her the messages.

"Wow, Jillian, it looks like those news stories are generating some interest for you. Good."

"The Lord provides, Cecilia. I really believe that."

"Jillian, it's just hard for me to…well…listen. You told me you prayed that they would find Simon alive and he was murdered. You also said you prayed that Mark Russell would pull through and he didn't. It doesn't seem like God is listening. Why do you keep putting so much faith in Him?"

"That's a tough question and one that eventually most people have to come to terms with. I've known people who have prayed for certain things to happen and when they didn't happen just the way they prayed, they stopped believing. But with God, a prayer is answered one of three ways: yes, no, or not now. With me, God has never been late on an answer. It always comes just at the right time. Sometimes the answer has come instantly, like when it seemed Leah was going to kill us both. God provided that car to block our path.

"I always pray for someone to be healed, like Mark, for instance. But when death comes instead of healing, that's an answer. For Mark, it was *no* here on earth, but it was a *yes* because he lives in Heaven now.

"I told you about the man who wanted the letter read at Mark's funeral. He believed the accident involving his wife and daughter was an answer to his prayer, although a painful one. That's also how God works. Sometimes He uses circumstances in our lives to meet the needs of His other children.

"I don't know why God allowed Simon to be murdered, but sometimes people do bad things. God won't stop every bad thing from happening, but he can help us through it. Sometimes there's a bigger reason.

"Cecilia, I pray because I believe that He knows more than I do. He loves me and cares for me in every moment of my life."

"I wish I could have your faith, Jillian. I've always thought believing in God was for weak-minded people, but you're certainly not that."

"If you want my faith all you have to do is ask God for it. He looks on the heart. And when a person humbly asks forgiveness for past mistakes, He forgives. We Christians believe that God sent Jesus into the world as His only Son to show us how to live. God sends his Holy Spirit to live in us as our guide. It's really amazing how we can actually have access to Him, just by praying."

"It's that simple? Just ask and believe?"

"Just ask and believe. I can pray with you or you can pray all by yourself, but God will answer you either way, I promise."

Room service arrived and brought in our breakfast trays along with several bouquets of flowers for me. Arthur and Diana sent beautiful fall flowers wishing me a speedy recovery. The Hansens sent yellow roses for friendship and a note saying how glad they were I had survived the accident.

Tori and Richard sent a pretty bouquet of daisies saying how glad they were I was still in one piece! I was overwhelmed with gratitude that these friends thought of me with such warmth.

Cecilia and I enjoyed our breakfast, then she excused herself and went into her bedroom. I silently prayed for her to accept Christ as her Savior at the right time for her.

The phone interrupted my thoughts.

"Jillian, how are you?"

"Good morning, Detective. I'm glad to be alive. I'm a little sore, but grateful to be in one piece."

"Good. Just thought I'd let you know we're going to question Vincent Fontaine in about an hour. We're waiting for his attorney to get here."

"What about Leah? When is her psychiatric review?"

"She's being released from the hospital this morning and then we're transporting her over here to a holding cell. The psychiatrist will interview her right before lunch."

"I see. Did you look up Rene's and Richard's financial records yet?"

"Yes, we did. I'll show you what we found when you get here."

"Have you seen the news?"

"Yeah, I saw it last night and this morning. Actually, we're finally getting somewhere on this case."

"We'll know who our murderer is after today."

"I sure hope so. I have at least three other cases with no leads at all. Jillian, I can honestly say you've been a tremendous help in getting us as far as we are in this investigation. Why don't have your own detective agency?"

"I've never really thought about it. Wouldn't I have to fill out reports and go through police training and all that?"

"Probably. I know I did."

"Then I wouldn't be interested. My niece had to go through that training and it wasn't easy, especially the physical fitness part."

"I remember. She's right, it isn't easy, but if you want it bad enough you go through it. I wanted to be a detective more than anything else in the world. I didn't want to just sit behind a desk all day pushing paper."

"I admire you for being a detective. You're a good one. Listen, I'd better get going so I can meet you. I'll see you in a little while."

"See you, Jillian. Take care, and thanks."

Teddy hopped up on the sofa, turned around and lay down for his morning nap. I kissed him goodbye and told Cecilia I was leaving.

She was on the phone with Walter as she waved goodbye.

***

I decided to stop by the concierge desk on my way to my car to check on any package deliveries. Servers and workers alike spoke to me as I passed and called me by name.

"Good morning Mrs. Bradley...."

"Glad you're okay, Mrs. Bradley...."

"I saw you on the news. Glad you're all right."

I thanked everyone and finally reached the concierge desk. She rose to meet me and came around to the front of her desk.

"Oh, I'm so glad you're all right after that awful car accident. I saw it on the news and couldn't believe it!"

"I'm fine, thank you. Those news reporters do a terrific job, don't they?"

"Is there anything you need?"

"Well, I would like to know if you received any packages last week on Thursday or Friday for anyone. Would you be able to check on that and let me know? You can reach me on my phone. I'm going to police headquarters right now."

She was more than anxious to help and sat down at her computer right away.

"Oh, it won't take a minute. This is so exciting! Let's see, I'm pulling up the dates and checking. Hmm...there were only two deliveries by carrier for those days. One was for a guest on Thursday, but it looks like it was a manila envelope, and the other one was for Thursday as well. There weren't any deliveries on Friday that I can see."

"The other one for Thursday, who was it sent to?" I held my breath.

"It says here there was a package for Dr. Leah Fontaine and the return address is in Florida. I can give you the dimensions and weight if you wish. It's all in the receipt information."

"Thank you. I may need it later. You've been a big help."

"Not at all, Mrs. Bradley. Let me know if you need any more information."

She was clearly thrilled at being a small part of the investigation.

The valet brought my car around, and opened the door for me. "Glad you're still with us, Mrs. Bradley."

I smiled. "I'm glad I'm still with you, too."

The drive went smoothly and soon I arrived at headquarters.

I was lost in my thoughts. What could have caused her to do it? Had Rene treated Leah poorly? It would be interesting to find out. Perhaps he had hurt her, cheated, or said something. Or, she could be out of her mind.

It was hard to picture that though, despite what had happened in the car with her talking in a strange voice. By all rights, Leah was a brilliant scientist. Nevertheless, there are brilliant scientists who have gone insane. It made me think of Dr. Frankenstein and Dr. Jekyll and Mr. Hyde. I blushed at being so silly.

I would try to think the best about Leah until I heard the psychiatrist's report.

Just coming through the entrance of police headquarters, I could tell the place was buzzing. I asked for Detective Noble.

The officer sitting at the front desk asked me to wait.

I took a seat.

All manner of people were coming and going. There were young teens dressed in T-shirts and cutoffs, young women with worried faces, men dressed in work clothes bringing in papers.

I glanced down the hall and saw several men in line waiting for the police to take their fingerprints. Poor Vincent. What humiliation, all the criminal procedures he'd already had to endure.

Detective Noble walked into the waiting area and welcomed me. He took my arm and ushered me down the opposite hall from the fingerprinting area. He was impressed with my tenacity when I told him about the package and its arrival to Leah's room, not Vincent's.

"Now, tell me, Detective. What did you find out about the financial records?"

"Bottom line is that Richard's records look clean. We found nothing out of the ordinary, just usual payroll direct deposits all for the same amount. Now Rene's was different. We found periodic deposits of questionable origin that corresponded with the documents Leah Fontaine gave you."

"So we can surmise Richard Sanchez is innocent?"

"That's correct. We're in the process of discharging him as we speak. Tori is on her way over to pick him up. I just talked with her."

"I'm so glad for both of them. You know they're in love, don't you?"

"Really? I never would have guessed." He laughed.

I smiled to myself. One more answered prayer.

We reached the interrogation rooms. Detective Noble

asked me to wait in one of the adjacent rooms with a two-way mirror until he brought in Vincent and his lawyer. All I could do was silently pray. I wanted a happy ending for Vincent in the worst way.

He entered, handcuffed, followed by his attorney. Vincent looked disheveled. I was embarrassed for him.

Detective Noble had them seated and then I heard him ask Vincent if he wanted me to be present during the questioning. Surprisingly he said he did!

Detective Noble motioned for me to come into the room with them and I followed an officer who let me in.

"Hello, Vincent."

Detective Noble introduced me to the lawyer. He stood and shook my hand.

"Let's get underway," said Noble.

Vincent kept looking at me, half-ashamed and half-delighted to see me, I thought. I smiled at him letting him know I was supporting him all the way, no matter what.

"I'm going to ask you some personal questions to begin with, Vincent. Jillian, if you wish to ask anything just give me a signal. Are we ready?"

We all nodded our heads.

Detective Noble began.

"Do you know a man by the name of Ray Ackermann?"

Vincent's eyes widened. He was physically taken aback. His face contorted in surprise and disbelief. For a second, he couldn't say a word and looked to his lawyer for guidance. The lawyer told him he didn't have to answer according to the Fifth Amendment.

Vincent pondered before speaking. "I'm going to tell the truth. I didn't kill anyone. But yes, I did know a man by the name of Ray Ackermann. It was a couple of years ago. Why do you want to know?"

"It seems we have evidence that links you and Ray Ackermann to Rene Parker."

"Evidence?" Vincent sounded disbelieving. "What possible evidence could you have?"

"We have a video of a conversation between you and Ray Ackermann that took place in Ocala a few years ago regarding a poaching arrangement. It was recorded by Rene Parker. We also have receipts that prove you were there on two occasions. We've looked into Ackermann's financial records and found deposits of checks written by you from the Florida Department of Agriculture for what we believe were for the poaching of rare ghost orchids."

Vincent sat back in his chair looking stunned. He didn't even glance at me.

"Do you deny these allegations, Dr. Fontaine?" Noble pressed for an answer.

His lawyer gave him counsel again that he did not have to answer the question.

"I told you I would tell the truth. And the truth is just as you say. I was intent on cloning the ghost orchid, not just for monetary reasons, but also scientific ones. If the truth be told, I was finding any excuse to be working in my lab. After the divorce, I found it easier to be at work than at home.

"Cloning orchids was as good as an excuse as any and I enjoyed the thrill of doing something that might, just might, bring me some notoriety I really needed in my life. When I was home all I had was an ex-wife who constantly called to berate or get more money.

"Jillian, I'm sorry you have to hear all this, but you know I wouldn't kill Rene even if he blackmailed me."

"Did he blackmail you, Vincent?"

"No. I never heard a word about blackmail from Rene Parker or anyone else. I'm telling the truth."

I looked at Detective Noble. "I believe him, Detective."

He sighed, then asked Vincent about the gun.

"If that's my gun, I don't know how it got here. The

last time I saw it was when I took the boys out shooting a few years ago. After we finished, we cleaned all the guns, put the safeties on, and put them back in the locked box where we kept them."

"Who has keys to the box?" I asked.

"I have one and the housekeeper has one."

"No one else?"

"No. I didn't want them to be a temptation for my boys to use without me."

"You said you took Leah out to shoot?"

"She came with us a time or two, but not usually."

"But she knew how to use the gun and where it was kept?"

"What are you inferring, Jillian?" Vincent looked puzzled.

"Vincent, I'm saying that Leah knew how to shoot. She knew where the gun was and she...."

"No! No! Jillian, I know what you're trying to do but that can't be true, Leah couldn't have shot Rene."

"And why is that, Vincent?" Detective Noble interrupted.

"Because, because she's my little girl, she's my little girl...."

Vincent broke down at the realization of what he'd probably known subconsciously. Leah had access to his gun, she had the opportunity, and she had the mental instability to commit murder.

He cried.

I excused myself. Alone in the hall, I cried myself, deeply touched that in spite of everything, Vincent loved Leah as his own child. He had just now realized it under the most painful of circumstances.

Vincent knew nothing about the porcelain orchid and it became obvious as they questioned him further. No one brought it up. It was the one trump card left to trap the killer.

Vincent's lawyer left the interrogation room first,

followed by Vincent and Detective Noble.

"We're discharging Vincent on his own recognizance to report to the Florida authorities when this investigation is over," Detective Noble said. "We have your cooperation in this matter, don't we Vincent?"

"I'll cooperate in any way I can, Detective. You have my word."

"Thank you, Dr. Fontaine. Jillian, I'll meet you in fifteen minutes, all right?"

I nodded in the affirmative as he left, leaving Vincent and me alone together.

Looking at the floor he asked, "Did you get my e-mail, Jillian?"

I knew he still felt ashamed and embarrassed by everything that had happened.

"Yes, I did. It was touching. I was flattered by your opinion of me."

"I'll bet you're disappointed in me, aren't you, Jillian? I know I would be if I were you."

"But you're not me. I'm just sad, not disappointed. I can understand the desire to take science to a new level with cloning. You got the idea from the conference you went to in Chicago, didn't you?"

"You don't miss a thing, do you?"

"Vincent, what's going to happen to you? Have they told you?"

"My lawyer says the Florida law is pretty lenient when it comes to poachers. And since it's my first offense, I'll probably just have to pay a fine of some sort and they'll warn me never to let it happen again. Like I'd ever do something that stupid again! It's true what they say about the long arm of the law. It sure reached me, didn't it?"

"Yes, it did. But after you pay the fine your slate is clean, and you can go back to doing what you love — finding ways to preserve endangered species. That's worthwhile."

"We'll see what happens. Right now, all I want to do is get out of these clothes and take a shower. I know they're going to question Leah but they won't let me be present. I'll come back as soon as I've cleaned up. Are you going to be there?"

"I'm not sure if she'll let me be in the same room, but I can watch from the two-way mirror. Detective Noble and I have decided how to question her. I think he'll do fine without me in the room with him. He's a good detective, you know."

"Yes, I know. Jillian, would you please pray for Leah? I know you're a believer and…."

"Don't worry, Vincent. I've been praying for both of you all along. And look—you're pretty much a free man. Richard Sanchez has been exonerated, too. That's another answer to prayer. Everything is going to be all right. There isn't anything too big for God to handle."

"Thank you, Jillian. I know you've done everything you could to help all of us. When you get a moment, I want you to answer my e-mail, would you?"

"I will, I promise. When all this is over. Now I have to go and sit in on the interview. I'll stay in touch."

Vincent took my hand and kissed it, then turned and walked away.

Detective Noble stuck his head outside the door looking for me. I joined him in the interrogation room. Leah had given her consent for me to be present while she was questioned, which surprised me after what I'd been through with her. She had a different lawyer representing her. The psychiatrist sat across the table from her. Two other chairs were placed next to him for Detective Noble and me to sit.

Leah looked normal as we walked into the room. Dr. Rehnquist, who made the introductions, certainly seemed skilled in his profession because he put us all instantly at ease. What would have been an awkward reunion felt like a family therapy session.

"We've already administered the written examination and I must say Dr. Fontaine passed it beautifully. Congratulations, Dr. Fontaine." He smiled deferentially since they were both doctors.

Leah smiled first at Dr. Rehnquist, then at me.

I smiled back.

"Now, Dr. Fontaine," he continued, "I'd like for you to tell us about your relationship with your mother if you would be so kind."

"Certainly, Dr. Rehnquist."

She proceeded to tell of a normal childhood up until the time her mother left her father for another man.

"And how did you feel about that, Dr. Fontaine?"

Leah stared at him for a moment with a frozen smile on her face. After a moment she answered him.

"Feel? I simply hated her."

"I see. Thank you, Dr. Fontaine. Now I would like to ask you about your relationship with your father."

"My father? I...I love him dearly. We're close, he and I."

"Good, that's good," Rehnquist said. "Would you please tell me about your relationship with Rene Parker?"

All the while, Dr. Rehnquist made notations on a yellow legal pad. Leah's demeanor changed dramatically at the mention of Rene's name. She sank down into her chair, no longer the formidable scientist. Instead, I saw the same Leah that was in the car with me, the Leah full of hate and revenge.

"I hated Rene Parker."

"I see," said Rehnquist calmly. "You hated Rene Parker like you hated your mother. Was it because Rene Parker did something to hurt you like your mother hurt you, Dr. Fontaine?"

Detective Noble and I stared transfixed at what took place next.

Leah slowly sat up and the officer in the corner stood

poised for action. In the childlike voice Leah had used with me in the car the night before, she answered Dr. Rehnquist's question.

"Hurt me? Yes, he hurt me! But not like my mommy hurt me, no, not like her. Mommy just left me alone, all by myself, to be with her boyfriend. She didn't want to be with me. I was scared when she left me. Mommy was bad. Rene Parker was bad, too. He made me do things with him I didn't want to do, but I was scared not to do them."

"Why were you scared, Leah? Won't you kindly tell us why you were scared of Rene Parker?" Rehnquist spoke gently.

Leah turned her face away from Dr. Rehnquist and looked toward me. *"Because Rene would hurt my daddy if I didn't do what he told me. He would hurt my daddy by telling on him — what he did was bad."*

"May I ask her a question, Dr. Rehnquist?" I asked.

"Go ahead."

"Leah, what did Rene say that your daddy did that was bad?"

"He said, he said my daddy was a dirty poacher and he would tell on him if I wouldn't be his girlfriend. I didn't want to be his girlfriend. I didn't, but he was going to hurt my daddy!"

Leah spoke with real fear in her eyes.

Dr. Rehnquist spoke again. "I think we should...."

"Just one more question and I'll be through, I promise," I said.

Rehnquist nodded and the officer sat back down.

"Leah, won't you tell us what happened on the night Rene died?"

The little girl in Leah seemed to vanish as she sat up straighter and looked at us.

"I'm sorry, what was the question again?"

"Leah, you were going to tell us about the night Rene died."

"I'm afraid I don't know what you're talking about Jillian."

"Leah, it's no use. We have enough evidence to prove you killed Rene. We don't need a word from you. But, you should tell us what happened. If you don't, your father is going to suffer tremendously. You wouldn't want to put him through a trial with cameras and people talking, would you?"

Leah must have reached the same conclusion. It would hurt her father if she didn't tell us. Her demeanor changed suddenly as if she were happy.

"Isn't it wonderful?" she said. "Rene's dead. He can't hurt my father anymore now, can he? I'm so glad he's dead. Do you know, I didn't mean to kill him that night. I really didn't. But you see, he asked me to meet him after everyone had left the party. He told me he had something special to show me. He told me not to let anyone know I was coming and to come to the back door and he'd let me in. Mark Russell had given him a key.

"It was all part of Rene's plan to rig the grant proposal. Rene was going to cheat to win. Cheat! After all the work we did getting our proposal together, all the countless nights of working overtime on it and he wanted to cheat to get it.

"When he told me to come look at what he was about to do on the computer I knew I had to stop him. I had brought a gun with me for protection. I took it out of my purse and pointed it at him. I told him to get away from the computer. He said he was doing this for *us* and to put the gun down. I told him there was no *us*. He got angry and came at me. He slapped me across the face and I was stunned. I fell backwards."

"And knocked over the chair." I could picture the whole thing happening.

"Yes. Rene tried to take the gun away from me. We struggled and I pulled the trigger. He fell backwards and landed on his back. I saw where I had shot him — right through the heart, just like daddy showed us."

"Then what happened, Leah?" I asked.

"Then I saw the blood starting to come from the wound and I realized it would get all over the carpet. I carried a porcelain orchid that Rene had given me. It was his way of reminding me that he could ruin my father's reputation any time he wanted to. I carried it with me wherever I went. It was a reminder of how much I hated Rene, and how one day, I would be rid of him.

"After I shot him, I thought how appropriate it would be to place the orchid over the wound that killed him. It was over. Rene Parker would never bother me or my father again."

"But then you had to get rid of the gun, didn't you?"

Dr. Rehnquist didn't stop me so I waited for Leah to respond.

"That was the hard part. I remembered the wren's nest from the tour I'd taken the day before and thought what a perfect hiding place it would be. I waited until the middle of the night before I went out. I wore gloves so there wouldn't be any fingerprints.

"After I hid it, I heard someone asking what I was doing there. It was the guard. He came over to me and I pretended to be looking for a bracelet I'd lost earlier. He got down on his knees with his flashlight to help me. I found a rock and hit him with it. I couldn't get caught with the gun, you see.

"I got his body into the golf cart, which wasn't easy, and then I took him up to the top of the mountain and buried him under some rocks. I'm sorry I had to kill him, but I couldn't get caught."

And then in her childlike voice, Leah said, *"Daddy would have said, 'Bad girl, Leah, bad girl!'"*

Detective Noble whispered something to Dr. Rehnquist, and thanked him for coming.

Rehnquist picked up his tablet and placed his pen back into his pocket. He smiled at Leah, then left quietly.

The lawyer had a few words with Leah and left. The officer seated in the corner came forward and placed handcuffs on Leah's wrists behind her back.

"Take care of daddy for me, Jillian."

"Don't worry, Leah. He'll be fine now."

"Leah Fontaine," Detective Noble began.

Leah's eyes narrowed as she faced him.

"*Dr.* Leah Fontaine."

"Dr. Leah Fontaine, I'm arresting you for the murder of Rene Parker and Simon Collier. You have the right to remain silent...."

Chapter 21

I drove back to the Sanctuary in a daze. The whole investigation seemed like a bad dream. The only consolation I had were those few wonderful days dating Vincent. Such a tragic ending. My heart went out to Vincent and his daughter.

I arrived back at the hotel and felt a little hungry as I made my way back to my casita. Eating in again seemed wearisome. Perhaps Cecilia would join me for lunch. We'd take Teddy with us this time. I had his dog tote for just such an occasion.

I slipped my card through the slot and opened the front door. The sadness of Leah's arrest weighed me down. I stepped into the hall and Teddy came running. Some of the sadness melted away. Still, it would take time for me to get over the ordeal.

He yipped a 'hello, I'm glad you're home,' and wagged his little tail.

"Come on Teddy, let's go find Cecilia and get some lunch, what do you say?"

Pricking up his ears, he yipped twice as if agreeing he thought it was a splendid idea.

Cecilia came out from her bedroom with her cellphone.

"Hi, Jillian, is it all over? I've been staying in touch

with the news. They have an interview with Leah and Vincent that's on in a few minutes."

"Everyone loves to hear bad news, don't they? People always seem so hungry for anything sensational. I have to watch it, of course, because they're friends, but I wouldn't otherwise."

"I agree. It's like people enjoy watching someone else suffer."

"Exactly. Have you had lunch yet?"

"I was waiting until you got back. What about Teddy?"

"He can rest in his tote while we eat. He'll be fine."

The commercial on TV ended and the live interview with the Fontaines continued with blaring music and a breaking news headline decorating the screen.

"The investigation into the murders of Rene Parker and Simon Collier reached a shocking conclusion today with the arrest of Dr. Leah Fontaine, Director of the Research and Preservation Society of the Florida Everglades. We spoke with the person in charge of the investigation, Detective Jack Noble, earlier today."

The camera cut to Detective Noble with a microphone in his face.

"We have made an arrest for the murders of Rene Parker, of Ocala, Florida and an Arizona resident, Simon Collier, of Mesa. Authorities have charged Dr. Leah Fontaine with manslaughter in both cases. She has been advised to plead guilty by reason of insanity, which in the state of Arizona carries a prison sentence of ten to twenty-two years. At this time, I wish to offer my thanks to a special person. Without her help, we would not have apprehended the killer in such an expedient way. Thank you, Jillian Bradley, and a special

*thank you to your dog, Teddy, who helped uncover
a vital piece of evidence. I think from this point on,
we'll be referring to Teddy as* Sleuth Dog *for that
indeed is what he is."*

The cameras moved to Vincent standing in front of a crowd of onlookers with his arm around Leah. Two officers stood at Leah's other side as the reporter put the microphone in front of Vincent and asked him questions. It was painful to watch.

Vincent told the reporters that Leah had acted in self-defense. She was only trying to protect her father. She would remain under the protection of a special facility in Florida and he would be by her side for the rest of her life. He thanked them and motioned for the officers to take them to the waiting patrol car.

Such a gentleman. He was going to sacrifice his life for a daughter who wasn't even biologically his. It would cause him pain for the rest of his life, and yet I knew Vincent had found peace knowing he was truly needed and loved.

"Goodbye, Vincent," I whispered under my breath. "I pray God will give you strength to stand by Leah in the days to come."

I turned off the TV and got out Teddy's tote and leash so we could go for lunch. My eye rested on the faded red roses Vincent had sent me. Their blossoms drooped and the leaves had begun to sag. Might as well toss them out.

Should I toss out my relationship with Vincent as well? Perhaps, on the exterior, I should. But that didn't mean I couldn't keep a small pleasant memory in my heart. No one would know if I did that. I hoped he would do the same.

***

The restaurant buzzed with customers. I'm sure it was due to the notoriety of the criminal guests. Surely, everyone was hoping for a glimpse of them. The maître d' seated us right away in one of the private booths overlooking the terrace. I placed Teddy comfortably in his tote on the seat next to me and gave him a little treat.

"Now I expect you to behave yourself and be quiet, Teddy."

He looked at me with those warm brown eyes as if to say, "Would I ever give you trouble, mistress?"

After he settled down and we had a chance to look over our menus, we ordered lunch. We both had a grilled chicken Caesar salad. Our minds were not on food.

Cecilia was thinking about her and Walter and I couldn't stop thinking about how much I was going to miss all the attention I had received from Vincent. It was certainly nice while it lasted, but I might as well put it behind me and start thinking about the future. We left our salads half-finished and walked slowly back to the casita.

I hadn't realize how exhausted I was from the accident and the interrogations. I decided to take a nap and at last slept peacefully.

I heard a knock on my door. Teddy sat up and pricked up his ears.

"Jillian, sorry to disturb you, but I just got a call from Herbert Jamison."

"Herbert Jamison? I shook off my drowsiness. "Did he leave a message or does he want me to call him back?"

"Actually, it was a personal invitation from Paul and Elise Hansen. They've invited you and some other guests for a final reception tomorrow morning before everyone has to leave. It's going to be a brunch in their private quarters here. I'm supposed to R.S.V.P. as soon as possible."

"By all means tell him I'll attend. What time does our flight leave tomorrow?"

"It's not until 3:30 pm so we should have plenty of time. And by the way, they've invited me and Teddy as well, wasn't that thoughtful of them?"

"I'm sure they're happy this investigation is over. It will bring much-needed closure for all of us. It's a wonderful idea, actually. I'm glad you two are coming. Care to join me for some tea, Cecilia?"

She went to the desk and picked up the phone.

"It will be twenty minutes. Would you like to watch the news, Jillian?"

"I really don't think so. I'd rather just talk if you don't mind. I haven't had a chance to vent since the accident."

"You've been through a lot these past few days, haven't you?"

"A lot more than I bargained for, I'm afraid. The main thing I did was help find Rene's killer and Simon's, too."

Teddy barked a single bark.

"I'm sorry, Teddy. You helped too, didn't you? We certainly couldn't have found that gun without you leading us to it."

"He certainly lives up to his name, doesn't he?" Cecilia smiled.

"What name is that?"

"Don't you know that everyone around here is calling him *Sleuth Dog*?"

I had to laugh. "I remember now. Detective Noble gave him that name, didn't he? But a four-and-a-half pound sleuth?"

Teddy cocked his head and looked at me as if to say, "And what's wrong with that?"

"I'm sorry, Teddy. You really are an amazing little sleuth."

"Did you figure out what really happened, Jillian? I

THE GHOST ORCHID MURDER | 299

mean, how did Rene get so far with his blackmail when all Leah had to do was tell her father what was going on?"

"Leah thought she was protecting her father against any kind of exposure. I'm wondering what Detective Noble is going to tell Yvette. I'm sure she'll want to know why Leah killed her son. He'll have to tell her that Rene held the evidence of the poaching over Leah's head."

"What do you think caused Rene to go as far as he did? Do you think he just wanted money, or power over Leah because he couldn't get her any other way?"

"It all started with Rene wanting to protect his mother against Ray Ackermann. If he had evidence against him, he could use it to keep him away. But it went beyond protecting his mother. Rene went looking for Vincent Fontaine. He got a job working for him, and at first, he only wanted to keep tabs on Vincent and explore the possibility of blackmail. Rene didn't earn a large salary, but he was ambitious. When he saw Leah, things changed. Now what he wanted was Leah. He thought he could have her by threatening to blackmail Vincent if she didn't comply with his demands."

"But didn't he take a chance? What if Leah turned him in after she learned what he was up to?"

"That's a chance Rene took. He could always deny it. And he figured Leah would want to protect her father. I talked with Dr. Rehnquist and he told me Leah has an emotional imbalance. Vincent never accepted her as his daughter because of his wife's unfaithfulness.

"Leah tried to win Vincent's love by excelling in school and becoming a scientist. It surely affected her mental health...as did hearing those things about her mother.

"Vincent told me the harder she tried to get his attention, the farther away it pushed him. He couldn't help it. Leah was a constant reminder of his wife's adultery.

"Leah really believed if she spurned Rene, he would expose her father and he would be ruined. Before she would let that happen, she killed him."

"You said she showed no remorse, not even for killing poor Simon."

"That's when I knew she was insane. Mentally, she had crossed over from being a rational scientist to becoming the irrational savior of her father. She finally got what she always wanted, which was Vincent's full love and attention. Now she'll have it for the rest of her life."

"I guess Vincent's all right in my book. That really takes an act of unselfishness on his part. Does Leah know he's not her real father?"

"No, and I don't believe Vincent will ever tell her. That's what makes it all so touching to me. He really is an amazing man, Cecilia."

"Yes he is, Jillian. I'm sorry it didn't work out between you two."

"So am I, but life goes on, and my life is full of wonderful possibilities, I can assure you. Look at the blessings that are coming out of this mess! I've had two offers of syndication for my column and I just received an e-mail from my editor saying he's lifted the salary cut. He even apologized for doing it in the first place!"

"That's wonderful, Jillian." Cecilia bowed her head and looked up again smiling. "I have something to tell you."

"Is it about Walter?"

"No. It's that I did what you said. I prayed and asked the Lord to come into my heart and be my Savior."

"Cecilia! I'm so glad!" I hugged her. "You won't be disappointed."

"I know. I told God what I felt was wrong in my life and asked Him to forgive me. A heavy weight lifted off my shoulders. I was thrown into a sudden rush of enthusiasm for the future. I was happy. It was different than when Walter told me he loved me and yet it was like that in a way."

"It's because God loves you, Cecilia. All the angels rejoiced in Heaven when you prayed for salvation."

"Does that mean I have angels watching over me now?"

"I'm positive you do. The Bible says He gives them charge over us to help us and protect us and after this week I can tell you for sure that it's true!"

"No kidding, Jillian? Angels? Really, Jillian, how can you be so sure?"

"Angels are with us, Cecilia. God gives them to us for protection and provision when there are no other means to see us through difficult situations. I've read about them and have actually felt them on a couple of occasions before this."

"That's amazing. I've never heard anyone talk about them before. But you've actually witnessed them? When did you see angels?"

"It was when my husband and I were driving home late one night on an empty freeway coming home from Los Angeles. We started to have car trouble and the engine sounded like it was coming apart. We prayed to God for help and just as we said, 'Amen,' we felt something grab the roof of our car and guide us off the freeway at the next exit to a gas station. We made it to the garage but saw a *No Checks Please* sign. Our hearts sank because we had no other means to pay."

"What happened?"

"We told the attendant we were honest Christians — we promised our check would be good. He said he'd look under the hood. After a few minutes, he came back and told us that the timing belt had slipped. Evidently, the last person who had worked on our car hadn't replaced it properly. He put it back in place and the car ran fine. He only charged us $25 and took a check. We knew it was an angel who'd guided us to that station because without the timing belt in place the engine would have stopped and we'd have been stranded."

Cecilia sat down in the armless chair next to the fireplace and slipped off her shoes. "That's quite a story, Jillian. I'd believe in angels, too, if something like that happened to me."

We laughed and it felt like we were almost back to normal again, although it would take me a lot longer to forget Vincent.

Lord, you'll just have to help me forget.

The tea finally arrived, this time with homemade oatmeal raisin cookies and a fresh fruit and cheese plate. We enjoyed the fare immensely and talked about other things. The investigation was over and we both had begun to think about returning home.

***

"Let's watch a movie tonight, Jillian, what do you say?"

"Okay, but you choose. Why don't we order a pizza? I haven't had one in weeks."

Teddy barked that he thought it an excellent idea.

"I'd better feed Teddy while you order the pizza or he'll try and mooch ours."

It was a good way to end the day. After Teddy ate his supper, he jumped up on the sofa next to me, turned around twice as he always did, and settled.

We relaxed and watched the movie while we ate pizza and drank soda. The fatigue slowly melted away. I glanced outside and enjoyed a marvelous sunset of brilliant oranges, reds, purples, and gold slowly fading behind the dark-peaked mountains. It would be the last one I watched before going home tomorrow. I would miss seeing them.

Before I readied for bed, I remembered. Vincent was

waiting for an answer.

"What should I say, Lord?" I prayed. "You know my heart, but I want to end what we had on a positive note."

Then the Lord told me what to say.

Dear Vincent,

It's been quite a journey this past week, hasn't it? You know how sorry I am about Leah. I am impressed with what you're doing for her — standing by her no matter what. That's real love, Vincent.

You said in your message that you believed having me in your life would make you whole. I know what you mean. I felt the same way about you, but then I realized that being whole doesn't need to be about being a couple with someone. To me it means that having God in my life is what makes me whole. I can turn to Him any moment of the day or night and He's always there for me. He's been a faithful friend and guide all my life because I chose Him as my Lord and Savior when I was just a little girl.

If you don't know Him personally, I pray you ask Him to be your Savior and Lord, too. He promises to hear you when you call. I'll always keep what we had as a fond memory. I wish you both the best.

Jillian

After I clicked the send button, I felt true closure.

It was time for a final bubble bath in this resort. As I sank beneath the fragrant foam I began to think about Peter and Elise's upcoming brunch tomorrow. Hopefully, it would bring closure as well to both of the competing teams.

I would have to groom Teddy tomorrow morning so he would be at his best when he saw Lila again. I felt my life was returning to normalcy and I looked forward to seeing all my friends before returning home to Clover Hills tomorrow afternoon.

I helped Teddy up on the bed, then I slipped between the cool, clean sheets.

***

I'd set the alarm for eight o'clock the next morning. It would be a brand new day. No suspicions or dangerous threats to my welfare. I stretched my arms overhead and reached down to my toes slowly so I wouldn't get anything out of kilter.

I greeted Teddy as he stretched his front paws out in front of him and then his back paws. He shook himself all over and, after I threw on my robe and slippers, followed me into the living room where Cecilia was sitting at the desk, already at her computer.

Teddy looked at me as if to say, "Do you have treats for me?"

I picked him up, gently hugging him to me. "Let's get you some treats, Teddy."

I kissed the top of his head and carried him to where I kept his dog cookies in one of the kitchen drawers. He jumped down to wait while I gathered some in my hand.

"Here." I tossed him one.

We practiced a few commands.

Sit.

Stay.

Shake hands.

Roll over.

Play dead.

He gave a flawless performance.

"What a good dog you are, Teddy! Such an excellent dog."

Feeling pleased with himself after his achievement, he found a sunny spot under the picture window and settled in for a little rest.

The brunch began at ten o'clock so Cecilia and I just ordered a pot of coffee from room service instead of a full breakfast. I was going to miss the incredible menus, not to mention someone else preparing the meals and cleaning up afterwards.

Soon, our bags were packed and all we had to do was check out. Cecilia's phone rang. When she looked at the screen, her face lit up.

"Jillian, it's Walter, excuse me for a minute while I text him back."

I smiled, nodded my head in understanding, then sat back and enjoyed my steaming cup of delicious coffee. Cecilia didn't text too long. I asked if everything was all right.

"Walter says he can't wait to see me and I can't wait to see him."

I was looking forward to seeing them together for the first time since they had confessed being in love. However, I couldn't help feeling a brief moment of pain at the thought of their newfound relationship. I had lost love twice now.

Stop feeling sorry for yourself, Jillian. Today is the first day of the rest of your life and you have a great one.

I smiled. It was time to go. I gathered Teddy, his leash and tote, and with my passkey in hand started out the door with Cecilia following.

Maria Vargas had finished cleaning the casita next to ours. I was happy to see her.

"Mrs. Bradley! I must tell you that we owe you our thanks for helping to solve Simon's murder. A terrible cloud has lifted for us. Are you leaving today?"

"We're leaving this afternoon. Maria, I want to thank you for coming forward with that evidence you found. I've left something for you on the desk. You've done an outstanding job taking care of our needs while we were here."

"It was my pleasure, ma'am. We'll all miss seeing Teddy around here. He really brightened up our day."

Teddy yipped at the mention of his name.

"It's like he understands, doesn't he?"

"Yes, he's an intelligent dog. And he's a sweet dog, too, I must say."

Teddy looked at me and yipped again as if to thank me for the compliments.

Cecilia, Teddy, and I said goodbye to Maria and started on our way to the brunch.

***

Everyone else was already at the Hansen's magnificent private quarters when we arrived. Elise greeted the three of us and graciously escorted us inside. The brunch table was set up by the pool in the backyard. Lila came running when she saw Teddy and the two ran all over the place in sheer ecstasy to be together. After about two minutes they were tired out and laid down at one end of the yard under a mesquite tree.

Elise offered us a glass of delicious tropical fruit punch and said she had a surprise for us. An attractive-looking man, dressed in a nice pair of casual slacks and sport shirt, walked out from the house. He had a nice tan and striking blue eyes. Cecilia put her hand on my arm, and said under her breath,

"Jillian, that's Lila's dog walker! I talked to him before when I was out walking Teddy."

Elise took the man by the arm and introduced him.

"Everyone, I would like for you to meet my husband, Peter Hansen."

Peter walked over to each guest and introduced himself, saving Cecilia for last.

"It's nice to see you again, Cecilia."

He reached for her hand.

Cecilia was speechless at first, but then she took his hand. "Yeah, nice to finally meet you, Mr. Hansen."

"Please call me Peter. Everyone does." He smiled.

Cecilia acted dazed by the fact that now she knew a millionaire!

"Sure." Her face shone.

I spoke to Arthur and Diana for a few minutes until Elise asked us to fill our plates and have a seat in the living room. She certainly didn't have to ask me twice. I was famished!

Besides the regular breakfast fare of made to order omelets by a waiting chef, there was also every kind of breakfast meat imaginable, fresh fruit, pasta salads, eggs Benedict, hash browns, pan-fried potatoes with rosemary and thyme, huevos rancheros with rice, beans, guacamole, and salsa. As much as I wanted a spoonful of everything, I used restraint and only had the huevos rancheros, one of my all-time favorites.

A server refreshed our drinks when we sat down in the living room. Peter and Elise stood in front of the fireplace and smiled until we got settled. Other than Arthur and Diana, there were Richard Sanchez and Tori DeMarco, Warren Burkett and his wife Sylvia, Helen Morningstar, and the Hansen's facilitator, Herbert Jamison.

"Please enjoy your food while Peter and I say a few words."

Elise began by thanking everyone for coming on such short notice. "I know this has been a trying week for all of us. Peter and I are shocked and saddened at the outcome and our hearts go out to everyone who has been directly involved in this highly stressful investigation.

"Peter and I have struggled with the grant presentation since the unfortunate death of your colleague. But, now that the case has been resolved, thanks to the Scottsdale police and Jillian Bradley's tireless efforts to uncover the truth, we have reached a decision."

Elise looked at Peter signaling for him to continue.

"Ladies and gentlemen, after meeting with several of you in private, Elise and I have decided to award $1,000,000 dollars to each team. Both of the proposals were impeccably presented and we've agreed that both projects should be funded."

Elise spoke again as she looked directly at Richard Sanchez. "We've met with Richard and discussed at length his vision for the Research and Preservation Society and have come to the conclusion that he is the right person to take over for Dr. Fontaine as the society's new director."

Everyone began applauding. Tori placed her arm through Richard's and held it tightly, smiling and looking at him lovingly.

Richard beamed and gazed at her in the same way. He stood and said, "Thank you, everyone. I appreciate the appointment that the Hansens have bestowed. I will work diligently in the days ahead to merit this honor. Thank you, Peter and thank you, Elise." He paused. "Before I sit down again I have an announcement to make."

Everyone smiled and looked at Tori who blushed as she continued to look at Richard.

"The first order of business is to fire Tori."

Everyone in the room gasped at the unexpected announcement.

"Because," he continued, "I'm asking her to be my wife."

Everyone sighed, chuckled, and wished them well.

It was such a beautiful fall day. We moved outside, and sat by the pool on comfortable chaises and padded chairs, shaded by white square umbrellas.

Everyone came up to me with kudos and words of thanks for my role in solving the murders. I gave credit to God for the wisdom and discernment I had asked for, because He truly provided it. I also gave my *sleuth dog*, Teddy, credit for finding the murder weapon, but I had to spell his name when I mentioned it so I wouldn't disturb him.

He was lying fast asleep under the mesquite tree with Lila happily twitching her tail beside him.

Chapter 22

Cecilia was quiet on the plane ride home. She certainly had Walter on her mind. That and beginning her life with him.

I was in the process of clearing my mind of the past week and looking ahead to what awaited. Teddy slept the whole time in his carrier under the seat in front of me. He was a regular little traveler and it made me happy I was able to take him with me. The flight went quickly and before we knew it, we had landed at Oakland International Airport.

Walter was waiting for us at the baggage claim. When he saw Cecilia his face lit up. She hurried to meet him and I almost cried when I saw them embrace each other. Walter reached down and kissed her briefly before he acknowledged Teddy and me.

"I'm so glad you're both back. I was worried, you know. Cecilia kept me briefed. You have to tell me everything as soon as I get your luggage."

"I'll let Cecilia tell you the whole story, Walter. I'm actually trying to forget it. By the way, Cecilia tells me you've completed your police training. Congratulations!"

"Thanks, Mrs. Bradley. I can't wait to get my first case. Chief Viscuglia says I'm going to be a great detective."

"I think you are, too. Would you mind taking me to my car? I'd really appreciate it."

"It's just like the old days, huh, Mrs. Bradley?"

The old days...Walter had been my valet at the Ritz-Carlton in Half Moon Bay some years ago. I fondly remember that darling brown-eyed boy who'd confided in me so openly upon my first meeting him.

Yes, I'm home.

***

It was dark by the time I arrived at my house. However, I had some lights set on timers so it wasn't completely dark.

I carried Teddy inside and let him out of his crate. He was so happy to be out of the confinement he rolled all over the carpet, then barked to go out on the lawn. I let him into the backyard and began taking my bags from the car into the house.

It would be lovely just being home. Since Walter and Cecilia were finally together I didn't want to encroach on the two lovebirds so I hadn't suggested dinner.

Although I knew I would feel terribly lonely tonight, I wanted to get home as soon as possible. I didn't stop to eat anywhere — there would be something in the fridge.

After being with people all week, I found the house excessively quiet. Soon though, Teddy's barks filled the silence. He was chasing a bird. I swallowed the small lump that had grown in my throat. Teddy was here. I wasn't alone. Everything would be fine.

I let him back in.

He followed me into the kitchen and I pulled open the fridge and peered inside.

"Well, it looks like we're having bacon and eggs for dinner."

He yipped as if to say, "That sounds fine to me."

I made us a nice breakfast along with a pot of freshly brewed decaf coffee. After I did the dishes we went into the living room together. I sat in my favorite leather recliner, pushed it back as far as it would go and enjoyed drinking my after-dinner coffee.

Teddy lay down across the room and put his head on his front paws.

The coffee tasted delicious and I felt happy to be home. Bedtime would come early tonight. First came unpacking, then, of course, a hot bubble bath. Was life just what happened between soaking sessions?

It was wonderful to slip slowly into the hot sudsy water and let it soothe my tiredness away.

On with my silk pajamas, off with all of the lights in the house, and I was ready for bed. Teddy waited for me to pick him up and place him on his towel at the foot of my bed.

I complied. Who was I to stand against ritual?

"We've had a busy day and we're both ready for a good night's sleep in our own bed. Thank you again, dear Lord, for getting us through this past week and for a safe trip home."

Now that I was back, thoughts of Vincent began to fade.

***

The doorbell rang the next morning with a delivery from the gallery in Scottsdale where I had purchased my paintings. Teddy barked instruction at me as I opened the boxes and pulled out my purchases.

"All right, all right, Teddy. Give me a moment. Now let's see...."

No, they probably would never hire me to hang paintings at the museum – it took me more than a few tries. Eventually though, Teddy bounced in approval and I stood with a cup of tea and a plate of cookies admiring the effect the sunny pair of paintings brought to the room.

Lovely! Now my conservatory was complete. All the décor was perfect. Wherever I looked I saw the beautiful things I had collected over the years. I felt happy and blessed. Another package arrived later that day. My Capodimonte Rose?

I took a pair of scissors and opened the package. Carefully, I took the red fabric box out of the packaging and unfastened the latch. It was beautiful, and yet, where would I put it? It would come to me, I was sure. I nibbled the rest of the cookies, finished my tea, and placed the empty cup and saucer back on the tray.

My gardens...yes I loved them, too. Even though it was fall, thanks to the mild California climate, my yard looked spectacular at this time of the year with my liquid ambers arrayed in their glorious shades of reds and gold and the grass still a vibrant green.

The purple and yellow pansy borders I had put in before I left were coming along quite nicely. It was truly a lovely yard. I would enjoy being in it whenever I could.

The sun began to set. I would have to return to Arizona just to see those sunsets again. They had been so wide and beautiful—such a big sky. But here there was green. I loved that too. Maybe I would treat Arthur and Diana to lunch at ZuZu's. There were dishes I still wanted to try.

The day seemed to be growing longer but there were still plenty of things to do. E-mail. Yes, e-mail would save me. Comfortably seated at my Chippendale secretary, I opened my computer and read them all. I was amazed at the number of messages I had received asking about the investigation.

This definitely called for a dinner party, and the sooner the better.

Dinner that night consisted of a grilled chicken breast

seasoned with taco seasoning, fresh broccoli steamed with butter and lemon pepper, and a small baked potato with a little butter, cheese, and sour cream. For dessert, I made a small sundae with a scoop of yummy chocolate ice cream topped with chocolate syrup, whipped cream, and a maraschino cherry. I also enjoyed a cup of decaf, of course.

I happily responded to my editor's message that he was not only reinstating my salary, but was giving me a 10 percent raise for the increase in my notoriety. I graciously thanked him. As to the two new syndications of my column, I happily accepted them as well, thereby increasing my income by another 200 percent. All I had to do was to forward the same column two more times each week.

"Thank you, Lord, for provision. You never cease to amaze me."

After dinner, I took the Capodimonte Rose in my hand and began to look for a place to put it. I settled on the mantle where I could view it from wherever I sat in the room. It looked lovely there between the two crystal candleholders. After lighting the gas logs and placing my cup of coffee next to me, I sat down in my recliner to relax and reflect on my day.

Teddy lay down in front of the fireplace and closed his eyes, content to be home again.

The transition from resort to home was always a sad, but necessary, one. However, I could be happy in whatever environment God placed me. The Lord had helped me to create a lovely sanctuary here. It wasn't so much the things, but a feeling of restfulness, of peace.

Now for that guest list. I took out a notebook and began thinking of whom I would like to invite to the dinner party. The holidays were fast approaching so I decided to make it a Christmas theme. I began listing the names and my eyes wandered around the room. They stopped and rested on the rose. I thought of

Yvette, trying bravely to carry on in her little convenience store and gas station in Ocala. Yes, I have been blessed.

"Dear Lord, thank you for the wonderful life you have given me."

The End

If you enjoyed *The Ghost Orchid Murder*, please leave a review on your favorite reading site.

Thank you!

Visit http://www.nancy-jill.blogspot.com

Also by Nancy Jill Thames

MURDER IN HALF MOON BAY
Book 1

FROM THE CLUTCHES OF EVIL
Book 3

THE MARK OF EDEN
Book 4

PACIFIC BEACH
Book 5

WAITING FOR SANTA
Book 6

THE RUBY OF SIAM
Book 7

THE LONG TRIP HOME (2014)
Book 8

ABOUT THE AUTHOR

Nancy Jill Thames has published Christian fiction since 2010. The author of seven books in the Jillian Bradley Mystery Series, she is an award winning blogger and listed numerous times on the Author Watch Bestseller's List. In addition she won first place in her church's 4th of July celebration for her chocolate cream pie.

When she isn't plotting her next book, she spends time with her six grandchildren in two states, tags along with her husband on business trips, and plays classical piano for her personal enjoyment. She is an active member of the Leander Writes' Guild, American Christian Fiction Writers (ACFW), CenTex Chapter of ACFW and supports the Central Texas SPCA with a portion of her book sales. She resides with her husband in Leander, Texas.

Made in the USA
San Bernardino, CA
04 May 2014